MW01280013

FRAMED SHADOWS

SHADOWS LANDING #6

KATHLEEN BROOKS

All Rights Reserved. No part of this book may be used or reproduced in any manner whatsoever without written permission, except in the case of brief quotations embodied in critical articles and reviews.

This book is a work of fiction. The names, characters, places, and incidents are products of the writer's imagination or have been used fictitiously and are not to be construed as real. Any resemblance to persons living or dead, actual events, locale, or organizations is entirely coincidental.

An original work of Kathleen Brooks. *Framed Shadows* copyright @ 2021 by Kathleen Brooks.

Kathleen Brooks® is a registered Trademark of Laurens Publishing, LLC

❀ Created with Vellum

Forever Concealed

Forever Devoted

Forever Hunted

Forever Guarded

Forever Notorious

Forever Ventured

Forever Freed

Forever Saved

Forever Bold

Forever Thrown (coming Aug/Sept 2021)

Shadows Landing Series

Saving Shadows

Sunken Shadows

Lasting Shadows

Fierce Shadows

Broken Shadows

Framed Shadows

Endless Shadows (coming Oct 2021)

Women of Power Series

Chosen for Power

Built for Power

Fashioned for Power

Destined for Power

Web of Lies Series

Whispered Lies

PROLOGUE

Budapest, Hungary, 1944 . . .

Dezo Alder's body was shaking with fear. He knew what was coming as he walked into the local leader's office. All of his instincts told him to stop wasting time and to run. His palms were sweaty as his longtime friend, Gellert Balogh, gestured to the chair across from his desk.

"Thank you for coming, my friend," he said as Dezo's heart rate increased.

"Is this about the Germans?" Dezo asked as he fought to keep his voice even.

Gellert nodded his head slowly. "Our national leaders had been close to Hitler since he took power. They wanted him to get back some of the lands we lost when the Austro-Hungarian Empire was broken up after the Great War. We got our land, but at a price. Since Stalingrad and other battles, we've lost tens of thousands of Hungarians. Some of our leaders have been trying to find a way out of our alliance with Germany."

Gellert had been Dezo's friend since childhood. They'd grown up in the same small neighborhood in Budapest, but the war changed everything. Gellert Balogh rose to power and Dezo Alder had been placed on the Jewish list as Hungary became an Axis Power. Dezo lost his standing in the community and he'd been forced to close the doors to his family's art gallery. They'd gone from being a prosperous family to a poor one. However, Gellert had saved him more than once. He kept Dezo and his family safe from deportation and forced military service. Dezo's oldest son, Elek, had been forced into manual labor but at least he was still able to live at home.

Dezo hoped Gellert was going to tell him Hungary had changed sides in the war. That they'd negotiated with the Allies. That help was on the way. However, the resignation on Gellert's face told him that hope was futile.

"Hitler found out about our attempts to reach out to the Allies. The Germans are here. Hitler's troops are moving toward the city as we speak. I'm sorry, dear friend. Your family's name is on the list of prominent Jews that will be turned over to the SS when they arrive. They'll be here within the hour. I tried to get your names off of it, but not everyone in my office is sympathetic. I can no longer keep you safe from being transported to Auschwitz. If you don't escape Budapest, you will most likely be taken away. Take Rozsa and your children, dear Elek and Sandor, and get to Switzerland as fast as you can."

Dezo felt the impact of the words reverberate through his whole body. He stood on wobbly legs as Gellert handed him a thick envelope. "Papers to help with your escape. I don't know how long you can get away with using them, but I had to try. I'm sorry, dear friend."

Dezo took the envelope and then shook his friend's hand. "Thank you. I will always remember your kindness."

Dezo tried to walk from the building calmly. He didn't want to draw any attention to himself even though he wanted to tell all of his people to run for their lives.

He heard shouts in the distance. The earth shook as the road was filled with German military vehicles and tanks rolling through the outskirts of town on their way to downtown Budapest just a short distance away.

Dezo stopped walking and stared in horror as people on the street clicked their heels together and raised their arms into the air as the troops drove by. Dezo was in grave danger. His family was in danger. His people were in danger. He couldn't depend on anyone but himself now. He patted the papers in his pocket and picked up his pace.

"Papa!" Sandor yelled the second Dezo unlocked the door to their gallery. They'd been forced to sell their house in a well-to-do neighborhood for a small fraction of what it was worth and had moved into the small apartment above his family's art gallery—a gallery that had been in his family for generations that he was now forced to abandon.

Dezo's throat tightened as his wife and son ran into his arms.

"We saw Nazis," his wife cried into his neck.

"Rozsa, where is Elek?" Dezo asked of their fifteen-year-old son.

"He's working down by the river," his wife responded. "Dezo, what's going on?"

"We've fallen to Germany. Gellert can't protect us. He gave us fake papers and told us to run for Switzerland. Take only what we can carry. We must leave now."

"But we've been safe until now, even as others have been deported," Rozsa protested.

"We are safe no longer, Rozsa. Pack for me, my dear. Only what we can carry. Sandor," he said, looking at his ten-year-old son. "Pack your things and some for Elek. I'll meet you all upstairs in ten minutes."

"My sister," Rozsa gasped. "I must warn her."

"There is no time, Rozsa. I'm sorry, love. We must leave the house in fifteen minutes."

Dezo left his family in tears as he made his way to the gallery. Masterpieces hung on the wall from Dali, Monet, Munch, Rembrandt, Picasso, Caravaggio, Renoir, Degas, Vermeer, and so many more. How could he abandon this history? How could he leave this part of him and his family's legacy for the Nazis to take or destroy?

His heart broke as he grabbed what paintings and sketches he could. He felt his soul rip apart as he cut them from their frames and shoved them between the pages of his ledger books. He wanted to take more, but he couldn't. Some were too large to pack in the bags they had to carry.

The door to the gallery shook as someone pounded on it. His time was up. Dezo raced up the stairs and ordered his family out the back door to the car. "Meet me down the block," he told his wife. Together they walked downstairs, his wife and son carrying all they could take with them before they turned and went out the back. The gallery door was about to be kicked in when Dezo answered it. A young man in Nazi uniform stood looking annoyed.

"Heil Hitler," he said, his arm shooting up.

"Heil Hitler," Dezo forced out, the words making him nauseous.

"We have reports that this is a Jewish-owned gallery. I

need your papers." Dezo looked behind the soldier to find three more young men and a truck. "Are you the owner?"

"No," Dezo said, reaching into his pocket and pulling out the papers Gellert had given him. "I'm just an assistant. The owner left this morning."

The Nazi soldier looked over the papers and then handed them back. "You may leave. We are taking all the art for der Führer. Heil Hitler."

"Heil Hitler," Dezo mumbled as he allowed himself one last look at the art his family had collected over generations. He vowed to himself, to the paintings, and to his ancestors that he'd come back for them one day. One day his family's collection would be complete again.

Dezo walked out the door and didn't look back. "Hurry, we must find Elek," he said as soon as he got into the car.

Chaos erupted all around them as they drove through Budapest toward the Danube River. People were running in the street in a blind panic. Nazi soldiers were shooting anyone who defied them. Rozsa smothered her cries as they approached the river and a group of Nazi guards held up their hands to stop them.

"Pretend to be supporters of Hitler," Dezo ordered his family as he rolled down his window.

"Heil Hitler!" the guard shouted as he saluted.

"Heil Hitler," Dezo responded as his stomach turned in revulsion.

"Where are you going?" the guard asked.

"We are returning home from a trip from the country. Our house is on the other side of the river," Dezo lied.

"Papers?"

Dezo took a deep breath and handed him the envelope

from Gellert. As the guard examined them, Dezo watched as two men were dragged from a house and shoved to their knees. When they refused to submit to the soldiers, they were shot in the head.

The guard turned to his fellow guards. "Let them through."

Dezo drove slowly through the now German-occupied Budapest toward the river. "Papa! It's Elek!"

Dezo slowed the car at the sight of his son walking with his head down along the buildings. He was hidden in a group of well-to-do teens rushing home. "Rozsa, don't create a scene. Just call him over to the car." Even as Dezo's whole body shook, he tried to appear calm as he stopped the car.

Rozsa opened the car door and stepped out. He could see her skirts swaying as fear shook her body. "There you are, Elek. Now, get in the car so we won't be late for dinner."

Elek's head shot up and he ran for the car until he saw his mother motion for him to slow down. Dezo's heart pounded as his son closed the distance between them and finally slipped into the car.

"They're killing people, Papa," Elek said with his face streaked with tears. "They killed hundreds and just tossed them in the river."

Dezo put the car in gear and did what he had to do to save the Alder family. He lied, he stole, and he prayed.

It took two days to reach the farthest western border of Hungary. Dezo and his family parked the car in the small village and prepared to make the rest of the trip on foot. They'd seen all cars attempting to leave the country turned away. This was now their only option. They ate in silence as Nazi guards patrolled the street around them. Dezo pocketed a loaf of bread and ordered his family to do the same before they strolled to a nearby park with their backpacks containing everything they now owned.

The west end of the park sat next to a forest and mountainous region. Dezo's plan was to stroll through the park to the forest at the border. They would lay out their blanket and pretend to have a picnic dinner until the park cleared. Then it would be a 600-kilometer hike through the forest and mountains of Austria that were filled with Nazis to reach the Swiss border. They would have to hurry, yet hide the entire way. Dezo knew they were likely to be killed, but he had to try to save his family.

As the sun set on Hungary, the Alder family slipped into the darkness of the trees, never to see their home country again.

1

Spring, present day, Shadows Landing, South Carolina . . .

Tinsley Faulkner's long, wavy brown hair had paint in it. How did that happen? She'd had it tied back when she was working on her latest painting, but of course she didn't see the cobalt blue paint until she was feet from her cousin-in-law's art gallery.

Tinsley stood on the cobblestone sidewalk of downtown Charleston, trying to pick the paint from the tips of her hair. That's when she noticed the white paint on her forearm.

"I'm hopeless." Tinsley sighed as she gave up. If anyone would understand her paint-splattered appearance, it was Ellery.

Tinsley opened the door to the gallery and felt as if she'd just walked into her home. She had her own gallery in Shadows Landing in which she displayed her pieces as well as those by some other, lesser-known, artists. Ellery's gallery in downtown Charleston was the opposite. She had some local artists, and of course insisted on carrying some of

Tinsley's paintings, but she also got the big names of the art world. However, a gallery was a gallery and the paintings, sketches, and statues instantly calmed Tinsley as she smiled at them all.

"Aren't you a lovely one," she murmured to a painting.

"That she is. I, however, am not."

Tinsley looked up at Ellery making her way slowly toward her. Ellery was nine months pregnant and ready to go at any moment.

"You're stunning," Tinsley said as she hugged Ellery. "I only wish I was talented enough to capture this maternal glow you have in a painting."

Ellery rolled her eyes. "I can't see my feet. I can't wear heels. I go to the bathroom every five minutes. I swear this kid is playing kickball with my bladder."

"And you've never been happier," Tinsley said with a knowing grin.

Ellery nodded as she rubbed her hand over her baby bump. "And I've never been happier."

"Ready to get that pedicure?" Tinsley asked.

"I can't wait." Ellery went to close the door, but before she could reach it, two men came in.

What struck Tinsley as odd was not their jeans and baggy T-shirts, nor the fact that their tennis shoes were unlaced and appeared too big for them, or even that they had large tattoos on their upper arms. What struck Tinsley as odd was that they didn't take even a second to look at the art on the walls.

"Can I help you?" Ellery asked.

"Yeah," the first man said. He was tall, over six feet, and had what looked like a snake tattooed around his arm. The second man stood back with his hands held in front of him. He didn't look around either. He just stared at Tinsley and

Ellery. "My brother and I are looking to sell some art. Do you do that here?"

"We display and sell for select artists and private owners. We also work with other galleries across the country to display prominent artists," Ellery answered.

"See," the guy started to say before clearing his throat and standing up straighter. "Our grandmother has this painting that she's looking to sell. She's really sick and needs help with her medical bills."

"Who is the artist?" Ellery asked as the man pulled out his phone.

"I'm sorry, I'm not very knowledgeable on this sort of thing," he admitted as he showed her the painting.

Tinsley looked over Ellery's shoulder and frowned. She knew that artist. "That's a Hamburg. Where did your grandmother find it?" Tinsley asked.

Ellery glanced at Tinsley in surprise. Hamburg paintings were notoriously hard to come by.

"I don't know," the man admitted.

"Well, I'd be happy to sell it for her," Ellery said slowly. "However, I'd need to get it appraised and also see all of the paperwork on it."

"There's paperwork for art?" the man asked.

"A Certificate of Authenticity," Tinsley explained. "It's proof of the chain of ownership going back to the artist. It's the artwork's provenance, used for insurance purposes to prove who the artist is and the list of owners is in date order to help with appraisals and stop forgeries, prevent ownership disputes, and such."

"Yes, it's standard in the art industry," Ellery told him.

"I don't know if my grandmother has that. Can't you sell the painting without it?" the man asked.

Ellery shook her head. "No gallery or art buyer will buy

a piece of this value without it. I hope you find it. Many people keep those papers in a safe deposit box or a safe."

"Yeah, I'll check those out. I didn't know they were needed. Thanks a lot. You've been very helpful."

Tinsley and Ellery watched the men leave before turning toward each other.

"That was strange, right?" Ellery asked. "Did you notice they never looked at any of the artwork?"

Tinsley nodded. "Very strange. Think it was a forgery?"

"Has to be. No one has a Hamburg without guarding the provenance with their life."

"They didn't even know who Hamburg was." Tinsley shook her head. Unfortunately, art forgery was more common than people thought. "Well, are you ready for your pedicure?"

Tinsley looked at Ellery and saw her face wrinkle in confusion.

"You know, where someone rubs your feet and makes your toes pretty?"

The grooves in Ellery's forehead deepened before her eyes shot wide open. "Dammit!"

"What?" Tinsley asked.

"I'm not going to get my pedicure," Ellery said as a tear rolled down her face.

"Why not? We're going right now."

"Because I just went into labor," Ellery cried.

Tinsley looked down at Ellery's stomach as if expecting the baby to pop out right this instant. "What do I do?"

"Call Gavin," Ellery said as she made her way to her office as quickly as she could while Tinsley fumbled with her phone.

"Gav, Ellery is in labor!" she yelled the second her cousin answered his phone.

Ellery came walking back out with her hands supporting her lower back and walked to the front door. She flipped the sign to Closed and locked up before cringing again.

"Get her to the hospital. I'll tell them you're on your way. I'll be there soon. How is she holding up?" Gavin asked.

"She's pissed she didn't get her pedicure."

"I'll work something out. Take care of her, Tins."

"I will," Tinsley swore.

"Just look at them. They're mocking me." Ellery glared at her toes from her hospital bed.

A nurse was waiting for them at admitting and whisked Ellery up to the maternity floor, leaving Tinsley to handle the registration. They'd gotten Ellery changed into a hospital gown, hooked her up to all these devices, and examined all before Tinsley arrived from the land of endless paperwork. Ellery was five centimeters dilated and had just gotten what she called her happy juice.

The door to the room burst open and Ryker Faulkner was standing there in a thousand-dollar suit with a look of pure panic on his face. "I'm here!"

Tinsley looked at her cousin and tried not to laugh. "That's nice of you to come support Ellery and Gavin."

Ryker shook his head and held up a drug store bag. "Gavin called and said it was an emergency. I left a very important and sensitive negotiation to get this to you. He said you couldn't have the baby without it."

Tinsley stood up and walked to the door where Ryker seemed stuck. She grabbed the bag and opened it. "This is very nice of you, Ryker."

"What is it?" Ellery asked.

"It's nail polish for your toes," Tinsley said, bringing the bag to the bed. It wasn't just nail polish—it was a whole collection of nail polish. Ryker had bought one of every color.

"Ryker! You're amazing!" Ellery said before bursting out into tears.

Ryker's pale face paled even more. He started to back slowly out of the room, but Ellery motioned for him to come to her bedside. Warring emotions of fear, panic, and Southern manners slid across his face. In the end, manners won and he stepped forward slowly. Ellery reached for his hand and Ryker looked as if he were sticking it in a vat of acid as he tentatively put his hand in hers.

"Thank you so much. I know it's silly, but it's important to me."

"You're welcome," Ryker said slowly, still acting as if someone were about to jump out and scare him.

"What color should I do?" Ellery asked as she began going through the bottles.

"This one," Tinsley said, picking up a bright red. "It's called Red Hot Mama."

"Perfect," Ellery said as she clapped her hands. Ryker tried to sneak out, but Ellery stopped him. "Will you stay for a bit, Ryker?"

"Don't you need something else? I can run and get you some food or maybe some bourbon. I feel bourbon would be helpful right now."

Tinsley hid her laugh at her cousin. Ryker had changed so much since that night long ago. His laughter and carefree attitude had vanished in a single moment. Ryker had turned into a stone-cold business tycoon. However, every now and then, flashes of the old Ryker came through.

"Baby!" Ellery cried out suddenly.

"Where?" Ryker jumped up, looking at where Tinsley was painting Ellery's toes.

"I think she means me," Gavin said with a laugh as he walked into the room with Ellery's bag and the biggest smile Tinsley had ever seen. "I guess I'll need a new term of endearment or it could get confusing."

"Oh, thank God you're here," Ryker said with relief as Gavin hurried to Ellery's bedside with the rest of the family right behind him.

Tinsley kept right on painting Ellery's toes as the rest of the Faulkner family entertained Ellery.

Ryker had silently slipped from the room within seconds of their arrival, but now four hours later he was back in the waiting room with the rest of the family. Ellery was progressing, and the family had taken up half of the waiting room.

Tinsley sat next to her brother, Ridge, and his wife, Savannah, and talked to pass the time. Her cousin Wade, and his wife, Darcy, sat talking to Gavin's sister, Harper, and her husband, Dare. Trent was off to the side talking with Ryker. As the hours passed, people rotated around the room until Tinsley had talked with everyone.

The elevator doors opened and a woman with brown hair and a blood-splattered shirt raced out. "Did I miss it?"

Trent shook his head at his wife, Skye. Skye Jessamine was a famous actress and currently shooting her first action movie in Atlanta. Luckily, the blood on her shirt was fake and part of her costume.

"No, the baby isn't here yet. You had time to change." Trent kissed his wife as the other people in the waiting room gaped and rushed to ask if they could take her picture.

Skye agreed to photos then politely, but firmly,

disengaged from her fans so she could focus on her family. "Tell me everything."

"A nurse told us that she's started pushing," Trent told her.

They turned as the door to the labor room opened and out came Gavin with a bundle in his arms.

Tinsley gasped and felt tears rush to her eyes. She was a softy and didn't care who knew it as Gavin showed off the chubby-cheeked baby.

"I'm an auntie," Harper whispered in quiet wonder as she ran a finger down the baby's cheek. "How's Ellery?"

"She's perfect. She was simply amazing. And this little bundle came out bright-eyed and ready to meet everyone. This is our son, Chase."

2

The summer heat in Charleston was worse than in Atlanta. Paxton Kendry would never give Charleston the satisfaction of complaining, but the ocean breeze did very little to lower the humidity.

Paxton rubbed his chest where three bullet wounds had healed and scarred over as he looked at his computer in the FBI's office. Six months ago, he was working deep undercover in Atlanta as second-in-command of the Violent Gang Task Force and now he was stuck sitting behind a desk in a freaking suit looking at art crimes. He'd taken three bullets on the job in Atlanta, but instead of moving up to head the task force when his boss retired, Paxton had been shipped off to Charleston where he was dealing with several complaints about forged paintings. On top of the lack of excitement, so far none of the galleries had actually purchased or sold said forgeries so there was no evidence for him to examine. Just gut feelings of several art gallery owners.

"Kendry, are you working on anything right now?" his

boss, Peter Castle, asked from the door to Paxton's small office.

"Nothing important. What have you got?" Paxton said a prayer that a new gang had moved into town or something equally threatening to get him out of the office and back on the streets.

Peter stepped into the office and took a seat at the one chair across from Paxton. He held out a file and Paxton took it. He flipped the file open and began scanning the documents. "Home burglary really isn't our thing, but sure, why not? I'll take it."

"It's not your run-of-the-mill burglary. There have been three break-ins in very upscale neighborhoods where only jewelry and artwork have been taken. And," Peter said dramatically, "not all artwork. Only very specific, high-value, artwork."

Okay, that got Paxton's attention. "Interesting. Any suspects?"

Peter shook his head. "Local police couldn't find any common denominators. They all use different service providers, from house cleaners to yard maintenance. They are all in different neighborhoods, have different jobs, and donate to different charities, as far as we can tell. Nothing is the same except they have very expensive taste in art. Hence, local police have asked for our help."

Paxton finished reviewing the file. "Well, jewelry can be melted down, but artwork is different. Was it insured?"

"Yes. They were all insured."

"Have they been ransomed? Lots of art thieves ransom the artwork back to the insurance companies so they end up paying out less than the claim. It's a quick turnaround for the thieves, and the insurance companies usually agree to it because it's cheaper than paying out the claim."

"Nope. Not a single ransom or a hint of any contact whatsoever," Peter told him.

Paxton looked at pictures of the artwork taken and groaned. "I know my art but I don't know it well enough to know if there's some hidden connection to the artwork."

"Good thing we have an FBI consultant when need be." Peter smirked and Paxton wanted to groan. "How can you not like Tinsley Faulkner? She's literally one of the sweetest people I know."

Oh, it wasn't a matter of not liking her. It was a matter of liking her a little too much. Over the years, he'd been told that all good things come in small packages. Well, Tinsley was a perfect example of that. She only came up to his chest and had curves that he dreamed about. She was sweet as the apple pie she'd brought to welcome him to Charleston. Only Paxton didn't do *sweet* and this attraction bugged the hell out of him. He was used to controlling everything and everyone around him. You didn't get as far as he did in Violent Gangs without pushing people around.

He'd tried to push Tinsley around when she'd helped on a case. Tried to shunt her off to the side and retain control of the case and his feelings. Then the worst thing happened. Tinsley hadn't backed down. She'd poked him in the chest and told him if he wanted to solve the case, he either needed to listen to her or go back to school to learn about art. It was the sexiest damn thing he'd ever seen. He'd wanted to pick her up, have her wrap her legs around his waist, and . . .

"I never said I didn't like her," Paxton pointed out.

"I can take these to her when I go home tonight if you don't want to. Maybe you're a big elephant afraid of the little Tinsley mouse," Peter said, interrupting Paxton's thoughts.

"No, I've got it. I know how much you enjoy your time

with Karri. How is she doing? Tell her I really loved the
meal she sent me last week."

"She's doing great. Her partnership with Harper Reigns
is taking off. Their specialty paired meal and drink menu is
even attracting people from Charleston to drive out to
Shadows Landing," Peter said proudly. Paxton had met
Peter's girlfriend on the first day in the Charleston office
when Peter had taken him out to dinner at Karri's restaurant
in Shadows Landing. The two of them were totally in sync
and completely in love.

"I'll have a flyer sent to the galleries so they'll be on the
lookout for the stolen paintings before I talk to Tinsley,"
Paxton said, turning to his computer.

Peter left his office as Paxton's fingers flew over the
keyboard. He'd send his notes to his assistant and have him
mail out the graphic to all the galleries in a hundred-mile
radius after he uploaded the artwork into the stolen art
database.

Paxton was working even though his mind was on
Tinsley. He didn't mean to always get into debates with her,
but she was just so damned sexy when she parked her hands
on her hips and told him what's what. Her intellect was sexier
than those curves she had, and that was saying something. If
Tinsley loved with the same passion she debated with, she
would rock Paxton's world. That is, if Tinsley ever let him into
her bed. However, Tinsley struck him as a long-term
relationship kind of woman, and one thing Paxton wasn't was
a long-term kind of guy. He never knew when he'd be
transferred, and he fully intended to get back to the Violent
Gangs Task Force in Atlanta as soon as possible. That meant
instead of wrapping those legs around his waist and pushing
her up against the wall, debating Tinsley would have to do.

Tinsley stepped back to look at her canvas and frowned. How did that man get there? Why was he kissing that woman? Why did the man look suspiciously like Paxton Kendry and the woman look shockingly similar to her?

Tinsley let her head fall back on a groan before she moved to turn off the music in the back room of her gallery. She had been free painting and apparently her subconscious was tired of being shut out of her thoughts.

She'd overheard two tourists trashing all the art in her studio and needed to refresh her creative soul which had been crushed at the unnecessarily cruel criticism. She knew it was part of life, but that didn't mean it didn't hurt when she heard them laughing and saying nasty things about her work. So, Tinsley had turned off the lights, lit a roomful of candles, and turned on her favorite music. Then she'd gotten lost in the world of color, music, and unconscious movement. Her mind told her that Paxton was a pain in the ass, but her subconscious was connected to her heart and painted a different picture. This painting showed how strong and protective Paxton was. His storm-gray eyes were closed in the painting as he clutched her to him. Her back was curved into the shape of a C as Paxton bent her back and kissed her.

Tinsley had been annoyed because Paxton liked to dominate every conversation they had, even when they weren't arguing. And while she was petite, she wasn't a pushover. However, her annoyance had shifted recently when she realized his whole body came alive when they were together. The storm clouds cleared from his eyes. His body language wasn't intimidating, but proud. He leaned toward her when they talked, he smiled at her, teased her, and that's when her annoyance turned into anticipation.

Everyone around her treated Tinsley like she was some kind of fragile flower. She was the smallest and the youngest of all the Faulkners and her family tended to think of her as a child still. Then a couple of years ago, she'd been attacked when she was trying to protect her best friend, Edie Greene Wecker, from the man who had killed Edie's husband and was trying to kill her brother.

Yes, Tinsley had been injured. Yes, she'd been scared. That didn't mean she was broken, though. She'd fought back. She'd been taking self-defense lessons not only in Charleston, but also at the church in Shadows Landing. Only when she felt fully capable of handling a weapon safely herself did she go out and buy Tina, a paint-splattered handgun she kept for safety at her house. Tinsley's gallery was in downtown Shadows Landing, but her house was out in the country. She felt better knowing she had Tina when she went home alone at night.

Tinsley looked at the painting and smiled. Paxton might be pushy and refused to admit he didn't know the difference between Monet and Manet, but he didn't treat her as if she'd break if he looked at her cross-eyed. Instead, he treated her like an equal. He constantly pushed her intellectually, and she was finding herself looking forward to their next debate. Maybe looking forward too much if her painting told her anything.

"Tinsley."

Tinsley spun with her paintbrush out like a dagger as a deep voice interrupted her thoughts.

"Are you going to paint me to death?"

Tinsley rolled her eyes at the object of her fascination.

"Agent Kendry, what are you doing here and why didn't you knock?"

Paxton's lips turned up into a slow smile and Tinsley bit the inside of her lower lip to prevent herself from staring. "I did knock, but you were lost in thought. I'm sorry to interrupt your work."

Paxton moved to look at the painting and Tinsley jumped in front of it. Would he notice she'd painted them kissing?

Paxton looked down at her and chuckled. His eyes were alive as he kept his smile in place. "You're cute when you're self-conscious about your work, but it doesn't do much good to try to hide it when I'm taller than you by a foot."

"Then you should respect my obvious wishes for no one to see it and look away," Tinsley said, putting her hands on her hips and glaring up at him. Unfortunately, her eyes never made it past his lips until his smile widened after he noticed where she was staring.

"I'd be happy to oblige your curiosity." Paxton's voice dipped lower as he leaned toward her. "If you're not afraid of the big bad wolf."

Tinsley rolled her eyes. "Oh please. You don't scare me. You're all bark and no bite."

"You're the only person to ever say that to me. And for the record, I do bite, and you'd love it." Tinsley tried to act nonchalant but failed miserably when she couldn't form a comeback. "Nice painting."

Paxton stepped around her to get a closer look, and Tinsley hurried forward to try to block him, but failed when he shot his arm out to the side to barricade her from getting by him. "This is different from your other paintings. Romance isn't really my thing, but this may be my favorite of yours so far. Your landscapes are excellent, but you hardly ever put people in them."

Tinsley was filled with warmth at the compliment. The negative comments from the tourists were forgotten. She knew Paxton well enough to know he wouldn't hold back with his opinions. So the fact that he liked it meant a lot to her. Now, she just had to stop him from realizing it was the two of them kissing in the painting.

"I'm not very good at people. What did you need or did you realize you hadn't met your quota for torturing people for the day and decided to visit me?"

Tinsley moved to wash her brush, forcing Paxton to turn his back to the painting.

"There are all kinds of torture, you know. The kinds that are painful and designed to hurt, and then there are the kinds that leave you begging for more," Paxton said, his voice growing rougher as he spoke.

Holy smokes! Tinsley's body was on fire because she knew exactly what kind of torture he was talking about and looking at his eyes staring at her left her with no doubt he'd be very, very good at it.

What was happening here? Did he feel the same as she did? That these little skirmishes were just foreplay before the main event?

"So, what did you need?" Tinsley asked, proud that her voice didn't crack or that she hadn't stripped naked and jumped him.

"I have a case that I need your opinion on," Paxton told her. Then to her horror, her stomach rumbled. He smirked at her again and all sexy thoughts flew out the window at her embarrassment. "How about we discuss the case over dinner?"

Her stomach liked that idea, but she didn't. "If we go out,

we won't get any work done. Everyone will stop by the table to chat. It's what I normally love about my small town, but if I need to look at files and examine paintings, I need to be able to focus."

Paxton looked around and nodded. "Okay. You clean up and I'll grab something from the Pink Pig. What do you want from there?"

The Pink Pig was one of two barbecue joints in town and the one closest to her. There was a friendly but intense rivalry between the Pink Pig and Lowcountry Smokehouse. It was a rivalry where there were no losers because both places were so good. Just thinking about them had her stomach rumbling again.

Tinsley gave him the order and watched as he walked out of the backroom. Oh boy. What was she getting herself into and could she get herself out of it if need be? She couldn't wait for Paxton to get back, but even she knew he wasn't the staying type.

3

Paxton thanked the waitress and grabbed the large brown paper bag filled with food. The entire time he was waiting for his order, his mind was on the painting at Tinsley's. It had been them. She may say she wasn't good at painting people, but she was wrong. It had felt as if Paxton had Tinsley bent back in his arms and was kissing her the second he had seen the painting.

Paxton smiled to himself as he walked by the Shadows Landing Historical Society. He wasn't the only one thinking of them together. He picked up his pace, excited to get back to Tinsley and it wasn't just because of the painting. Paxton had to be tough when dealing with dangerous gangs, but Tinsley would just roll her eyes and his tough act dissolved in a heartbeat. The question was, did he want to see what would happen if he pushed her in another way?

Yes, he wanted to see that very badly. But, even though he acted otherwise, he did have a heart and he wouldn't hurt Tinsley for anything. That meant even protecting her from him. He couldn't risk them starting something only to have him leave on assignment. That would be cruel and he'd never do that to Tinsley.

"Hello, young man."

Paxton smiled at the polar-opposite pair of old ladies walking toward him. One looked like a plucked chicken, all pale, thin, and wrinkly. The other was darker-skinned and perfectly rounded. Yet, they both had the same curious look in their eyes as they took him in.

"Good evening, ladies." Paxton smiled at them as he continued walking. He might be a tough as nails federal agent, but he wasn't stupid. There wasn't anything scarier than a granny gang. They would trip you with their sweetness, then cajole you into spilling your guts for a casserole. There was one such granny gang in Atlanta who had served as his confidential informants. And he wasn't fooling himself to think only he got information from them. No, they strangled every last bit of information from him with the pretty scarf they'd knitted for him.

"We were just coming from knitting club when we saw someone new and thought we'd see if you needed any help," the chicken said as the warning bells went off in his head.

Danger, danger, danger flashed through his mind. Dear God, they had knitting needles and he smelled a chicken and cheese casserole.

"That's very nice of y'all, but I have to get going. Have a nice night, ladies."

Paxton faked to the right and rolled to the left before slamming into a lady with a blouse embroidered with cats all over it.

"I'm so sorry," Paxton muttered.

"He's new, Mitzi," the chicken lady called out.

"Oh, you're new!" Mitzi said, her eyes lighting up like a

cat that spotted a little red laser dot smack in the middle of Paxton's forehead.

Paxton looked up and saw more old women, a hulking mountain of a man, and was that America's Sweetheart stepping out of the church's front door? The granny gang was growing. He was out of time.

"Lovely to meet you," Paxton said and then he ran.

He zigged and zagged like a professional running back, outmaneuvering the defense until he slammed through the front door of the art gallery. He was breathing hard as he turned to look out the door. They were all shuffling toward him like a mob of zombie grannies. Paxton felt no regret at flicking the deadbolt closed, turning off the lights, and racing to the back room.

"Is everything okay?" Tinsley asked worriedly when he shut and locked the door behind him.

"Yeah, didn't want the food to get cold." Paxton set down the bag and moved to the Bluetooth speaker. He turned up the music to hide the sound of the granny gang knocking on the front door. "Love this song," he said with a bright smile when Tinsley looked questioningly at him.

Tinsley unloaded the bag of food as he blared the music. Once the song was finally over and he didn't hear any more knocking, he turned the music down.

"There have been some robberies in Charleston," Paxton began to explain as he sat across from her at the artist table covered in smudges of old paint.

"I'm guessing art was the target since you're here," Tinsley said sarcastically.

Paxton smiled before biting into his sandwich. Sassy Tinsley was his favorite so far. "Ding, ding, we have a winner." Tinsley rolled her eyes and Paxton placed pictures of the art stolen in front of her as he explained their dead ends. "I'm hoping you know of some connection that we're missing."

Tinsley took the pictures and studied them closely. Paxton finished his sandwich and tried to guess what she saw in the pictures. "Can I see pictures of the houses and crime scenes?" Tinsley asked finally.

"Sure," Paxton said, handing her the photos she'd asked for.

He watched as she leaned forward and nibbled on her bottom lip as she examined the photos. Then she nodded to herself and sat back in her chair. "They were targeted art thefts. The jewelry was just a bonus. This was all about taking these specific paintings."

"What? How do you know that?" Paxton asked, looking down at the photos again. How did she know that?

"These are quality paintings worth a lot of money, but they're not the only paintings these people owned." Tinsley picked up some of the photos and turned them around. "You can see where the stolen art was, but look around. There's other art left behind. The pieces that were taken are worth over ten thousand dollars each. The paintings left behind were between two and five thousand. Also, see this Manet here?"

Paxton looked at a Manet painting and then looked up at Tinsley. "Are you sure it's not a Monet?"

Tinsley reached across the table and punched his shoulder. Paxton couldn't keep the laugh in. He tossed his head back and laughed out loud. "I'm sorry, beautiful, but you're just too cute when you're mad so I couldn't resist."

He watched as her mouth dropped open and her eyes went comically wide. "Oh my gosh. You've been teasing me this whole time, haven't you? You knew the difference between Monet and Manet." Paxton grinned and Tinsley punched him again. "I can't believe you!"

"If you want to touch me, you're more than welcome to. You don't have to keep hitting me. Now, what were you saying about the Manet?" Paxton looked down at her small hands. What would they feel like running over his body?

"It's a reproduction. A very good one as I'm sure you know, but what's interesting is that they knew it, too. They specifically targeted the high-value paintings and left everything else behind. So, the question I would be asking is, who knew these three couples had these three very valuable pieces?"

"That is a very good question, Tinsley."

He had been teasing her. Unbelievable. Tinsley sat back as Paxton began looking over the case file. "Why did you tease me?"

"Hmm?" Paxton murmured as he looked back up at her. She hadn't meant to ask the question out loud, but now she was curious.

"Why did you tease me? Is it because you don't like working with me?" Tinsley's heart pounded as she waited for Paxton to answer.

His gray eyes locked onto hers and he frowned. "I did it at first because I didn't think we'd work well together and I wanted to put an end to it."

Tinsley's stomach dropped at the same time her temper soared. "Why would you think that? I can work with anyone!"

"But I can't," Paxton admitted. "I worked on violent gang cases. I don't play nice. I do what it takes to get the job done. I thought I'd send you running off in tears, but you stayed.

You challenged me. I respect that about you, Tinsley. I respect more than that. I respect all of you. Plus," Paxton leaned forward as if sharing a secret, "you're really sexy when you're fired up."

Tinsley felt herself blush from head to toe. When she looked into his eyes, it was like everything she thought she had known had been turned upside down. She realized that what she'd seen in his eyes wasn't annoyance. What Tinsley saw in Paxton's eyes was desire.

"Understand now?" Paxton asked. His deep voice seemed to reverberate through her whole body, sending off delightful sparks of lust.

Tinsley nodded before awkwardly clearing her throat. "So, what can I do to catch this art thief?"

4

Paxton had nothing on the thefts. The insurance investigators hadn't found anything either. That's why Paxton was in the office at six in the morning trying to figure out what these families had in common. They were all wealthy enough to afford expensive artwork. They had all been on vacation at the time of the thefts. But how did the thieves know about the art and the vacations? There were no common connections. They didn't attend the same churches, they weren't in the same charities, and none of them worked in the same industry.

Paxton pulled up the social media accounts for the owners of the first house. The husband's account was private, and Paxton couldn't see anything except for some photos he'd been tagged in. Okay, maybe he could find a connection between them there? Paxton opened tabs on all the homeowners looking for common friends or photos.

He began scrolling through the week of the robberies for each person and that familiar feeling on the back of his neck when he was onto something began tickling him. All the families who had been robbed had posted pictures of them on their vacations and tagged their locations. Sometimes it was the husband, sometimes it was the wife, and most of the time it was both. The wording, too, made it clear they were on vacation—not at home—and even gave the date they were coming back.

Paxton moved to the week before the robbery. There were public posts about counting down the days for their upcoming vacations. The further he scrolled back, the clearer it became. Photos of the owners with the expensive jewelry they just got, the rare painting, the new cars . . . they'd posted a picture of anything worth a good deal of money to social media.

Paxton gathered all the photographs from one couple and he was able to get an almost total view of their house. Each room and the valuables in them were right there for the world to see.

"Peter!" Paxton called out as he flung open his boss's door without knocking. "I got it."

Paxton was already back at his seat pulling up all the information by the time Peter walked to his desk. "Look, their whole lives are on social media. Most of these posts are public. Look at them collectively and what do you see?"

Peter looked over all the images and shook his head. "It's everything a thief needs to know, even a barely competent thief could clean them out. What time they have their morning coffee. What time their exercise classes are. When and where they're going on vacation and the whole freaking layout of their house with every valuable asset chronicled for the world to see."

"I've asked IT to run a scan for all Charleston residents on social media who have tagged themselves in certain locations," Paxton told him.

"Good. Let me know what you find."

. . .

It didn't take long for Paxton to get a list of people who were actively posting their current vacation photos. Now it was up to him to see if they had any art of value to steal.

Paxton's eyes were crossed, but two hours later he'd found two promising leads. With Peter's blessing, he was off to check them out. He drove over the bridge and into Mount Pleasant. It didn't take long to reach Sullivan's Island and the four million dollar beach house whose owners were currently away.

Paxton stopped across the street and looked at the sprawling house with sweeping staircases and a circular drive with a large water feature in the middle. A brand new Mercedes-Benz Sprinter was backed up to the garage. The sign on the side read in clear print *Palmetto Luxury Contractors*. A phone number and website were also listed. Paxton pulled up the website on his phone and saw a passable enough page. He then called the number listed. It rang but then he got the voicemail for Palmetto Luxury Contractors. Lots of people had construction done when they weren't at home, but something felt off to him. It was too coincidental.

Paxton checked his gun and then approached the house as casually as possible. He made it to the garage before seeing the first person. The man had on pressed khaki pants and a gray polo shirt with the company name embroidered in red across his heart. It wasn't the professional outfit that caught Paxton's attention. It was the sight of the snake tattoo on the man's arm. It was the same tattoo Paxton had painted onto his arm to prove his membership with the Myriad gang when he was undercover with them in Atlanta. This man was not part of the Atlanta gang, at least not someone he'd ever met. But that didn't mean he wouldn't know Paxton. He had hoped his scruffy appearance while undercover versus this clean-cut look was enough to confuse anyone.

"Can I help you?" the man asked as he walked out with a friendly smile on his face.

"Hey," Paxton smiled easily back at him. "I'm the Havishes' neighbor. They asked me to come water their plants while they're on vacation. So, are they finally re-doing their bathroom? They've talked about it forever."

"Yes. We're taking our measurements now. Maybe you can come back once we're done?" the man asked easily enough to Paxton.

"Can't. I have to get to the city for work. I won't be but a minute and I'll keep out of your way," Paxton began to walk past the man who was now looking a little nervous. He didn't look back as he took the stairs from the garage up to the first floor. Paxton's hand was already on his gun as he approached the open door.

The sound of boots walking toward the door in front of him and the sound of the door at the bottom of the stairs opening had Paxton pulling his weapon. He was trapped with someone coming up the stairs from behind and someone coming toward the door a few steps above him.

Paxton hurried up the last two stairs and put his ear to the door. The second the footfalls stopped on the other side, Paxton flung the door open as hard as he could.

The door slammed into the man on the other side as Paxton rushed through the open door, shut it, and threw the deadbolt while a second man groaned and held his hands to his nose.

In a blink of an eye, Paxton took in his surroundings. He was in a hallway. A guest room was to the left, and to the right was the rest of the first floor. The man going for his weapon had the same uniform as the man Paxton had locked downstairs and the same snake tattoo. Myriads in Charleston? Paxton didn't have time to think about what that meant.

The man moved for his weapon and Paxton aimed his gun at him. "FBI. Don't move or I'll shoot you," Paxton warned.

Leaning against the wall next to the man was a painting that had been taken down. That split second it took for Paxton to see the painting was all the man needed. The gang member pulled his weapon and aimed it at Paxton. Paxton didn't hesitate. He fired. The dead man dropped to the ground with the gun still in his hand.

Paxton heard the sound of the man in the stairwell take off for the garage and Paxton gave chase. The wooden stairs in the enclosed stairwell echoed as he ran down them, gun at the ready.

He burst into the garage in time to see the van speed out of the driveway. The man wasn't going to hang around hoping his buddy had killed Paxton and not the other way around. He was out of there, and Paxton heard the distant ringing of a cell phone from the top of the stairs. The getaway driver was getting whatever they'd already stolen free from the house and would then find out if his partner was alive.

Paxton raced down the long driveway to his car. The van slid to a stop down the road. Paxton heard the tires squeal against the hot asphalt. Then he heard a series of gunshots and the sound of the van peeling out.

Paxton reached the end of the driveway with sweat from the humid morning rolling down his face only to find his car shot to pieces. Both tires were flat and he looked up to see the van turning the corner and driving out of sight.

"Damn!" Paxton cursed as he pulled out his phone and called it into Peter.

Tinsley looked in the mirror and dabbed on concealer to cover the dark puffy bags under her eyes. She hadn't slept at all last night. Every time she closed her eyes, and even when they weren't closed, she thought of Paxton.

She'd been so excited to meet him that first time. Then let down because he'd been kind of a jerk. Not in the mean way, but in the arrogant way. It was like he enjoyed pushing her buttons, so she'd written him off as an annoyance she'd have to deal with since he was friends and coworkers with Peter Castle.

If you want to touch me, you're more than welcome to.

Over the hours of tossing and turning, Tinsley had realized something about herself. She'd always been the sweet one. Harper teased her about it, but her family always turned to her when they needed a kind word or help.

Tinsley stepped into the strappy, bright green sundress with just a tiny splatter of paint at the hem. Tinsley knew her life had changed because of what she'd learned about herself last night. She'd learned she wasn't just sweet. Not with the thoughts she had about Paxton last night.

There wasn't a single sweet thought to be had about him. No, there had been the urgent tearing of clothes, battling tongues, and demanding hands as Paxton seemed to push her harder and higher than she'd ever gone before. Sweet Tinsley was also very passionate Tinsley and there was no denying it.

Tinsley wasn't new to relationships. She'd been to college and had a few steady boyfriends in the past. She wasn't terribly experienced with sex, but she wasn't a novice either. That's why it surprised her when her dreams had been so . . . *charged*.

Before Harper married Dare, the two of them would talk about the men in their lives. Harper was a take-charge, no-embarrassment type woman. Tinsley had been envious of her sexual confidence. Harper had once asked her, "You paint with so many colors and so many emotions, how can you be so *vanilla*?"

Tinsley would bet if Harper had seen her dreams last night, Harper would faint with shock. Just thinking about the way they'd squeezed every bit of pleasure from each other in her dream left some of Tinsley's concealer running.

Tinsley fanned herself off and blamed it on the summer's heat and humidity as she left home for the gallery. There was one thing she couldn't wait to do—paint. She'd get all her feelings out on the canvas and then she'd stop thinking of Paxton Kendry.

Late that morning, Tinsley heard the soft chime go off in the front room of her gallery and set down her paintbrush. She looked at the canvas covered with bold colors. She could feel the energy leaping off the canvas.

"Hello?" a voice called from the front room.

"I'll be right there," Tinsley called back as she pulled the smock from her dress and rushed from the room.

She smiled as she walked into the front of the gallery to find a man looking at the art. His arms were clasped behind him. He was in slacks and a button-down shirt with the sleeves rolled up, exposing muscled arms.

"Can I help you with anything or answer any questions?" Tinsley asked from behind the man's back. He turned slowly and Tinsley blinked. She recognized him, but why? He was in his twenties with a pleasant smile, but then she saw it. The bottom of a snake tattoo on his upper arm was peeking out from the rolled-up sleeve and then the nagging memory became clear. He had come into Ellery's gallery the day Ellery went into labor.

"I sure hope so. I travel a lot for work and have always driven by here so I decided to stop and check out your gallery. It's beautiful," he said as he stood tall and smiled kindly at her. Normally it would put Tinsley at ease, but he was acting completely different from the last time she saw him and that sent off some warning bells.

"Thank you. I'm Tinsley Faulkner. I'm the owner." Tinsley held out her hand and he gently clasped her hand and shook it. The gentle clasp was completely unexpected from someone so muscled.

"Maurice. Maurice Smith."

"Nice to meet you. Are you looking for anything in particular?" Tinsley asked, getting ready to show him around the gallery. It was clear he didn't remember her, so she wasn't going to make him feel awkward about mentioning the last time they saw each other.

"Actually, I'm looking to sell some pieces. My grandmother is very ill and requires a full-time nurse. I'm unable to do it myself since I travel for work. However, my grandmother has an extensive art collection and has given me power of attorney to sell some of it to pay for her care."

Red flags, warning bells, and the sound of her instinct screaming "Stop!" went off all at once. *What is the painting he's selling?* The thought went through her mind right before she was going to tell him, "Thanks, but no thanks," to selling whatever it was. Then, suddenly Paxton popped into her mind and she knew what she was going to do.

"May I see the painting? I can tell you if it's something I could sell and what kind of price to expect from it." Tinsley stepped forward prepared to see the Hamburg he'd shown Ellery. Instead, he held out his phone and she looked down at a Castille. Not just any Castille either. It was one Ellery had sold from her gallery for a hundred thousand dollars a year ago.

"It's a Castille," Maurice said.

"Yes, I'm familiar with the artist." Tinsley tried to keep calm as she looked up at Maurice. "It's stunning. Do you have the provenance papers for it?"

She was expecting the interview to end now, but Maurice reached into his pocket and pulled out an envelope and handed it to her. Tinsley opened it up and looked for Ellery's signature, but it wasn't there. The papers were forged. The scary part was that they were forged very well. If it wasn't that she personally knew the provenance of this painting, she'd never have known it was stolen.

"Can you sell it?" Maurice asked.

Tinsley stared at the papers, trying to decide her next course. Timid Tinsley would say sorry. She couldn't. Maybe it was the lack of sleep or maybe it was because she wanted to be seen as more than nice, safe, predictable Tinsley, so she nodded her head.

"Yes, I can sell it. I'd be honored to."

"Do you think you can sell it fast? We need to buy a hospital bed and the nurse said she'd only wait a couple of weeks for us to decide if we can hire her." Tinsley glanced up at Maurice. He looked so sincere that it angered her.

"I think so. I have a large base of private buyers who have me keeping an eye out for special pieces. We can sign the paperwork if you wish to move forward."

"Paperwork?" Maurice asked as if he weren't prepared for that.

"Yes," Tinsley smiled pleasantly at him. "It authorizes me to sell it on your grandmother's behalf and keeps the provenance nice and clean. It also lays out a timeline, such as I have ninety days to sell it, and it also states what you're willing to sell the painting for as well as what my commission is. No gallery can sell artwork without it. Thanks, lawyers," Tinsley laughed.

"Of course. Let's do it. I really like you and think you'll treat this piece of my family well."

"Then follow me to the desk back here and I'll get everything in order." Tinsley walked to the sales desk and fought her desire to call Granger, the town's sheriff, or to text Paxton to get over here right away. Instead, she'd hand them their case with the thief literally signing on the dotted line.

"My commission is twenty-five percent of the sale price," Tinsley said as she reached into the folder to pull out a listing agreement. "If you could fill in all the contact information, I'll copy the provenance for you. I'll also need your power of attorney."

"I keep the provenance, right?" he asked as he took a seat.

"I keep the original to pass along to the buyer, but you'll keep the copy."

Maurice nodded as he picked up a pen. "I haven't done this before. I'm not familiar with how it works." He gave a self-deprecating laugh and Tinsley would have thought charming if she didn't know he was scamming her.

"I'm here to help. Fill that out and grab the painting while I try to figure out a sale price."

Maurice nodded as he went to work on the form. Tinsley took the paperwork and went into the office. She sent a text to Granger but didn't hear back so she sent one to Kord, Granger's deputy. Still nothing and now the bell had chimed twice, meaning Maurice was back with the painting.

"I have the painting," she heard Maurice call out.

Tinsley rushed from the office with the copies made. "Oh, it's just stunning. Castille is so bold that it just moves you."

"What do you think you can sell it for?"

Tinsley knew what it would go for. One hundred thousand or more. "Well, it depends. Do you want me to hold it for the best price or the fastest price?"

"Fastest," Maurice answered instantly.

"Castille goes from sixty thousand to four hundred thousand. This one would go for a hundred thousand, give or take twenty thousand, at top price."

"And for the fast price?" Maurice asked.

"Seventy or so."

"So, on the contract I'll authorize a sale from sixty thousand up?" Maurice asked as Tinsley took the painting from him and set it on an empty easel.

"I think you can get more than sixty, but if you want to put that as your bottom price, I will do everything I can to stay away from it. After all, the more I sell it for the more you make, plus the more I make." Tinsley thought he'd appreciate that and his broad smile showed he did.

"Deal. My grandma could really use the money so if you can sell it fast, that would be best."

"Bless her heart. I'll pray for her. If you need any more paintings sold, please let me know. I have a big database of private buyers who would love the first shot at paintings like this."

"That would be great. Thank you, Tinsley." Maurice shook her hand and left the gallery with a little pep to his step. Tinsley watched him go and felt a surge of satisfaction that she was going to take him down. Even though he was very polite, the fastest way you could get on Tinsley's bad side was to steal art. She locked the front door after him and pulled out her cell phone.

"Tinsley, I can't talk right now. I'm at a crime scene," Paxton said the second he answered the phone.

"Does this crime involve a stolen Castille?" Tinsley asked with a smile on her face. She knew by his silence she'd surprised him and that was just plain fun.

"How do you know that?" Paxton asked slowly. She heard the background noise fade as he walked someplace more private.

"Because I'm looking at it."

"I'm coming."

The line went dead and Tinsley's giggles evaporated into lust-filled clouds that stormed through her body. Paxton didn't know that what he'd just said had been featured prominently in her dreams last night. Or did he?

5

How the hell did Tinsley Faulkner have the Castille painting stolen from the Havish house he was still standing in? The Havish family had been called and given a tour of the house over videoconference. They confirmed that some jewelry and a Castille painting were missing. When Paxton stopped the Myriad member, he'd saved a million-dollar painting by Soulages from being stolen.

Paxton gunned the FBI SUV he'd taken from Peter out of Sullivan's Island. It wasn't only to get to Tinsley quickly because of his case. Last night Paxton had dreamt of nothing but her. What freaked him out was the fact they weren't lust-filled dreams. Well, some parts of them were, but the majority of his dreams had them in a relationship. He dreamed of them snuggled up on the couch, of him watching her paint, of him being . . . romantic. Then came the lust-filled part of the dream right before he woke up.

Honestly, he didn't know what to make of it. Then he'd heard Tinsley's gleeful voice saying she had the painting he was looking for, and he knew the man who stole it had probably been with her. Now his body and mind demanded he get to her immediately.

So he drove as fast as he could and only when he saw her through the gallery windows was he able to calm down. Paxton's breath caught in his throat when Tinsley's eyes locked on his through the windows and she smiled. He wanted her all for himself. He wanted to be the only one she smiled at in that way.

Now was not the time for his demanding side to come out. No, he wouldn't do that to Tinsley. First, she was just too sweet to be with someone like him. She'd probably run screaming from the room if he told her a quarter of the things he wanted to do with her. Second, even if he could be abrasive at times, he wasn't an asshole. He would never purposely hurt a woman. He wasn't going to be in Charleston much longer, if he had his way, and the last thing he wanted to do was lead Tinsley on about a possible relationship then hurt her when he transferred back to Atlanta. Too bad his libido wasn't listening to his brain.

Paxton headed into the gallery to find Tinsley practically bouncing from foot to foot. He wanted to groan with frustration because she was so freaking beautiful. She was practically glowing with excitement.

"What did the man look like who came in here?" Paxton demanded. Fear that he was still nearby or that it could be someone who had recognized him from his undercover work made the question come out harsher than he intended.

"About this tall," Tinsley said, holding up her hand to indicate his height, which was a good six inches taller than the man at the Havish house. "Clean cut. His hair was black and tightly trimmed to frame his face. No facial hair.

Business casual dress. Oh, and he drove a luxury sedan, but I didn't get the plate number."

Definitely not the same man from earlier in the day. The painting must have been handed off to this man and the jewelry to another. Both would then be sold immediately to increase the chance of getting money before a police report could be filed.

"Here it is." Tinsley moved aside as she pointed to the Castille painting behind her.

"Tell me everything," Paxton demanded as they stood in front of the painting.

Tinsley told him about Maurice, the sick grandmother, and the fact she'd seen him pull this act before with a Hamburg in Charleston. "Did Ellery sell the Hamburg?"

Tinsley shook her head. "He didn't have any papers and Ellery went into labor. I don't know what happened to it."

Paxton turned his phone around. "Was it this one?"

"Yeah, how did—it's stolen, right?" Tinsley was bouncing again from foot to foot as she put the pieces together.

"Yeah, it hasn't been seen since March. Now, please tell me you got a phone number or something for this guy."

Tinsley reached down onto her desk and handed him a bunch of papers. "I got all of his information. Though I don't know if any of it's legit. I have copies of the fake power of attorney for this sick grandmother, but more importantly, I got the original faked provenance. And the best part? I set myself up as his art dealer for the stolen goods. I'm the inside woman!"

Paxton's head shot up from where he was reviewing the documents. "No."

"Yes! It's perfect. Maybe I can recover all of the stolen art."

Paxton felt nerves fire warning signals all through his body. "This isn't a game, Tinsley. I just came from a shootout with the man who is probably working with this Maurice guy. Just because it's stolen art and not drugs doesn't mean it's not dangerous. You've done a great job, but now it's time for you to sit at home and let me do my thing."

He saw her hands go to her hips as she stopped bouncing from foot to foot. "Excuse me? Did you just tell me to go home and twiddle my thumbs while the men take care of this?"

"Did you miss the part where I just had a shootout and had to kill someone? Plus, if you were at my home, the last thing you'd be doing is twiddling your thumbs." Crap, he was losing it. She flushed red and Paxton had to take a breath because that came out way too suggestive. "It's dangerous, Tinsley. I want to protect you. That's all."

"That's not all you want."

Paxton groaned and Tinsley sputtered.

"That's not what I meant!" Tinsley's hands were back on her hips and her face was cherry-red, but she wasn't backing down. "I meant you don't think I'm strong enough to pull this off. Well, screw you. I am. I'm not sweet little Tinsley. Well, I am, but I'm so much more than that. I had Maurice Smith eating out of the palm of my hand because everyone thinks of me as you do."

"I hope not. I don't know if I could beat them all up," Paxton muttered.

"What?"

"Nothing. Go on, Tinsley. Tell me, how do I think of you? Be descriptive," Paxton challenged.

"That I'm not strong enough, that I'm not smart enough, that I'm not tough enough, and that I'm not brave enough.

Well, I am. I am set up perfectly for this sting and I'm going to do it. If you don't let me, I bet Peter will."

Paxton felt his brow crease as he looked down at Tinsley. "That's what you think I think of you?"

"You told me so yourself."

"I admit that's what I first thought, but it took all of twenty seconds to throw that impression out the window. Tinsley," Paxton said, stepping close enough to her that she had to tilt her head back to look up at him. He reached out and gently clasped her upper arms, almost willing her to believe him. "The only reason I don't want you involved is that it's dangerous. I don't want anything to hurt you, ever. I think, *I know*, you're perfectly capable of pulling this off. You're one of the smartest people I know. I just couldn't live with myself if you were hurt in any way."

Her mouth opened, then closed, then opened again. "Oh." Then the stubborn look was back. "I still want to do it."

Paxton's mind went through all the scenarios until he landed on one he could live with. "Fine, sell the painting. But you just hired a new employee. You won't be alone for one minute. Deal?"

The bright smile Tinsley showed him warmed his heart. He wanted more—more smiles, more Tinsley. No, what he wanted was his old job in Atlanta. Wasn't it?

Tinsley watched Paxton leave and immediately went to paint. Emotions swirled like the colors on the canvas. She understood Paxton now. He was like her cousin Ryker. Ryker had changed so much after what happened all those years ago. He didn't share his thoughts or feelings. Instead he thrived off living in the shadows as someone so tough and powerful that no one dared to cross him. Well, except the family. They still teased him. And they still loved him. And they still waited for that day the old Ryker would come back.

It was the same with Paxton. Underneath that gruff voice and hard stare was a kind heart who wanted to protect the innocent, just like Ryker. Everything made so much more sense now.

Her painting became less chaotic as she smoothed out the rough edges and added just a hint of lightness to the darkness. She stepped back and smiled at herself. She knew what she was dealing with now, and she almost felt sorry for Paxton. Almost.

Day after tomorrow, their adventure would start and she'd find a way to slip in under Paxton's defenses so she could get to know him. It was a desire that took root in her heart and wasn't about to let go. She needed to be the one who saw the real Paxton because she had a feeling when she did, it would change their lives.

She'd give Paxton a couple of days to get used to the town and the gallery. Then she'd call Maurice and tell him they had a buyer. It was the perfect plan.

Tinsley took a deep breath and looked at the clock. The sun had set long ago, but she'd been lost in painting. Time ceased to exist. She had a finished painting and, hopefully, with her emotions on the canvas, she had a full night's sleep ahead of her, too.

"You think it's a good idea to bring Tinsley in like this?" Paxton asked Peter as he shut down his computer for the night.

"I do. She knows the art business better than anyone. If the thieves look into her, she's legit, and she's so sweet no one would guess she's helping gather evidence to take them down. Plus you'll be there to keep her safe," Peter reassured.

Paxton shook his head. Peter wasn't supposed to let a civilian consultant help. It was Paxton's last shot at keeping Tinsley out of the operation. "Would you let Karri help in this situation?"

Peter shrugged. "Karri doesn't know anything about art so I don't think she'd be very helpful."

"You know what I mean."

"I do, and that makes me curious as to why you equated Tinsley to my long-term, very serious girlfriend." Peter crossed his arms over his chest and waited for an answer. When Paxton didn't answer, Peter grinned. "You like her. Unbelievable. I thought you couldn't stand her."

"She's a distraction and I don't plan to be in Charleston long enough to be distracted."

Peter snorted. "Sorry, Pax, but you're not going back to Atlanta. I know you think you will, but the writing is on the wall. You've been kicked out of VGTF permanently. This is your life now."

Paxton muttered a curse word under his breath. He wasn't going to give up. That promotion should have been his. "It doesn't make sense. I was closing in on the biggest up-and-coming gang leader on the Eastern seaboard. That promotion was mine."

"Maybe you pissed off the wrong people." Peter paused before asking, "Is it really so bad here? You're not getting shot at . . . well, that often. You have a pretty awesome boss. Plus, now you can have the girl. Think about it. I'll see you in the office tomorrow to get everything ready for you to take to Shadows Landing. Goodnight."

Paxton leaned back in his office chair. Was it so bad to be in Charleston? The food was outstanding. The people were laid back. There was no confusion over which Peachtree Street to go down. But he'd built his entire career around being the biggest, baddest undercover agent around. He knew gangs backward and forward. He lived and breathed their way of life, their criminal activities, and their rivalries. He did it all to make the country safer. He enjoyed the intellectual challenge aspect of art crimes, but he wasn't advancing himself here.

Although, he could have the girl.

6

Tinsley turned on the soft music in her gallery as she got ready for the day. Paxton would start working for her tomorrow morning and today she was going to make a list of things she needed to be done.

With a smirk to herself, she got to work on the list. Changing the hard-to-reach light bulbs. There was a crack in the back wall that needed a touchup. Tinsley tapped her pen to her lip and wondered how Paxton was with plumbing. Oh, she knew he thought he was coming in here as a sales associate, but she had a better idea.

The bells above the door chimed, drawing her from her thoughts. She sat at the sales table in the back of the room that afforded her a view of the entire gallery. No, no, no. What was Maurice doing here?

"Mr. Smith," Tinsley said, standing up. "It's a pleasure to see you so soon. What can I do for you?" Tinsley's eyes went to the second man who entered. She recognized him as Maurice's partner that day in Ellery's gallery. Only, like Maurice, he'd received a makeover.

Maurice smiled and stepped forward to shake her hand.

"Tinsley, meet my brother, Murray, and please call me Maurice."

Tinsley shook the man's hand, but he didn't speak. Instead, he deferred to Maurice.

"Have you heard from your private buyer?" Maurice asked.

"I've sent the information to her and I'm just waiting to hear back. She was very interested." Tinsley tried to smile as if she were excited. It was one thing when she was here with just Maurice, but now she was outnumbered. If things went badly . . .

"Excellent. I told Murray I had faith in you and we've decided to sell some more paintings to hire an additional nurse for our grandmother. Would you be up for that?"

"Of course," Tinsley said as her heart galloped in her chest. More stolen art? How much more? Maybe Paxton was right. She was getting in dangerous territory here.

"Murray," Maurice motioned and Murray walked out of the gallery. Maurice turned back to her and smiled in a way that made her a little nervous because she felt as if he were testing her. "Now, some of these we've had appraised, but I'd like your take on them. I feel like we're a lot of old families —asset rich, cash poor. I hate to part with them, but it's the only way to pay for things."

Tinsley nodded. "You're not the first to hire me for that very reason. I'll do what I did the last time. I'll tell you the range you can expect to get for them. I may have to do a little research. As much as I wish I knew the value of every painting ever painted, it's not always the case."

The door opened and Murray came in carrying two portfolio cases. "Where should I put these?"

"Right here," Tinsley said as she moved to clear off the desk. Murray set them down and stepped back. Tinsley tried not to shake as she reached out to slowly unzip them. The instant she saw the first painting, she knew she was in deep.

Tinsley slipped on the protective white gloves she kept in her desk and carefully moved the paintings to examine each of them. It was strange holding the art she'd just seen in the FBI files. Now she just needed to pretend to have never seen them before.

"Your grandmother has an exquisite collection. I know some of these off the top of my head, but if you give me a moment, I can give you a range for the others." Right now all Tinsley wanted to do was get to her phone and text Paxton.

"Tell us what you know right now. Then we can fill out the paperwork while you do your research," Maurice told her. He tried to make it seem like a suggestion, but she knew it wasn't.

Tinsley looked from one painting to the next and told him what she knew of them. A couple of them she pretended not to know so it wasn't obvious she had literally just read about them in the FBI files.

"Excellent," Maurice said, satisfied after Murray gave a slight nod of approval. "We'd like you to sell these. Price them to sell quickly, but don't give up too much money. Nothing is too good for our grandmother. We want her to have the absolute best care."

"I'm honored you're entrusting me with this. I'll do all I can to get the best possible price." Tinsley handed the paperwork to Maurice and he handed over the forged provenances. "I'll make a copy and then get to work on the research. Feel free to take a look around the gallery while you wait."

Murray looked down at his watch and shook his head. "We can only wait ten minutes. We have to get to work."

"Do you two work together?" Tinsley then realized she

shouldn't have asked criminals what they did for a living. "I don't know if I could work with my brother." Tinsley gave a little giggle and saw the men relax. Yup, sweet, unassuming Tinsley is all everyone ever saw.

"It has its moments," Murray said as Maurice filled out the paperwork.

"I bet. I'll be right back," Tinsley said as she headed straight for the back office. She had just put the stack of papers onto the auto feeder when Murray filled the doorway. Tinsley wanted to curse because she'd been about to reach for her cell phone when the large shadow filled the room.

"Did you go to college for this stuff?" Murray asked as Tinsley was forced to take a seat and start the research on the couple of pieces she'd pretended not to know.

"I did. I just love pretty things and nothing is prettier than art." Tinsley felt stupid even saying it, but it was clear Murray was scoping her out. The last thing she wanted was for him to become suspicious of her. "I'm also an artist. That's my main focus. I paint."

"Then how do you have these private contacts?" Murray asked, not being able to hide the suspicion in his voice.

"If you can think of a cause, I'm on a charity for it. Being a debutante opens up a world of networking. Shadows Landing is too small to have a come-out, but I came out in Charleston and am very active in the charity scene there. You wouldn't believe the contacts I have just from the garden club," Tinsley told him with a conspiratorial wink. She saw Murray nod his head and then look back down at his watch. "So, what do you see for the two paintings?"

Tinsley looked down at her computer. "Both would sell from fifteen to twenty thousand."

"Good. We have a deal then, Miss Faulkner. My brother

said he was happy with your knowledge and contacts. If you can sell the Castille this week, we have a lot more art for you to sell. You may be a painter, but we can make you very rich as an art dealer."

Tinsley stood up with a smile and smoothed her skirt down. "I look forward to it. I have no doubt I can sell that painting by then. What other art would you have for me?"

"Our grandmother's entire art collection. She was an avid collector. Maurice and I don't know much about it. If it can help pay for her care, we'd rather sell it."

"I'm happy to help in any way I can."

Maurice appeared then with the signed contracts. The paperwork was concluded and before Tinsley could even reach for her cell phone, Murray and Maurice were gone.

Tinsley's hands were shaking with adrenaline and nerves as she picked up her phone and sent a text to Paxton. *How fast can you get here?*

Paxton texted back immediately. *I can be there in thirty if it's an emergency. Otherwise I'll be there tomorrow morning.*

Tinsley walked out into the gallery and snapped a picture of the paintings and sent it to him. She didn't have to wait long for Paxton's text. *I'll be there in two hours. Know of a place I can stay for the next while?*

Tinsley put her finger on the phone and was going to suggest her place only to start and stop typing no less than five times. *I'll ask around.*

See you soon, beautiful.

Tinsley stared at the text for way longer than she should. Then, taking a deep breath, she locked up the gallery and hit up the lunch crowd across the street at Harper's bar.

She had thought of the apartment above the bar, but Harper's bartender, Georgina, was living there. Then she thought of Trent's house, which was near hers. He'd moved out and into a home he'd bought with his wife on the other side of town. However, Karri Hill, Peter Castle's girlfriend, was renting it. Her cousin Ryker had a guesthouse, but that would take a lot of bribing and threats to get. The last option was the Bell family. They had an old family mansion that they had turned into a bed and breakfast.

Tinsley pushed open the heavy wooden door to the bar and was immediately overcome by air conditioning and the smell of freshly fried food. It made her mouth water as she looked around the bar.

"Howdy, Miss Tinsley," Gator said. He was a mountain of a man in overalls and a South Carolina COCKS hat. He was aptly named, considering the man was the town's alligator removal expert.

"Hi, Gator. Have y'all seen any of the Bells?"

"Gage is right over there," Gator answered with a nod of his head.

Gage and Maggie Bell were the children of the owners of the bed and breakfast. Gage was named after a twelve-gauge shotgun, and Maggie's full name was Magnum. Their parents were avid shooters and Gage and Maggie had followed in their footsteps. Maggie was an Olympic silver medalist, and Gage had made the men's Olympic team, but placed fourth in shooting.

Tinsley walked around the corner of the wall and found Gage sitting at a tableful of men. Several were in their early twenties to Gage's mid-twenties. Then there were a couple of men who looked to be in their thirties and finally a man who looked to be in his forties.

"I'm sorry to interrupt," Tinsley said, coming to stand near Gage.

"Tinsley, no apology necessary. Guys, this is my friend

Tinsley Faulkner. She's the artist who owns the gallery across the street. Tinsley, these are my Olympic teammates."

"Oh, wow. It's nice to meet y'all."

"Maggie and I are hosting the men's and women's shooting teams this week. We're getting in a ton of practice at the estate and then time for team building," Gage said proudly.

Tinsley smiled at the men even as she felt herself groan inwardly. "I take it you're all full up for the week then?"

Gage's smile fell. "Not a couch to spare. I'm sorry, did you need a room?"

"Yes, but don't worry about it."

"I'll text you some B&Bs that are in Charleston."

"Thanks, Gage. Y'all have a great retreat week."

Tinsley walked back to the bar and pulled herself up onto the worn barstool. She sent a text to Ryker but didn't hold out hope that he'd agree. He was very guarded about his privacy. He'd let Trent's wife, Skye, stay in the guest house. But that was an anomaly. And just as she thought, she got a text back from Ryker that simply said *No*.

"Here you go, Miss Tinsley," Skeeter said from the stool next to her. He slid a shot glass toward her. Tinsley looked down at it and back up at Skeeter. He was a skinny guy who wore clothing two sizes too big for him. "You look like you need this."

"Skeeter, it's too early for vodka."

"Georgie," Skeeter called out as the young bartender came over with a beaming smile that seemed way too happy, considering her living in the apartment upstairs was causing Tinsley the pain she was in right now. "Orange juice, please."

Georgina poured a glass and handed it to him. Skeeter

poured the vodka into it. "There. It's one of them fancy mixed drinks now."

Tinsley laughed. What else was she to do? In less than two hours she was going to tell the man who burned up her dreams that he was going to be staying in the bedroom next to hers. She wasn't going to sleep again until Paxton Kendry was out of her house. Even then it was debatable, considering the way he took over her dreams.

"Thanks, Skeeter." Tinsley took the drink and chugged it down.

She slid from the barstool and pulled her shoulders back. She was walking into war. Not with the thieves, but with her heart.

7

"What do you mean I'm staying at your place?" Paxton asked again. He'd been working for the past hour setting up hidden cameras in the art gallery when Tinsley dropped that little bomb. It wasn't bad. In fact, it was an answer to his prayers. However, he had a case to solve and lying in a bed just one thin wall away from Tinsley—who made him question everything he thought he knew about his life goals —wasn't going to make things easy.

Tinsley plastered on a smile that was way too perky to be real. "The B&B is all filled up for the week. The Olympic shooting team is there. It would be unpatriotic to kick them out. The only other place is my house. I have a guest room. It's not like we'd have to share a bed."

Paxton raised an eyebrow and watched as Tinsley turned bright red. "That's too bad. Are you sure you have the spare room available? I don't mind doubling up."

Tinsley sputtered. He could see her struggling between being shy and not backing down from him. Paxton eagerly waited to see which side won out.

"I'm sure you wouldn't want me to be on top of you like that. Personal space-wise, I mean." Tinsley blinked her eyes innocently and Paxton wanted to simultaneously groan in sexual frustration and applaud her for not backing down from him. It was seriously the biggest turn-on of his life when a woman got him. Most didn't. Tinsley did. The fact that she was so nice only turned him on more. He wondered if anyone else knew she had this naughty, playful side. Then he realized he hoped they didn't. He wanted to be the only one to see this side of her.

"I don't mind. I'm flexible. I can be on top, too." Paxton loved the way her eyes dropped down and then flew back up. What she was thinking was written all across her face and he'd be happy to fulfill every single thought she had.

Finally, Tinsley shook her head. "You're teasing me again."

"More like feeling you out."

Her mouth dropped open and then she snapped it closed. "And they say women are confusing," she muttered before walking away.

Tinsley closed the office door and looked at her phone. She bit her lip and finally reached for it. "Hey, Tins. What's up?"

"Hi, Ridge. I have a question for you," she said to her brother.

"What's up?"

"Do you have a spare room for someone to stay?"

"Well, I have a spare room, but it's filled with a whole bunch of things Savannah bought for a house she's decorating. There's about a two-foot-wide path through it. Why?"

"No reason. Just a friend needing a place to stay."

"You have a guest room," Ridge pointed out.

"I do. I guess he can stay there."

"He?"

Tinsley rolled her eyes. "Yes, he."

"Wait! Is this the same guy seen going into the gallery late last night?" Ridge asked.

"What?"

"The knitting club was letting out and Dare said some of them cornered a guy with takeout. He ran into the gallery and locked them out."

"He did what?" Tinsley screamed loud enough for Paxton to come bursting into the room. "You ran from the knitting club and then locked them out of the gallery last night?"

"The granny gang? Hell yeah, I did. There is nothing scarier than a granny gang. They rip confidential information from you faster than waterboarding," Paxton told her.

"Is that him? Tinsley? Who is this guy you're with?" Ridge yelled over the phone.

"Um, bye, Ridge. Love you." Tinsley hung up the phone and grimaced. "So, my brother might be a problem. He still thinks I'm ten and the idea of a guy staying with me as gotten him a little ... miffed."

Paxton didn't look worried. "It'll be fine. He'll like me. I'm a guy's guy."

"You're scared of a knitting club," Tinsley reminded him.

"And you aren't?"

Okay, he might have her there, but he didn't need to know that. Tinsley was about to deny it when the front door flew open so hard it slammed shut on its own.

"Tinsley! Ridge called me and told me to get over here."

"I'm back here, Harper. I'm fine."

Her cousin charged in with her long hair in a ponytail, jeans, and boots that could kick a door down. She looked at Tinsley standing behind her desk and then over at Paxton standing next to her. A slow smile spread across her face. "Gotcha. Dinner tonight at the bar. Both of you."

Then she spun around and left. It was then Tinsley noticed the knife in her hand.

"What was that about?" Paxton asked.

Tinsley shrugged and batted her eyes innocently. Her brother had now brought in the whole family to save Tinsley from the big, bad man sleeping in her house. Good thing she didn't tell Ridge about the whole "being on top of each other" thing. "No idea. Now, what else needs to be done before dinner?"

Paxton and Tinsley worked for the next two hours getting everything set up for this undercover operation. Hidden cameras were aimed at each door. Alarms were installed on all of the doors and windows. More hidden cameras covered the entire interior of the gallery from multiple angles. Tinsley would be safe. The second Maurice and Murray returned, they'd be on camera from enough angles to make a 3-D rendering of them.

However, the closer to dinnertime, the more and more nervous Tinsley acted.

"Hey, Tinsley," Paxton called as he stepped down from the ladder.

"Yeah?" she said as she turned off the lights in the back of the gallery.

"Does everyone call you Tins?"

"My close friends and family do. Do you have a nickname?"

"I've had several undercover identities so if I happen to run across anyone from a past investigation, I have to be ready to answer to anything. Most of my coworkers call me Kendry."

"Harper, my cousin who told us to come to dinner, is married to Dare who was undercover with the ATF when they met. I'm sure you'll meet him tonight. However, you might be afraid of him."

Paxton scoffed. He wasn't afraid of much. "I'm not too worried about an ATF agent."

"He's in the knitting club."

Yikes.

Paxton followed Tinsley into Harper's bar. When he opened the door for her, his eyes widened at the bullets still lodged in the thick wood. What the heck happened here? Shadows Landing wasn't a hotbed of crime, was it?

"Hey, Tins!"

Tinsley waved at the young bartender, but the welcoming committee at the Faulkner table wasn't so friendly. Everyone just stared at Paxton. Even when they hugged Tinsley, they were staring at him with narrowed eyes. What the heck had she told them about him?

"So, you must be the guy scared of a couple of old ladies," a large man with dark hair asked as he smirked at Paxton.

Paxton didn't say anything. Instead he looked for a friendly face. The friendliest was Harper, who sat next to the man who had just spoken. That must be Dare.

"Harper, it's nice seeing you again."

She smiled at him, but it wasn't welcoming. It was like a cat toying with a mouse. "And here I sit not knowing your name."

"Oh, sorry," Tinsley said, jumping in. "Y'all, this is Paxton Kendry. He's the art crime agent who works with Peter. Paxton, you've met Harper. That's her husband, Dare Reigns, next to her. Then that's my cousin Gavin. He's the only doctor in town. His wife, Ellery, is holding their sweet boy, Chase. Then there's my cousin Trent and his wife, Skye."

Paxton nodded his hello. Peter had told him all about Trent and America's Sweetheart, Skye Jessamine. She was best friends with Peter's girlfriend, Karri.

"Then this is my cousin Wade. He's with the Coast Guard and his wife, Darcy, is a treasure hunter. Then this is my other cousin, Ryker Faulkner," Tinsley continued.

Paxton noticed she didn't mention what Ryker did. She didn't need to. Ryker's name was quietly whispered as one of the most powerful businessmen in the world.

"Then this is my brother, Ridge. He's a builder of amazing designs. And this is my sister-in-law, Savannah. She has the interior decorating business above my gallery."

"It's nice to meet you all. I feel as if I already have from what Peter's told me," Paxton said as Tinsley took a seat next to Dare, leaving Paxton to sit next to Ridge. Great. The glare he was receiving from Ridge didn't take a detective to figure out. Ridge was not happy that his sister had a man in her life, even if he wasn't technically with her like that yet. Wait, yet? Paxton paused and thought about. Yeah, yet. Atlanta was suddenly not looking like the ultimate goal. The agitated woman sitting next to him was looking a lot more interesting.

"What are you doing with Tinsley, and why are you staying at her house?" Ridge asked bluntly.

"Ridge," Tinsley hissed, but her brother ignored her censure.

"I'm here on a case. That's all I can say."

"What does my sister have to do with it?" Ridge asked. It was clear he wasn't going to let anything go.

"She's helping me with the case. I assume you know how smart your sister is and how knowledgeable she is about art. She's a big asset to the case."

It was the truth and the look on Tinsley's face—as if he'd just hung the moon—was worth expressing more feelings than he was used to doing. It also helped that Savannah smiled at him and Darcy sent Ellery a not-so-subtle grin. He was winning over some of her family—a family he knew meant everything to her.

"I know all about how wonderful my sister is. Any man would be lucky to be with her, but a man who is just using her for a case—" Ridge didn't get a chance to finish. Tinsley slammed her hand on the table and Paxton found it interesting that everyone seemed surprised by her reaction. She'd slammed things, yelled at him, and then looked at him as if she wanted to devour him. Tinsley was full of passion, so why did her family look so surprised?

"Stop it! Nothing is going on between us. This is for work. I'm trying to catch an art thief here. So knock it off," Tinsley ground out between clenched teeth as she tried to keep her voice low so people didn't overhear her.

"Yet," Paxton added, knowing he had a death wish. Ryker's cold gaze slid over him. Paxton was pretty sure the devil himself couldn't produce such a stare. Ridge, on the other hand, looked like he was ready to explode.

Tinsley turned slowly to stare at him with heat in her

eyes. He loved it. She was a mixture of disbelief and a little bit of hope.

"What did you say?" Tinsley asked slowly.

"I said yet. Nothing is going on between us . . . *yet*."

"You do not touch my sister!" Ridge grabbed Paxton's arm and then suddenly a sharp whistle silenced the entire bar. Paxton looked over at Ellery as she stood with the baby in her arms and smiled sweetly.

"Ridge, let go of Paxton. Ryker, call off the assassin you probably just ordered. The last time I checked, Tinsley is an adult. She can do whatever, or *whomever*, she wants. She'll ask for our help if she needs it. Now, Paxton, Chase is a little fussy. Can you take him for a little walk around the bar to calm him down?"

Ellery made it sound like she was asking, but she wasn't. She shoved the baby into his arms and then made a shooing motion with her hands. What the hell would he do with a baby? Maybe carry it like a rifle? Paxton shifted the baby in his arms and secured him before standing up. He looked down and saw a look on Tinsley's face that knocked him over. Pure desire.

"Chase, I think you and I are going to be great friends," he murmured before strolling off with the baby.

Sweet magnolia, Tinsley had never seen a sexier sight than Paxton at that moment.

"Now that the distraction is gone," Ellery said, taking the seat Paxton had vacated, "Tinsley, what's up and what do you need us to do?"

Tinsley sent an appreciative smile to Ellery before telling them about the case. Everyone listened with frowns on their faces until the end. No one looked happy, and it made Tinsley fidget with her fingers.

"You're telling me those criminals have been in your gallery twice now?" Ridge asked with anger lacing his voice. "And you didn't call me?"

"I called the FBI, Ridge," Tinsley reminded him, as patiently as she could manage.

"And you're sure they're the same two who were in my shop when I went into labor?" Ellery asked.

"Yes."

"So, Paxton is going undercover in your gallery so that he can keep you safe and catch these guys?" Savannah asked.

"Exactly. There are hidden cameras all over the place. And now that Paxton is staying with me, I'll be protected at all times."

Ryker looked up from his phone and glanced over to Paxton bouncing a happily gurgling Chase in his arms. "He was undercover with the FBI's Violent Gangs Task Force, Tinsley. He's not a nice man. Nice men can't slip into gang life. Hell, he was shot three times when his cover was blown. His file is riddled with complaints against him for not listening to his superiors."

"Did you just run a background check on him? How did you get into his work file?" Tinsley was upset on Paxton's behalf. "No one in the family questioned when Dare started dating Harper, and Dare is in the same line of work. Why are you doing this when I'm not even dating Paxton?"

"Because he wants to date you," Ridge said angrily as he leaned around his wife to look at her. "And because he's not good enough for you. Dare and Harper fit. They have the same no-nonsense personality. You're too sweet for Paxton. It's like he's the big bad wolf eyeing Little Red Riding Hood to gobble her up. You're the nice one, Tins. You deserve a nice guy who won't bring criminals to your doorstep."

"You do know that Little Red Riding Hood was a story to scare women into what men decided was good moral behavior, right?" Tinsley told her brother. "That the only way you'll stay pure is to stay on the path, otherwise you die? However, before the modern take on it, there were some stories where Little Red Riding Hood outsmarted the wolf. So, do you think I'm the dumb one who can't tell a wolf in a hat or the other one who can use her intelligence to escape the bad guy?"

"You know what I mean, Tinsley," Ridge said with a roll of his eyes.

"Tinsley," Harper said, leaning toward her. "You don't need anyone's permission to be with Paxton if that's what you want. I just want to make sure you're safe from these criminals. What do we need to do to make sure you are safe?"

Tinsley shot an appreciative look at her cousin. "Paxton is going undercover at the gallery. I need you all to act as if he's been working there all this time so the guys don't get spooked before we can get our hands on the entire stolen collection."

"I'm happy to help in any way," Darcy told her with a wink.

"Me too. I can be sure to stop by as much as I can. If you need me, I'll be right upstairs."

"I don't know if you'd need it, but I'm good with makeup or getting you any kind of movie prop," Skye offered.

"Thank you all." Tinsley smiled at the women in her family. At least they had her back.

"I don't like this," Ridge muttered.

"Me neither," Ryker said, crossing his arms over his

chest. "However, you're always the first to offer help, so it's time we all paid you back for that. I'm here for you, Tins. Anything you need at any time. Well, except for my house. I have business associates coming in tomorrow."

"Thanks, Ryker." Now Tinsley had her family on her side, she just needed to get everyone else on it. Tomorrow was the Summer Shadows Street Fair. That would be the perfect time to introduce Paxton to the town.

8

Paxton was quiet as Tinsley showed him around her place. It suited her. It was warm and cozy with a bold side, just like Tinsley herself. She hadn't said anything about her family except they were all willing to help if Paxton needed it. However, she'd been contemplative since they settled down for the night.

Paxton stepped into the living room and on to the couch next to her. Tinsley might be quiet, but there was a stubborn set to her face that let him know that the wheels in her mind were turning. Her family was overprotective of her. He knew that, but surely they knew Paxton would never allow anyone to hurt Tinsley. If they'd known the things he'd had to do while undercover with the gang in Atlanta, they'd realize he'd do anything to keep her safe.

Or maybe that was it. He was too rough, too demanding, too everything for Tinsley. He knew what it was. "I take it your family isn't thrilled about me being here with you?"

Paxton slid his arm along the back of the couch and cupped her shoulder with his hand. He gave her a little nudge, and it surprised him when Tinsley instantly reacted and scooted closer to him. She leaned against his side and rested her head on his shoulder as she stared out the living room windows.

"You could say that. They think there's more going on than there is," Tinsley admitted. "They're also worried about my safety."

"I'd never let anyone hurt you, Tinsley."

"I know," Tinsley said instantly, and Paxton felt a calming warmth settle over him. She trusted him. It made him feel like a superhero.

"It's strange," Paxton said.

"What is?" Tinsley asked.

"Your family made the same mistake I made, but I figured it out in less than a minute and yet they still haven't figured it out after twenty-eight years."

Tinsley turned toward him so that her hand rested on his chest as she looked up at him. "Figured what out?"

"That you aren't some fragile little flower. Underneath the sweet smile, the kindness, and the caring, you have a backbone of solid steel. You didn't wilt when I challenged you at our first meeting. Instead, you challenged me back. You didn't crumble when Maurice came into your gallery. No, you used your intelligence to get more information about the case than I've been able to gather for the past three months. I'm just surprised your family doesn't see it."

"You see that when you look at me?" Tinsley asked.

Paxton nodded as he used his finger to push back a lock of hair from her face. "I see that and more, Tinsley."

"You know what I see when I look at you?"

Paxton shook his head. He didn't know if he wanted to hear this. He'd taken years to craft the hard exterior he showed the world. He knew he could come off arrogant and demanding. It was necessary for his survival.

"I see someone who will do anything to solve a case. Not just any case, but the most dangerous cases to keep the most dangerous criminals off the streets. However, underneath that is just a man afraid of the knitting club. And any man afraid of the knitting club has to have a kind heart. Otherwise, you'd just tell all those little old ladies to get lost. You're also a man who, when he says he'll do something, he does. You said you'd protect me. I know you will. You're smart, capable, and dare I say, sweet."

Paxton snorted with disbelief. "No one has called me sweet. Ever."

"Maybe I see something others don't, just like you see a part of me others don't. While you've teased me, it's never been done meanly. It's been your way of showing that you respect my knowledge of art. When I called you for help, you came. When you held baby Chase, he smiled. I'm sure that's hard for your ego to handle, but I see it. There is kindness underneath the hard exterior. You're actually not all that different from Ryker."

"Ryker? The billionaire?"

"There's more going on there than he ever shows, but that's his story to tell. Just know I see you. All of you."

Paxton felt as if he'd been punched in the gut. He wanted to pull her tight against him and kiss her with all the feelings swirling through him, but he couldn't. "You say you trust me, and trust me when I say I wish I could kiss you right now. I promised I wouldn't let anyone hurt you and that includes protecting you from myself. I want you, but I'm still planning on going back to Violent Gangs."

He felt Tinsley's body sigh against his. "See, I told you that you were a sweet guy." Tinsley lifted her face toward his and placed a slow, soft kiss on his cheek before standing up. "Goodnight, Paxton."

"Goodnight, Tinsley." Paxton watched her head upstairs to her room and a sense of panic almost overtook him. He was watching his future slip away from him, and he'd been the one to send her away.

Tinsley had spent another sleepless night in bed. Her eyes were puffy and she resembled a raccoon with dark circles under her eyes. This morning it took three layers of concealer to hide the exhaustion. Before last night, she'd had a physical attraction to Paxton. Now it went much deeper. The more time they spent together talking, the more she fell for him. She wasn't trying to fall for him, but here she was, walking by his side down the closed Main Street, laughing and getting deeper and deeper into trouble.

"I've never seen anything like this," Paxton said as he took in the Summer Shadows Festival.

"It's one of our fundraisers for the church. Twenty-five percent of all sales go to fund our self-defense classes and to hire a specialized metal worker to come in and sharpen all the weapons. You have to be careful with swords that are hundreds of years old," Tinsley told him as they stopped to get an iced tea for him and a lemon shake-up for her.

"Weapons? Why does the church have weapons?" Paxton asked, and Tinsley laughed.

"It's not a normal church."

Paxton shook his head in wonder. "I'm beginning to think there's nothing normal about Shadows Landing."

Tinsley smiled up at him and winked. "I knew you were a smart one."

They strolled down the street and stopped at each table, checking out decorations made from coconuts or palms. They bought baked goods, looked over artwork and furniture made from reclaimed wood. But then Tinsley's steps faltered as her hand flew to cover her mouth. Paxton instantly went on alert next to her and even moved to block her from danger.

"What is it? Is it Maurice?" Paxton asked as he scanned the people around them.

Tinsley shook her head as a giggle escaped around her fingers. She lifted her other hand and pointed. She knew when Paxton saw it because he smothered a laugh under a cough.

"Why is there a huge banner with a picture of your cousin Trent naked except for an apple pie over his package?" Paxton asked slowly as he worked to control his laughter.

"That's Miss Winnie and Miss Ruby. They make the best apple pie and Trent isn't the only one in my family who has posed nude with their pie," Tinsley laughed as they approached the stand. It was only then that she noticed Paxton go stiff. "What is it?"

"They're the ones who stopped me after knitting club."

"Are you telling me you're so scared of two little old ladies that you won't even go over there to get a piece of the best apple pie ever?" Tinsley crossed her arms and stared him down.

"Yes," Paxton said with a nod of his head. "That is exactly what I'm telling you." Tinsley clucked at him like a chicken and he rolled his eyes at her. "I have lived through very dangerous situations by being smart. It is not smart to go over there. No, Tins, don't!"

Tinsley smirked at him and waved to Miss Winnie and Miss Ruby as she walked toward them. She saw their eyes light on her and then lock onto Paxton, who was trying his best to hide behind her. The older women shared a look and suddenly Tinsley was worried she'd made a mistake.

"Tinsley, sweetie, how are you doing? Did you come for a slice of our famous pie?" Miss Ruby asked as she cut two pieces for them.

"We sure did. I told my new employee, Paxton, that your pie is the best around," Tinsley said with a smile that fell slightly when they zeroed in on Paxton with mischievous eyes.

"Employee, huh?" Miss Ruby didn't sound convinced.

"Here you go." Miss Winnie handed him a slice of pie and a fork. "Pie so good it's been known to make people's clothes fall off. I sure hope it's that good in your case."

Tinsley gaped at Miss Winnie as the lady winked at Paxton. Okay, maybe Paxton was right. They'd walked head first into an ambush.

Paxton took a bite and groaned. "I can understand the picture now. I'd probably strip naked for a pie, too."

"Tell us, young man," Miss Ruby said, holding up a second slice of pie. "What are you really doing in Shadows Landing with our sweet girl here?"

"Sweet?" Paxton laughed before taking another bite. "I mean, she is sweet, but there's a naughty side, too."

Tinsley felt her face flame with embarrassment.

"Not like that," Paxton hurried to supply. "I don't know about that yet. I meant she doesn't back down from anything or anyone."

"You should see her with a rapier," Miss Winnie told him proudly.

Tinsley saw Paxton look confused, but then shrug it off as he finished his pie.

"So an FBI agent is working for Tinsley and just what,

exactly, are you doing about keeping her safe?" Miss Ruby asked as she held out the second slice of pie to him.

"I didn't say I was with the FBI," Paxton said as Miss Ruby made his eyes cross by slowly bringing the pie right under his nose so he could take a deep breath of it.

"No, but we've already heard about you. Trying to stop an art thief. That's very good of you. But how much danger is our girl in?" Miss Ruby asked as she teased handing the plate over to Paxton's outstretched hand.

"That's why I'm working with her. So I can keep her safe."

"Where are you staying while here?" Miss Winnie asked, and Tinsley just shook her head. Paxton broke like a thin sheet of glass at the first hint of pie. Now she understood why he feared the granny gang.

"He's staying with me. Now stop interrogating him and give him the pie."

Paxton grabbed the pie and sighed. "I cracked like an egg, but it was worth it. You're right. This is the best pie I've ever had."

"So you want to become our new poster boy?" Miss Ruby asked, brightly, and Tinsley had to drag him away. He was just one more piece of pie away from stripping down on Main Street.

"I told you they're dangerous," Paxton muttered around another bite. "I'd totally strip for a whole pie."

"Good thing you didn't tell them that or you'd be naked right now."

"Would you sneak a peek?"

"I'm used to the nude male form. I was an art major after all." Tinsley tried to pull it off, but her mind was saying, *just a peek?*

"Fibber," Paxton said before taking his last bite of food.

Tinsley couldn't form the denial. She was already lost in a daydream of Paxton posing nude as she drew him.

Paxton continued to flirt with her as the day wore on. After last night, she didn't think he would, but by the end of the festival he reached out for her. His large hand covered hers as they walked back down Main Street. Today had been the best day. Tinsley had forgotten about the case. She'd forgotten about Paxton wanting to go back to Violent Gangs. She'd forgotten they weren't a real couple. Instead she got lost in the feeling of what could be.

What could be if Paxton didn't leave? What could be if they were a real couple? What could be if he stopped holding back and they both took a leap of faith? If today was a glimpse of what could be, it was worth fighting for.

Paxton drove her home after nightfall. They laughed, talked, and lived in the moment. They were still in that bubble when they arrived back at her home.

Tinsley felt her heartbeat with every step they took upstairs toward their bedrooms. They stopped at the top of the stairs with their hands interlaced as they gazed at each other. Paxton and his seriousness stood before her with desire in his eyes. The seriousness changed into playful banter. His roughness was still there. Only the edges seemed to have softened.

Tinsley reached out with her free hand and placed it on his chest. She felt the muscles go taut under her palm. When she let her fingers flutter over his pecs, up to his shoulder, and then to tease the back of his neck, she felt his breath hitch, coming as fast and shallow as hers as their eyes locked.

Paxton slowly lowered his head until his forehead rested

on hers. Together they simply breathed each other in.

"I'm sorry, Tinsley." Paxton's whispered breath flickered over her cheeks.

Tinsley opened her eyes and looked into his. "For what?"

"I told you I'd protect you," he whispered as his hand dropped hers only to come up and grab her hair gently. She felt the slight tug as his fingers fisted her hair at the nape of her neck. "But I can't protect you from me any longer. I tried so hard to do the right thing, but I can't stop myself. I don't want to stop myself."

"Stop yourself from what?" Tinsley's breath was a little more than a puff of air as she felt her whole body begging to be his.

"I can't stop from wanting you."

Paxton's hand tightened in her hair. He used his grasp to angle her head to his lips. His kiss wasn't the timid first kiss she normally experienced. No, Paxton kissed the way he lived—all in. There was no hesitation or self-doubt. Paxton took command of her mouth with his and together they sparred for control. He pushed and Tinsley pushed back. When the kiss finally ended, they were both clutching the other and breathing heavily.

"I should be sorry. I find that I'm not sorry at all. Goodnight, Tins," Paxton said as he brushed back some strands of hair from her cheek with his fingertips.

"I'm not either. Good night, Paxton." Tinsley rose up on her tiptoes and placed a soft kiss on his lips before slipping into her bedroom.

She fell onto her bed and stared at the ceiling as her fingers touched her mouth. Wow, that had been everything she'd ever dreamed of in a kiss. Paxton was worth fighting for. *They* were worth fighting for. Now Tinsley was going to show him just that.

9

Tinsley woke to the smell of brewing coffee. She heard Paxton in the kitchen and grabbed a hair tie on her way downstairs. By the time she made it to the kitchen she had her long hair in a sloppy bun and her robe tied.

"Good morning, Paxton," Tinsley said as she spied him making eggs.

"Right on time. Your breakfast is ready." Paxton set down a plate of eggs and toast and poured Tinsley a cup of coffee. "What is on the schedule today, boss?"

"I thought we could start laying the groundwork for our call to Maurice. What work do you need to do before we see him?" Tinsley asked.

Paxton took a seat across the small kitchen table from her. "I think I should be in contact with local law enforcement in case we need backup. Do you know them?" "Yes, I do. I can call them if you'd like."

"Do you trust them?" Paxton asked before taking a sip of his coffee.

"There's no one I trust more." Tinsley gave a little smile when Paxton acted as if he were wounded by her answer.

She pulled out her cell phone and sent a quick text to Granger, the sheriff of Shadows Landing. Within seconds he texted her back. "We can meet him at the sheriff's station in an hour."

"Eat up. Today we lay the groundwork to trap Maurice and Murray."

Paxton insisted on taking his own car in case he needed to run errands while Tinsley was at work. He followed her closely to the sheriff's station and soon they were chatting with the secretary as they waited for Granger.

"Show them back, please," Granger's voice sounded over the intercom.

Tinsley waved the secretary back to her seat. "I know the way. See you at self-defense."

Tinsley took the lead and Paxton followed her to Granger's office.

"Hey, Granger. This is Paxton Kendry. He's the FBI agent in charge of art crimes. He wanted to meet with you about the case we're working."

"That *you* are working?" Granger asked as he raised an eyebrow at Tinsley.

"That she's assisting me with," Paxton answered for her.

Tinsley put her hands on her hips and turned to face him. "Excuse me, but I'm pretty sure I've gotten you real, usable evidence and two suspects. What have you done so far?"

Granger sat back in his chair and grinned. "This sounds like Tinsley's case. Something super dangerous like a man in his basement who forges art?"

Tinsley saw Paxton's eyes narrow as they both measured each other's mettle.

"High-end art thieves involved with a dangerous gang, actually. I'm sorry I interrupted you doing . . . well, nothing."

Granger stopped smiling and glared. Tinsley rolled her eyes. "Paxton, don't be an ass. Granger, don't be a jerk. This is what we've got." Tinsley began to explain to Granger about the case until she could tell he was interested. Then she let Paxton take over as they discussed Tinsley's role, the security setup, what evidence he was hoping to collect, and what, if anything, Paxton needed from Granger. Granger called in Kord, the deputy sheriff, and they went to work detailing the ins and outs of the town. Tinsley took a seat and let the professionals finish making plans. It was her job to draw Maurice and Murray into the gallery for the sale. As soon as the sale was complete, Paxton would have the evidence needed to arrest them.

Paxton stood up and shook Granger's and Kord's hands. The three of them were smiling as they ended their meeting. Apparently the bond between law enforcement professionals had won them over, once they stopped acting like idiots.

"Hey, Tins. Can I have a private word with Paxton? It won't take but a second," Granger asked but it wasn't a request. Tinsley nodded and thanked them for their time. The door had just closed when she heard Granger's deep voice.

"What are you doing with her, Kendry?"

"That's none of your business," Tinsley heard Paxton snap back. Whatever camaraderie had formed was gone in a second as she shamelessly eavesdropped.

"She's my friend. That's what business it is of mine," Granger practically growled.

"Mine too," Kord added.

Men. Tinsley rolled her eyes again. Women didn't sit

around blustering and posturing for king of the hill. No, they smiled, threatened through compliments, and then served iced tea.

"Tinsley is sweet. She's an innocent about things like this. I'm not about to let some hardened agent come in here, use her, and then dump her once the case is closed. I know about you undercover gang agents. I know you saw some dark shit. Tinsley isn't like that."

"No, she's not," Paxton said seriously. "She's the light that eradicates the shadows. I'm not using her. I know her brother thinks I don't deserve her. The truth is, I don't. But that doesn't mean I'm not going to do everything I can to try to be the man she deserves. Now, you can report that back to Ridge *and* Ryker. I personally don't give a shit what you all think of me, but I do appreciate that you're looking out for Tinsley."

The room went quiet and Tinsley stepped closer to the door. She cupped her ear and held her breath, afraid she'd miss a single word.

"I don't know what to make of you," Granger finally said. "At least you're not Stephen. I think we were all worried Tinsley would end up with someone soft like him."

Tinsley stuck her tongue out at the door, hoping Granger felt her displeasure. Stephen Adkins? Did they really think she was such a weak, delicate flower that she'd go for the boring, safe, and totally pompous Stephen Adkins?

"Who is Stephen?" she heard Paxton ask with as much dislike in his voice for Stephen as she felt.

"Stephen Adkins runs the historical center in town. He went off to college and came back with no accent and a nose so far up in the air that birds land on it. He's had a thing for Tinsley for years. He sees her as his intellectual and cultural equal since she's spent time studying in Paris and Italy. We've all been worried she'd end up with him. Skeeter said he overhead Stephen practicing to ask her out on a date."

What? Tinsley couldn't hide her reaction and she was *horrified*. They really thought she'd go out with Stephen when he was so mean to her friends?

"Why would you think Tinsley would even consider going out with him?" she heard Paxton ask.

"As annoying as Stephen is, he's the only guy in town who can really sit down and talk about art without sounding as if he's repeating it from an Internet search," Granger told Paxton. "Look, we have your back on the case. Just know if you hurt Tinsley you might accidentally get caught in friendly fire. Nothing too serious. Maybe just a shot in the ass."

"I've already survived three to the chest. I think I can handle it. Thanks for your help." Tinsley heard Paxton shake hands as she jumped away from the door. Seconds later, when Paxton walked out, she was seated at a table a good fifteen feet from the door.

Paxton spent the rest of the morning watching Tinsley around her gallery. He saw how she processed orders, watched as she completed an online sale of one of her pieces, and then she showed him how she packed art for transport.

He delivered the package to the shipping company, and when he returned Tinsley was in her studio with music on. Paxton moved quietly to watch her paint. He crossed his arms over his chest and leaned against the doorway. He watched her back as she swayed to the music and at times she closed her eyes and let her head fall back as if she were picturing the creation she was about to make. Then she'd open her eyes and get back to work.

Paxton didn't know how long he'd watched her. In the beginning he couldn't tell what the painting was going to be. It seemed as if it were filled with random brush strokes. By the time his phone buzzed with an incoming text message, he could see that the painting was of a woman. For someone who claimed to only be good at painting landscapes, Tinsley was pretty impressive with the people she'd been painting recently.

Call me.

Paxton read the text from Peter and slipped from the room. He stepped to the far side of the gallery and called his boss.

"Do you have the money set up for the sale?" Paxton asked Peter.

"We do. We have a fake account set up ready to make the wire transfer for the artwork for up to a hundred thousand dollars. Tinsley can do it all over the phone with our financial guy so Maurice and Murray will believe there's a real buyer and will be happy when they see their account go up by the sales price. They shouldn't press Tinsley for any more information after that."

"Great. Tinsley is going to call them tomorrow afternoon to set up a time to complete the sale. We didn't want to appear to be too eager," Paxton told him.

Peter was quiet for a moment and Paxton could swear he could hear his boss smiling. "So I hear you met Granger and Kord. They're good guys. Use them if you need backup."

"I will. Why are you smiling?" Paxton asked.

"How did you know I was smiling?" Peter asked but then just chuckled. "I heard they told you at least you weren't Stephen Adkins. Quite the ringing endorsement. Funny how fast things changed from you tolerating Tinsley to you apparently living with Tinsley."

"I never said I didn't like her or that I only tolerated her. That was shoddy investigative work on your end," Paxton pointed out.

"Oh," Peter said, not bothering to hide his amusement. "You've liked her all along and didn't know how to handle it. You're right, bad work on my part. I should have seen that. What's the plan because I've fielded no fewer than five calls about you today and whether I think you're good enough for Tinsley."

"What?" Paxton yelped before quieting down. The last thing he wanted to do was disturb Tinsley as she was working. Plus, this was not the conversation he wanted her to overhear.

"What can I say? Tinsley is loved by all. Everyone wanted to make sure you were worthy of her."

"What did you say?" Paxton asked, sounding a little too much like a high school boy hoping the girl he had a crush on liked him too. He cleared his throat and took a deep breath. "Not that it matters. This is between Tinsley and me and no one else."

He didn't think it was a good sign when Peter snorted with amusement. "Don't worry. I told them you were better than Stephen."

"I need to meet Stephen."

Peter laughed again over the phone and Paxton wanted to shake him. "I'm sure you will soon. Seriously though, I told them you were a damn good agent and to give you a chance."

"I guess I owe you then." Paxton paused and looked back toward Tinsley's studio before dropping his voice. "Have you heard anything from Atlanta?"

"Already looking to leave? Not so serious about Tinsley then?"

"It's not that," Paxton admitted. "I put in for a transfer as you know, but now I'm not so sure what I want. One thing I do know— something isn't right. I should have been promoted. I was just curious if you've heard anything."

"Your transfer was denied an hour ago. It's one of the reasons I'm calling. The reason for it did strike me as odd. It said you weren't qualified. I looked up who got the promotion and you have five years of seniority over him. Plus you have more street experience. From what I can tell, you were blackballed. I'm curious as to the reason."

"Who was appointed?" Paxton asked as he clenched his fingers into a fist.

"Mark Trevino."

"That asshole? Something is definitely up." Mark was always the one to cut corners. Paxton had no evidence of it, but he thought it was Mark who had blown Paxton's cover, causing him to be shot.

"I tend to agree. What else is interesting is that your file has been changed. I have a copy from when you were transferred to me. I'm old school and printed it off. I pulled up the file online after I was told you weren't qualified. There's a ton of disciplinary actions that weren't there before. The question is: who is Mark Trevino and is he powerful enough to alter your file?"

"Pull his record," Paxton told him as his mind tried to understand this new development. He'd thought he was crazy thinking there was a conspiracy against him but now, it didn't seem so crazy at all.

"I could, but he'd probably get notice of it. I didn't think you'd want that yet."

"No, you're right." Paxton took a breath and focused his

mind. "Mark transferred in last year from the gang unit in the Boston office. He said he was tired of the cold weather when we asked why he transferred."

"Okay, I'll ask around to see if anyone has any contacts in the Boston office. See if we can find out the real reason for his transfer. Meanwhile, keep Tinsley safe and wrap up this art theft ring."

When Paxton turned around, he realized the music was off and found Tinsley standing in the door to her studio drying her hands.

"I didn't want to disturb your call since you looked upset. Is everything okay?" Tinsley asked.

"Yes, just Bureau politics. Peter has everything set up for a wire transfer. You'll call a number and talk to one of our agents. He'll send a wire with hidden software to trace it to the account number Maurice gives you. Then have Maurice sign over the sales papers and we'll swoop in to arrest him."

"Okay, I'll call him tomorrow after lunch and set it up."

Paxton nodded and then held out his hand. Tinsley walked across the gallery and slipped her hand into his. "Can I take you out to dinner tonight?"

"As in a date?" Tinsley smiled up at him. There was truly no better feeling in the world than that.

"Yes, as an official date. I'll even take you home and kiss you goodnight."

"I'd love that."

"I know this great place to eat and it happens to be right across the street. I have an in with the owner. I work with her boyfriend," Paxton teased as they locked up the gallery and headed to Karri's restaurant.

. . .

Paxton and Tinsley enjoyed shrimp and grits that were elevated way above any shrimp and grits Paxton had ever had before. The grits were made with a special cheese, then deep-fried to make grit cakes before being smothered with Lowcountry shrimp, sausage, and gravy.

Then there was the company. Tinsley had him laughing with stories of growing up in Shadows Landing, the pirate history of the town, and how they'd met their relatives from Keeneston, Kentucky.

"Wait, your cousin Greer is with FBI Hostage Rescue?" Paxton asked for clarification. He'd heard of a woman joining HRT but not her name.

"Yup, she's in New York City. Her father is retired FBI, her oldest brother is the FBI agent in charge in Lexington, and her other brother is with hostage rescue, too," Tinsley said proudly. It was clear that while the two families had only known each other a couple of years, they were already very close.

By the time they left the restaurant, it seemed second nature to slip her hand into his as they walked. Tinsley leaned against him as they took in the warm night air on the short walk to the cars. Paxton stopped by Tinsley's driver door as she opened it and tossed in her purse. She turned back around and smiled up at him. "This was fun. I'll see you at home?"

Home.

The thought of Tinsley at home waiting for him had him reaching out and grabbing her hips. He stepped forward and pressed her against the side of the car before kissing her. He let his desires take over as he speared one hand into her hair and deepened the kiss. His other hand pulled her flush against him. He felt the curve of her breasts, the way her breathing hitched in desire, the gentle rocking of her hips against his, and all thoughts fled from his mind.

His mouth devoured hers as his other hand ran up her hip and past her waist before cupping her breast. The little moan Tinsley let out vibrated straight through him like a dagger to the heart.

"What's that man doing to Miss Tinsley, Momma?" a little voice asked. It tore through the veil of desire and Paxton reluctantly took a step away from Tinsley.

"They're making babies," another little voice answered.

"They shouldn't be doing that on the street. No baby wants to be born on the street. It's dirty and icky," a little girl said.

Paxton turned to find a young woman surrounded by a herd of children, all staring at him and Tinsley.

"Good evening, Lydia," Tinsley said as if she hadn't just been caught clutching Paxton's shirt. "Hello, kids."

"Hello, Miss Tinsley," they all echoed back.

"Who's that?" the youngest boy asked.

"This is Mr. Paxton. He's a friend of mine," Tinsley said sweetly.

Meanwhile, Paxton just stared as he counted kids. "There's seven of them," he whispered to Tinsley in disbelief.

"Mr. Paxton, you look horny like Mr. Fuzzy Butt," the smallest girl told him with a giggle.

"Lindsey!" the mother admonished the little girl in pigtails who just shrugged off her mother.

"He does. He looks all horny with the way he's glaring. He's looking at me the way Fuzzy Butt does when I take his toy away."

"*Ornery*," the mother said quickly. "She means ornery."

The older boy crossed his arms and scowled at Paxton. "I think she had it right with horny."

"Landry Junior!" The mother smacked his arm. "How do you know what that word means?"

Paxton had to choke back a laugh as the boy who looked to be closing in on his teenage years let out an annoyed sigh and rolled his eyes in a completely adolescent way. "I'm twelve, Mom. I think I know what horny means, just like I know when you and Dad tell me to put on my headphones and listen to music in my room that I'll probably end up with another brother or sister in nine months. Duh."

The oldest daughter smacked her brother. "Landry, don't make Mom feel bad for being horny. If she's horny, then she's not ornery. Duh," she said, mocking her older brother.

"Shut up, Lacy. You think you know everything. I'm the older brother."

"Well, I know Mr. Paxton made it to second base while you probably think it's about baseball," Lacy shot back.

Paxton was going to lose it. He was trying hard not to because of the horrified look on the mother's face, so he pressed his lips tightly together to keep from laughing out loud.

"I like baseball," one of the little boys piped up. "I don't want to make it to second base though. I want to hit a home run!"

"I know I want to round second base, hit third, and slide home," Paxton whispered to Tinsley who smacked his arm. He saw the way her shoulders shook as she tried not to laugh.

"It's very nice to meet you, Mr. Paxton. Say goodbye, kids," Lydia ordered in an attempt to wrangle the kids up and escape the increasingly embarrassing situation.

Landry scowled at him. Lacy smiled at him. Lindsey said he didn't look horny anymore because he was smiling. The little boy was still talking about making a home run as Lydia herded them away. As they disappeared down the street, Paxton heard the youngest boy ask how babies were made and Paxton lost it. The laughter broke free and it wasn't just from him. Tinsley held tight to his arm as she bent over in a fit of giggles.

"They're going to tell everyone that you are horny and we were making babies on the street. Right now I'm just laughing too hard to care. But you may want to steer clear of my brother for a few days." Tinsley took in a deep breath to try to calm down, but it only resulted in more laughter.

"Come on, let's go home. I believe I'm up to bat."

"You sure you won't pop out on a foul ball?" Tinsley asked.

"I'm sure. In fact, I'm up for a doubleheader." Paxton placed a kiss on her forehead and held the door open for her to get into her car. "I'll see you at home."

He closed the door and watched as she drove away. Home. Nothing had ever sounded better to him than that.

Paxton followed Tinsley home. They met on the front porch and it was as if a spark had ignited a passion that was burning out of control. They came together in a clash, and before they were inside they were all hands, lips, and tongues. Paxton blindly reached around her to unlock the door. His heart was pounding, his body was on fire, and his mind was full of every little sound of pleasure Tinsley made.

That was until the sound of a car driving up the way entered his brain. "Are you expecting anyone?" Paxton asked as he moved his hand to the gun hidden at the small of his back.

"No," Tinsley confirmed as she looked into the darkness. Two headlights appeared and Tinsley groaned as the truck came into view. "It's my brother."

The truck stopped and Ridge pushed the door open. His wife got out on the other side and mouthed "Sorry" to them.

"Hey, you two," Ridge called out. "I felt bad about how the other night went so I thought we'd come over and get to know Paxton better."

Paxton knew better. He bent his head toward Tinsley and whispered, "Your brother is blocking the plate."

"So, Paxton," Ridge said with a smile as if he knew he'd interrupted them. "Do you want kids someday?"

"I am so sorry," Savannah muttered again as they all went inside for the longest, most frustrating night of Paxton's life.

10

Tinsley pushed open the door to the Lowcountry Smokehouse for lunch the next day with a little more force than necessary. It was all the pent-up sexual frustration from the night before.

Today she was both horny *and* ornery, and it was all her brother's fault. He'd kept Paxton talking until three in the morning. Tinsley gave up after Paxton had shared his views on children, marriage, monogamy, how many women he'd been with, his political views, how much money he made, if he went to church, and on and on. Her brother had been relentless and yet Paxton had just grabbed a beer from the fridge and sat back and answered everything.

At first it was interesting. While he didn't come off as the family man, he actually was, which only turned Tinsley on more. But then Ridge threw cold water on her feelings when he'd turned the conversation to Paxton's ex-girlfriends.

She'd zoned out after hearing his view of the current president and congress. Then she'd fallen asleep when he and Ridge started discussing movies. When she woke up, she'd had a pillow placed under her head and a blanket pulled over her. Now she was exhausted, had to call a criminal in two hours, and had promised to meet the girls for a lunch she knew she couldn't avoid.

Tinsley looked around the restaurant and found them around a big circular table in the back. Savannah was pouring coffee and as soon as she saw Tinsley, she poured her a cup. The rest of them stared at her with matching grins on their faces.

"When did y'all talk to Lydia?" Tinsley grumbled as she took the coffee from her sister-in-law.

"Probably while you were still getting felt up on the street," Harper said bluntly.

"You should talk. Remember I accidentally caught you and Dare behind the bar when I tried to take the shortcut to your house last month," Tinsley told her cousin with no remorse for sharing her and her husband's private moment.

Harper just smiled at the memory.

"Wade and I got caught on our boat deck by some college students on spring break. They tossed us a beer," Darcy admitted.

"I can't count the number of times Sadie has walked in on Gavin and me," Ellery told them. "In fact, we're so bad about being caught I've told Gavin he has to put a deadbolt on our door or we'll be explaining sex to baby Chase by the time he's three."

"Ryker caught Trent and me on our back patio," Skye confessed.

"Don't let Ridge make you feel guilty," Savannah told her. "We totally got busted by Reverend Winston after Ridge said we didn't need to lower the shades in the living room because, quote, 'Who would stop by?'"

"We're not here to give you a hard time," Harper told her. "We're here to find out how it was."

Tinsley didn't realize she'd sighed out loud until the table burst into laughter.

"Also, I put a hole in Ridge's tire after I heard what he did last night," Harper told her. "I actually like Paxton for you. He pushes you to be *you*. Not the quiet little mouse you think people want you to be. Plus, he's way better than Stephen Adkins."

Savannah spoke up sheepishly. "First, I am so sorry about last night. I tried to tell Ridge he was going overboard, but he said as your brother he had to protect you. Second, I agree with Harper. I actually like you two together. He's not the kind of man I pictured. But now that I see it, I realized how wrong I was before."

"What kind of man did you think I'd be with?" Tinsley asked. What did they all think of her?

"Honestly, someone like Stephen, just not so snobby. Maybe another artist or maybe a professor? I thought you'd end up with someone chill, safe, reliable, and maybe just a little snobby. That was where I was wrong. I like that Paxton is so intense. You two play off of each other in a way that makes it appear like foreplay," Savannah told her.

"I see that," Skye agreed. "I know I'm new, but he's brought out more confidence in you."

"I couldn't agree more." Tinsley turned to look behind her to find her best friend, Edie Greene Wecker, standing there. "I just came from the gallery where I chatted with Paxton for a moment. I never thought you should be with a pushover. You dated too many artists and collectors over the years who were all wrong for you. They either treat you like you'll break or they get jealous of your success. Paxton's too much of a confident man for that. I think he gushes over your ability as an artist more than we do. He thinks you're amazing. He thinks you're incredibly smart, and I think we all know after last night's Main Street porno that he finds you sexy. Sounds like a home run to me."

Tinsley choked on the iced tea.

"The only way he'd be better is if he had a motorcycle," Harper told the table as talk turned to gossip about their own men.

Tinsley left her girls' lunch feeling invigorated. She knew she liked Paxton and wanted to think it didn't matter what anyone else thought, but that was a lie. She was thrilled her friends and family liked him and encouraged her to go after a relationship with him. The men were a different story. In Ridge's mind, no one had ever been good enough for his little sister. That influenced the others, especially Ryker who also thought it was his place to be her protector after that night so long ago. Others had helped, but it had been Tinsley who had pulled him back from the edge.

She knew she and Paxton didn't have a defined relationship. However, there was a promise of one. Not just a casual one either. Once they'd opened themselves up, a deeper connection was made than she'd ever felt before.

Tinsley hurried into the gallery and was surprised to find it empty. "Paxton?" she asked as she moved into her office only to find it also empty. The sound of the door opening had her smiling. She couldn't wait to tell him about her lunch. Well, some of it. Girl code prevented full disclosure.

"Paxton! You wouldn't believe lunch," Tinsley called out as she walked quickly into the gallery only to stop short.

"Who's Paxton?" Maurice asked.

"He's my delivery man and he also helps out around the gallery." Tinsley smiled at him and tried to calm her nerves.

She'd been amped up because of lunch and now she needed to calm down and think straight. "Speak of the devil, though, I was just going to call you."

"Did it have anything to do with your lunch?" Maurice asked as he flashed what was supposed to be a flirtatious smile. Only it came across as predatory.

"Yes, it does. My buyer wants to purchase your painting. We just need to settle on a price. Congratulations, Maurice."

Maurice nodded and his smile widened. "That's very good news, Tinsley. I'd like to meet with the buyer for the negotiation. I'd like to see you work the sale in person."

Tinsley kept her smile in place only with the grace of Southern manners. "My buyer usually prefers to negotiate over the phone. Don't worry, I can put it on speaker and as soon as we reach a deal, I can email them the contract. The money will be wired as soon as they send the contract back."

"Maybe for future sales, but I need to see how this works. It'll make me feel better to know it's on the up and up. The best way to do that is face to face."

Tinsley's smile almost slipped. Was the criminal really questioning her ethics?

"Of course, Maurice. I'll make it happen."

"Tomorrow, here, two o'clock. This is a very promising start to what I hope is a long relationship, Tinsley. As I've said, my grandmother has a very large collection with some paintings by history's best artists. You seal this deal and we could make our own history together."

"I'd rather make money," Tinsley giggled. Where the hell was Paxton?

"That's why we make a good team. I'll see you and the buyer tomorrow."

Tinsley smiled and waved goodbye as Maurice left. The second he was out the door, she had her phone out and was calling Paxton. She heard the ring over the phone and then she heard it echo through the gallery.

"Paxton?" No answer, but the ringing continued. She walked past her office calling out his name, as the sound of ringing grew closer. In the small kitchen in the back she saw a half-eaten fried chicken sandwich from Stomping Grounds.

"Paxton!"

"Tinsley? Call for help!" Tinsley heard Paxton's muffled voice coming from outside. The back door to the small courtyard was closed, but she was sure that's where his voice had come from.

Tinsley ran to the door and yanked it open. Paxton's back was up against the twelve-foot brick wall. There were two ways out of the courtyard. One, the door Tinsley had just opened. And two, a decorative metal gate directly to her right that led to a small parking area and beyond that, down to the river. The only trouble was Bubba the alligator had parked himself right between both doors. The large gator's mouth was open as he hissed every time Paxton moved.

"What did you do to get Bubba mad at you?" Tinsley asked.

"He has a name?"

"Yeah. Everyone knows Big Bubba. You're lucky it wasn't Mean Abe or Bitchy Bertha," Tinsley told him.

"Will he bite me? I haven't moved in over an hour," Paxton asked while he eyed the massive gator.

"Um, maybe."

"*Maybe?*" Paxton was freaking out and Tinsley was highly amused.

"How did you become stuck with Bubba back here anyway?" Tinsley asked as she pulled out her phone and sent a text to Gator to help with a Bubba removal.

"I grabbed a chicken sandwich from the diner up the street. I was sitting in the back eating it when I heard a knock on the door. I went to open it, but no one was there so I took a step outside and *bam!* Bubba went after me. He was pressed up against the wall and cut off my escape back inside the second I stepped out. He almost bit me and I've been using this little statue to keep him back." Paxton held out the two-foot tall cement fairy Tinsley had painted when she was twelve years old.

"He probably smelled the fried chicken. It's his favorite. Gator's on his way. He'll remove him," Tinsley said before turning back inside.

"Where are you going?" Paxton shouted.

"To get him the rest of the sandwich. Maybe he'll leave if he's eaten."

Tinsley grabbed the sandwich and stood in the doorway looking out at Bubba. Bubba's nostrils flared and Tinsley tossed the sandwich. Bubba snapped the sandwich out of the air with a chomp so loud it echoed.

"Damn," Paxton muttered before looking up at Tinsley. "Maybe? *Maybe* he'd bite me? The damn thing would snap me in half!"

"Don't be so dramatic. It's just an alligator." Tinsley paused as Bubba made a low throaty growl. "Uh-oh."

"Uh-oh? What does that mean?" Paxton was near frantic as he pulled out his gun.

"I wouldn't do that if I were you," Tinsley warned. "Bubba doesn't like guns."

Sure enough, Bubba turned into a raging T-Rex as he growled.

"Okay, okay, I'm putting it away." Paxton slid the gun back under his shirt, but the damage had been done.

Bubba charged, Paxton shrieked like a soprano and just

as he hit High C, Tinsley pounced. She landed with a thud on Bubba's back. The boney, spiky scutes running down his back jabbed her bare legs and poked into her stomach and arms as she wrestled with him. Tinsley heard Paxton yelling, but she was too focused on not getting hit by Bubba's tail to pay attention to what he was yelling.

Tinsley squeezed her legs as she crawled up Bubba's back until she could cover his eyes with her hands. Bubba gave a couple of shakes, and began to settle down.

Letting out a deep breath, Tinsley finally looked up. Bubba had gotten within a foot of Paxton. Bubba's mouth was still open on a hiss, but Tinsley wasn't strong enough to close it.

"Step around here and lie on his tail," she instructed Paxton calmly.

Paxton hugged the wall as she scooted away from Bubba. He finally took a breath when he was beside Bubba. "You want me to do what?"

"A gator's tail can do a tremendous amount of damage. In case you haven't noticed, Bubba is over twelve feet long and probably a good eight hundred pounds. I'm not that tall and not that heavy. If he hits me with his tail, I'll go flying and end up with more than a few broken bones. So I want you to lie on his tail and hug it. Got it?"

"This is insane," Paxton muttered as he got into position. In one move, he had Bubba's tail wrapped in a tight hug. Paxton's head was pressed at the base of the huge tail while his legs wrapped around the tip. "Um, Tins?"

"What?" Tinsley asked as she kept a tight grip on Bubba.

"My head is really close . . . I mean, do alligators fart?"

"They've been known to let 'er rip a time or two," a deep country voice called out in amusement. "Miss Tinsley, you got a nice hold on ol' Bubba there."

"Just like you taught me, Gator," Tinsley called out.

"Why did you answer the alligator?" Paxton asked.

"Not Bubba, me. I'm Gator," Gator explained to Paxton. "Was that you screamin' like a girl a second ago? We thought it might be Miss Tinsley, but she's no wimp when it comes to Bubba."

Tinsley pressed her face onto Bubba's back and tried to smother her laugh in his scales.

Paxton cleared his throat. "We?"

"Yeah, if you open up your eyes you'll see everyone's here," Gator told him.

"I can feel you laughing through the alligator, Tinsley," Paxton said through clenched teeth. Tinsley lost it then. Tears—alligator tears at that—ran down her cheeks as she laughed and laughed.

"That ain't right, Miss Tinsley," she heard Skeeter's deep country twang saying from beside her. "It ain't his fault he screams like a girl. Some men are delicate. You'll hurt his feelings if you keep on laughin' like that."

Of course, that only made Tinsley laugh harder. She even heard Paxton smother a laugh from Bubba's tail. She bet no one had ever called Paxton delicate before.

"Skeeter's right, Miss T." A small face appeared in front of her as Turtle pushed Bubba's mouth closed and Skeeter wrapped it up so Bubba couldn't bite them. "It hurt my feelin's something fierce when people laughed at my pecker being bitten by a snapping turtle. But your cousin did a right good job sewing it up. I think he even gave me an extra inch. Wanna see?"

A snort from Paxton drew their attention as Tinsley tried to hide the tears of laughter rolling down her cheeks. "Don't you worry none, sir," Turtle said to Paxton. "I won't laugh at you for screaming like a girl. I mean, I didn't scream like a girl when I had a snapping turtle latched onto my pecker. But some men just ain't as tough, ya know?"

Tinsley couldn't see him but she could imagine what Paxton looked like as she heard him choking on his laughter right now. A lesser man would defend his scream and tease Turtle, but Paxton didn't. Instead he cleared his throat, literally pushing down his laughter.

"That's very brave of you. I believe I would have reached teen-girl-at-a-boy-band-concert-level scream if a snapping turtle latched onto my, um, pecker."

"Well, let's get this done so he don't have Bubba snapping off his pecker," Gator said in his booming voice. "Turtle, you got his mouth wrapped up?"

"I sure do."

"Skeeter, you get the rag over his eyes so Miss T can get up."

Tinsley waited until the rag was secure and then Gator reached down and literally plucked her off Bubba as Skeeter and Turtle knelt down on each side and pressed down on the creature to keep him still.

Gator placed Tinsley on the ground and she got her first look at the scene. The whole town was crowded into her small courtyard. Miss Ruby and Miss Winnie had their cell phones out and were taking pictures. Harper and Karri were hanging onto each other and doubled over with laughter. Then there was Paxton. Bless his heart, he had a death grip on Bubba's tail and his face was dangerously close to Bubba's butt.

"Gator, this is Paxton. Paxton, this is Gator. Just do what he says, okay?" Tinsley told him.

"You do this often?" Paxton asked as Gator stepped up next to him.

"Yup. Now I want you to sit up and straddle the lower end of Bubba's tail. Can you do that?" Gator asked.

"Yeah, I can do that." Paxton shimmied down the tail and then sat up. Gator was instantly down on the ground with the thick base of Bubba's tail wrapped in his arms.

"We could use some help liftin' him," Gator called out. Granger and Kord instantly stepped forward to help.

"We got a call about a girl screaming like she was being stabbed," Granger said with a smirk.

Granger and Kord moved to Bubba's middle. Then Paxton shifted off the tail and all together they lifted. Tinsley and the crowd moved out of the way as Bubba was carried to Gator's pickup truck.

"I'll just take him back home. Don't hesitate to scream if you need me," Gator said with a little snicker before driving off with Turtle and Skeeter holding Bubba down.

"I take it you haven't been around alligators much," Granger said to Paxton as Harper and Karri gave up their fight and burst out laughing.

"Not too many gators on Peachtree Street unless the University of Florida is in town. That was wild, though. Do you all know how to do that? Just jump on an alligator?" Paxton asked.

"Yeah, but we try to leave it up to the experts," Kord answered. "I'm too fine to lose a finger. Or pecker."

Tinsley took one look at Karri and Harper and the peals of laughter started again. "I hate to break this up because this was the most fun I've had in years, but Maurice stopped in to see me and we have a problem," Tinsley announced.

11

Granger and Kord joined Tinsley and Paxton inside the gallery as she filled them in on her meeting with Maurice. Tinsley saw her same worry reflected on the lawmen's faces. None of them looked pleased with this development.

"Peter could pose as the client," Paxton finally said into the silence that lingered in the aftermath of her announcement that Maurice wanted to meet the buyer.

"I thought about that," Tinsley told them. "But I worry. This is a big test. I would say just bust them, but Maurice keeps mentioning that his grandma has a huge collection and even said it could be historical. I wonder how many stolen paintings he has and how he came about them. We'll never know if you arrest him now."

"We can have Peter pose as the buyer and we can trace the money," Paxton said again. "Then we follow the money and that will, hopefully, lead us to the rest of the paintings."

Tinsley shook her head. "I don't think that's the right play here. I think we need to do something he'll never see coming."

"What are you thinking, Tins?" Granger asked.

"Mrs. Elijah F. Cummings," Tinsley said as she crossed her arms over her chest.

"Who?" Paxton asked.

Granger ignored the question as Kord shook his head. "You want to use Miss Tibbie in a sting operation with a dangerous criminal?" Granger repeated for clarification.

"I do. No one can question her knowledge of art in case this is a test. Plus, she'd be way above suspicion as an undercover agent. I need to prove I can bring in a quality buyer. Miss Tibbie is a quality buyer," Tinsley explained.

"Who is this Miss Tibbie?" Paxton asked again, this time a little more forcefully in hopes someone would answer him.

"She is *the* grand dame of Charleston society. Her husband, Elijah, is a very powerful man even though he retired decades ago. Miss Tibbie is your little old grandmother with pearls and an iron fist tucked inside her white gloves. She can ruin you with one word," Granger explained.

"Won't she be recognizable then?" Paxton asked.

"Her name will be," Tinsley admitted, "But I also know Miss Tibbie isn't a fan of her picture being in newspapers. Most photos of her on the Internet are of when she was much younger. So, you change her name, come up with a little disguise, and say we know each other through a fake charity and we'll be good to go. If it makes you feel better, have Peter act as her grandson. Let's see, her spoiled, *bored* grandson. Trust me, society matrons are always trying to make their grandsons act properly and give them culture while dangling access to their trust fund over their heads."

"It's not a bad idea," Granger said. "You think Miss Tibbie will do it?"

"Miss Tibbie is always up for a little fun. Call Peter and

see what he thinks. If it's a go, I'll call Miss Tibbie and get it all set up." Tinsley hoped Peter would agree. She worried that Maurice was testing her, and it wouldn't just be the art on the line if she failed. It would be her life.

Paxton endured five minutes of laughter on the other end of the line when he called Peter. Karri had already called to tell Peter about Gatorgate, and before Paxton could even tell his boss about the investigation, the jokes were flying.

Finally, when Peter gasped for breath after laughing at everyone thinking a teenage girl was in trouble, Paxton was able to squeeze in Maurice's visit. That stopped the laughter and the joking.

"Mrs. Elijah F. Cummings? Tinsley wants to bring in an eighty-something-year-old society matron to deal with an art thief?" Peter paused for a second. "Hmm. Actually, that's genius. He'd never suspect her working with us and I like the idea about being the bored, spoiled grandson of a very, *very* rich old lady."

"Is he in?" Tinsley called out from across the gallery as she hung a new piece of art.

"Tell her I'm in. Have her call Mrs. Cummings and see if I can meet with her," Peter instructed.

So it was on. Paxton would at least have Peter in the room to help keep both civilians safe. Within minutes, Tinsley bounded back into the room with a large smile on her face. "Miss Tibbie is in, but she has one request. She wants her alias to be named Bunny."

Paxton shook his head as he smiled. "What is it with people around here being named after animals?"

Tinsley shrugged. "I don't know. But she said she likes

Bunny because people think they're all cute and cuddly but they actually have a sharp bite."

Paxton smiled as he thought about it. "I'm looking forward to meeting Miss Tibbie. She sounds like my kind of lady. Now, how about we head home and I make you dinner?"

"You just don't want to go to the bar and have everyone laugh at you for screaming like a girl," Tinsley teased.

"You're right. *I'd much rather make you scream.*" Tinsley's laughter stopped instantly as she gulped. Her eyes widened and her cheeks turned a pretty pink. When her eyes dropped downward with clear fascination, Paxton wondered just what kind of guys Tinsley had been dating. Either they clearly didn't appreciate what they had or they had no idea what to do with her once they had her. Paxton smiled down at Tinsley. He didn't have that problem. No, if Paxton were lucky enough to ever get Tinsley to be his, he'd whisper all sorts of naughty things to her, and that wasn't half of what he'd already fantasized about doing to her.

Tinsley had excused herself to get cleaned up for dinner the second they'd reached her house. She had basically run inside and was hiding in her bedroom while Paxton cooked dinner. *I'd much rather make you scream.*

Just thinking about it made her breathing speed up and it was time to admit she'd been wrong. Harper had always invited her to come out with her when she was single, but Tinsley had told Harper all the time she wasn't into the kind of guys Harper was. Harper wanted to go to bars and dance clubs. Tinsley had wanted to go to art shows or literary readings. She touched her lips remembering the panty-melting kisses she'd shared with Paxton. No, the guys at those shows or readings would never shove her up against a car and kiss her like that smack in the middle of Main Street.

Maybe her softness, her quietness, and her way of playing things safely needed that edge Paxton had. She would never in her life have crossed the imaginary line that seemed to limit her risks without it. Paxton could push her over that line. Heck, he'd already kissed his way over it. It wasn't just sexual, though. While they set up her gallery, he praised her ability to paint people. He was nudging her toward another imaginary line she'd drawn thinking it was too risky for her career to paint outside her comfort zone.

Was it just her being affected, though? No, it wasn't. With Tinsley in Paxton's life, she'd noticed he'd relaxed his self-control a bit. He was laughing more, teasing more, and talking more. He was opening up and showing her the real Paxton more and more the longer she was with him. Tinsley took a deep breath. She was taking on criminals. She could take on Paxton Kendry.

Paxton was pouring the wine when Tinsley marched into the kitchen. Her face was set with determination and he worried something had happened. "What's wrong, Tins?"

Tinsley didn't answer him. Instead she grabbed the bottle of wine from his hands and took long gulps from the bottle before slamming it onto the counter.

"Tinsley? Did something happen?" Paxton was getting worried now. She acted like a compressed trigger ready to go off.

"Do you go after something when you know you want it?" Tinsley asked suddenly as she began pacing in the small kitchen.

"Yes. You won't get anywhere in life without taking risks and going for what you want. Why?"

"I realized something just now. I live my life playing it safe. I don't paint people because they're not in my comfort zone." Paxton was not sure where this was going, but it was clear Tinsley was working out something in her mind. He could practically see the gears turning. "But you're pushing me to see that some risks are worth taking."

"Isn't that what art is all about?" Tinsley stopped and stared at him with questions in her eyes. "You can paint anything you want. Express anything you want. Interpret your feelings, what you're seeing, in any way you want. If you don't like it, you can paint over it. You can throw it away. But art is about pushing boundaries and taking risks to try to connect with the world and how you see it and feel it. If you do that with art, you can do that with life."

Tinsley nodded even though she was now staring at the table as if it held the answers to life. "You're right. I need to learn to take risks. If an artist can't be true to herself about what she sees and feels, how can she grow as an artist?"

Paxton gave a little chuckle as he watched Tinsley. Her eyes shot up to him and he shook his head. "I'm not laughing at you. I'm laughing at myself. I usually don't even consider the risks. But I'm learning sometimes taking it slow and playing it safe has its moments."

Tinsley took a deep breath and then the look of determination was back. "Yeah, this isn't one of those times."

Before Paxton could ask what kind of time it was, Tinsley grabbed his shirt with both hands and was yanking him down so she could reach his lips. Sparks flew, heat flowed, and passion roared as their lips melded together. Paxton bundled Tinsley into his arms, holding her tight against him. She pushed her small hands against his chest so he dropped his hold on her. With their tongues tangling and their lips crushing together, Tinsley shoved him backward. He reached behind his back to find the table and the plates he'd set.

Tinsley stopped pushing against his chest when he backed into the table and made the silverware dance. She pulled back and he let her go. Her face was flushed. Her lips were swollen and parted as she breathed quickly and it all made sense to him now.

Instead of taking the lead, he waited. This was Tinsley taking a risk and he wanted to be there for every risk she ever took. Because if she failed, he wanted to be the one to catch her. And if she succeeded, he wanted to be the one to watch her soar.

Paxton watched hesitancy cross Tinsley's face. "You're so beautiful, Tinsley. Tell me what you want."

Her face flushed, but Paxton pushed her. He wasn't going to move until she told him to, but he was going to help her take the risk she clearly wanted to take on him. It was humbling that she trusted him enough to spread her wings with him.

"I want . . ." Tinsley stopped and swallowed hard.

"Tell me what you want, Tinsley." Paxton kept his voice low and coaxing, but his eyes were on fire for her.

"I want to scream," she finally said. That was all Paxton was waiting for. In two steps he was to her. His lips were on hers as he bent to grab her ass. With a quick lift, he had her arms around his neck and her legs around his waist.

He carried her up the stairs as her fingers tightened in the hair at the nape of his neck. She gave him a little tug and he gently bit her lip as he climbed the stairs. The door to her room was open and Paxton didn't let go of her as he made his way through the room. He lowered them both to the bed, still interlocked, and kissed her for all he was worth.

He broke away from the kiss to move his lips to her neck as he undressed her. Her hands were sure and steady as they yanked his shirt from his pants. Gone was any hesitancy or self-consciousness as they let all their walls come tumbling down.

"I've wanted you from the first time you put your hands on your hips and looked up at me," Paxton whispered against her skin as he moved his lips from her breast and traveled downward. Tinsley's fingers raked through his hair and held him to her as he made her scream for the first time that night, but definitely not the last.

Paxton felt like a man possessed with the way Tinsley's skin felt against his. Her sighs, moans, and screams were addictive. He wanted more of everything. Now that he'd had her in his life, he didn't know if he could ever leave. Not her bed or her life.

He grabbed a condom and then looked into her face as he braced his arms by her head. Her arms wrapped around his back and Paxton felt her run her fingertips down his spine. The world slowed until there were only the two of them. When he slid inside her, the world as he knew it changed forever.

12

Tinsley woke slowly with a smile on her face as the morning sun began to fill the room. Paxton was on his back with one arm thrown over his head while she was snuggled up to his other arm. Last night had been the best night of her life. It might have gone unspoken, but something had changed between her and Paxton. She'd made the decision to open herself up to him. She did it in ways she never had before. And not just in bed.

They talked over dinner and she opened her heart and shared her feelings, her fears, and her dreams. Even the ones she's never been able to admit to herself. Paxton hadn't laughed at her. He supported her, encouraged her, and then he confided in her. There was so much both of them had hidden from the world, but that wasn't the case any longer. She had someone to share these things with now.

Paxton had warned her about the possibility of him transferring to another FBI office. They talked about it— why he wanted to transfer back to the Violent Gangs Task Force and why he was now thinking about not transferring. "I'll support you no matter what you choose," she had told him. His shoulders had slumped as if a weight had been lifted. Then he'd shoved the empty plates to the floor and made her scream again.

"Are you awake?" Paxton whispered.

Tinsley opened her eyes and nodded. "I am. It's time to go to work."

Tinsley tried not to pace the gallery as she waited for Maurice and Tibbie, or rather Bunny, to arrive. She'd cranked the air conditioning up but she was still sweating.

Paxton was in the back of the gallery pretending to fix the air conditioning when the doorbell jingled. Tinsley pasted on a smile as she stepped forward. Maurice and Murray were early. She'd hoped to talk to Miss Tibbie first.

"Maurice, Murray, are you both excited for the sale?" Tinsley asked as she joined them in the middle of the gallery and shook their hands.

"We are," Maurice said, his eyes going straight to Paxton. "Who's that?"

"I told you about him. He's my employee and right now he's trying to fix my runaway air conditioning." Tinsley shivered and moved toward the desk closest to Paxton. "Come have a seat. Can I get you something to drink while we wait?"

"No, thank you," Maurice said as he eyed Paxton.

Paxton looked to the side and gave them a brief smile before getting back to work on the air conditioning wall unit.

The doorbell chimed again and Tinsley smiled with genuine happiness at Miss Tibbie who sailed into the gallery like she hadn't a care in the world. She looked every inch the epitome of a society matron, but nothing like herself. The wig she had was brown and cut into a short, shaggy bob. Her makeup was flawless, but not colors Miss Tibbie had ever worn. No, these were blues and silvers and Tibbie usually wore warm colors. However, they did match the ice blue suit she wore with tasteful yet gigantic diamonds. She carried herself into the gallery as if she owned it.

"Tinsley, darling," Miss Tibbie glided forward and lifted her cheek for Tinsley to kiss.

"Miss Bunny, thank you for coming today."

The doorbell chimed a third time and Peter strode in. Tinsley almost choked when she saw him. He had on fitted salmon-colored pants that hit at his ankles, showing off brown loafers with no socks. He wore a button-down shirt in thin blue and white stripes with the top two buttons undone and the sleeves rolled up. He also wore dark black sunglasses and his hair must have taken thirty minutes to style into the perfect "rolled from bed" look.

Tibbie sighed. "Graham, come meet Tinsley. She's the one I told you about."

Peter pulled his glasses off and sauntered forward. He smiled like someone who's always had everything in the world handed to him and Tinsley was just another tasty morsel to add to his collection. "Ah, the girl my grandmother wants to set me up with. It's a pleasure to meet you." Peter lifted Tinsley's hand and placed a kiss on her knuckles.

Maurice cleared his throat and Tinsley yanked her hand from Peter. "Miss Bunny, these are the men selling the painting. Maurice Smith and his brother, Murray. Maurice and Murray, this is Miss Bunny. We volunteer for the same charity in Charleston."

"Such handsome young men," Tibbie held out her hand

and played it up. Maurice looked as if he didn't know what to do and looked to Tinsley. Tinsley pursed her lips into a kissy face and Maurice looked slightly confused for a second before catching on. He took Tibbie's hand and placed a careful kiss on her knuckles.

"It's a pleasure to meet you, Bunny. This painting is part of our grandmother's collection, so it holds a very special place in our hearts. Can you tell us why you'd like to buy it?"

Tibbie turned to Peter and smacked his arm. "See, they're good grandsons. I bet they're not amusing their grandmother just to get at their trust fund."

Peter rolled his eyes and took a seat close to Tinsley.

"Castille is one of my favorites. I have three of his paintings already and Tinsley knows to grab any Castille she comes across for me. This is one of his lesser-known works. The brush strokes are his signature style with fluid strokes that hook just slightly to give the appearance of movement." Tinsley sat back and let Tibbie put on a master class in art history. "However, this is a lesser-known and a smaller canvas size than his other works. Therefore, I'll offer you fifty thousand for it."

Maurice looked to Tinsley who was trying not to laugh. Leave it to Tibbie to play hardball with criminals. "Bunny," Tinsley said, letting her amusement show. "You know this painting is worth much more than that. The sale price is a hundred thousand."

Tibbie cocked her head and examined the painting for a second. She motioned for Tinsley to turn it over. Tinsley stepped forward and carefully turned the painting on the easel. Tibbie pulled back the paper backing on the frame and clucked. "Frayed canvas edges, and while it is in good condition, it's not excellent. Whoever last framed it didn't pull the canvas tight enough and that's led to some bulk of the fold. You can see it here where there's a ripple in the canvas. I'll offer seventy thousand for it, but that's my final offer."

Tinsley looked over at Maurice who appeared to be happy with the offer, but she needed to impress him. "Seventy-five thousand and we'll sign the deal right now."

Tibbie looked as if she were thinking it over. Then she held out her hand to Tinsley. "You've got a deal. I always love negotiating with you." Tibbie turned to Maurice and Murray. "Gentlemen. It's been a pleasure. Now, tell me what else does your grandmother have in her little art collection?"

Tinsley almost sputtered. Tibbie wasn't supposed to do that. "Actually," Tinsley said, answering for the Smith brothers. "Here are a few others. You have the first look at them." Tinsley stepped back and showed some of the stolen art they'd given her the other day.

"She might also have some more pieces that will interest you. My grandparents were longtime collectors. She has close to eighty pieces in her collection. Let me talk to Tinsley and I'm sure she'll be in contact with you. We'd appreciate them going to someone who respects them," Maurice said as he signed the papers for the Castille and handed them over to Tibbie.

"That one, the Shezun, how much for it?" Tibbie asked, pointing to the one painting valued at twenty thousand.

"Twenty thousand," Tinsley replied easily.

"Hmm," Bunny looked like she was considering it. "Fifteen and I'll take it, too."

"Eighteen and I'll have Paxton wrap it up," Tinsley replied in the blink of an eye.

"Young man, wrap these two up and take them to my car," Tibbie said, snapping her fingers at Paxton before turning back to Maurice and Tinsley. "Call me the second the rest of your collection comes in. You know I'll be very upset if I hear you let Cissy see them before me."

"Of course, Miss Bunny," Tinsley said as she handed the routing number and account number for Bunny to wire the FBI's money to. Bunny waved it away.

"Make yourself useful, Graham. You know I don't know how to work that blasted technology. Not that way, boy," Bunny hissed at Paxton and took off to instruct him how she wanted the painting wrapped.

Peter grunted, but his fingers flew over Tibbie's phone as he made the wire transfer. "Done. Gram, can we go now? I promised the guys we'd take the boat out today."

Tibbie bid them goodbye and Paxton carried the paintings outside as Peter held the door for him. As soon as they were alone, Maurice and Murray stood.

"Let me just transfer you the money minus my commission," Tinsley said as they watched her make the transfer. "Done. Wasn't that easy?"

"I like how you work, Tinsley." Maurice grinned at her as Paxton walked back in.

Paxton nodded to the men as he walked by and went back to work on the air conditioning.

"I know Bunny said she'd be interested in some of my grandmother's pieces, but I already have some buyers lined up. I want you to handle all the sales for us. I don't have the time or knowledge to do it myself. Can you explain how you just made the payment?" Maurice asked.

"My gallery has an escrow account. Most of the time, the seller wires money or gives me a check. Wiring money has become more common since they can leave with the piece as soon as it hits my account. Otherwise, they have to wait for us to deliver it after the check clears. Then I take out my commission and wire the rest to your account or write you a check. Your call," Tinsley explained.

Maurice and Murray shared a look before Maurice nodded to her. "We'll take wire transfers. You can use the account number we gave you. I'll be bringing the collection to you soon."

"I can have Paxton come pick it up. That way he can make sure they're transported safely. I have a specialized van for just that reason," Tinsley said, trying to get Paxton close to the sellers.

"No need. My grandmother lives out of town. I'll bring it in the next time I visit her. I look forward to growing our partnership, Tinsley." Maurice shook her hand and then Murray did.

They walked out of the gallery and Tinsley spun around to Paxton the second the door shut. "Aren't you going to follow them?"

"Someone already is. We have FBI agents lined up along the road to follow them. Tibbie and Peter are in the courtyard. Let's go let them in. I need to talk to Peter."

13

Paxton hurried to the back door with Tinsley right behind him. He pushed open the door and found Peter and Tibbie sitting at the small table, laughing.

"Oh, that was so much fun! I have more wigs than Dolly Parton. It was fun to pull them out again. The seventies, you know? All wigs, all time. Maybe I'll bring them back into fashion."

"You were excellent, Miss Tibbie. The FBI thanks you for your assistance," Peter told her. "Now, let me introduce you to my art crimes agent, Paxton Kendry. Paxton, this is Mrs. Elijah Cummings, or Miss Tibbie to those lucky enough to call her a friend."

Paxton shook her hand and gave her a wink. "I'm happy to have you as part of my team. You didn't even bat an eye at dealing with criminals."

"Bah, they're nothing. You should come to the Arts Endowment Silent Auction if you want to see real action. No matter how hard criminal organizations try, they'll never be tougher than society matrons at a silent auction."

Paxton laughed. That wasn't true, was it? He'd make sure to ask Miss Tibbie later. She looked like she had great stories to tell, but right now he had a break in the case and he needed to follow that lead.

"I know who they are," Paxton said and everyone went quiet. "It's been nagging at me since I saw the first video footage of Maurice. He looks really familiar, but now that I saw Murray, I know. They're from Atlanta. They're from the gang I was undercover with. I recognized the partial tattoo that was showing. They are brothers but their last name isn't Smith, it's Spiller," Paxton told Peter.

"Did they recognize you?" Peter asked, all business now.

Paxton shook his head. "When I was undercover I had a big, thick beard that covered most of my face, long, shoulder-length hair, and I wore colored contacts. I went by a different name and was covered in temporary tattoos that looked so real I was surprised they eventually washed off."

Peter frowned. "I don't like coincidences."

Miss Tibbie shook her head and clucked. "As if it were a coincidence while at the fundraiser last week that Tex Thomas left to use the restroom thirty seconds after Titty Roberts did . . . excuse me, Kitty Roberts. Those two have been foolin' around for six months and still think no one knows. Well, what they don't know is Tex's wife and Kitty's husband are filing divorce papers at the same time on Monday. Coincidence? Ha! There are no coincidences. So, tell us about that gang you were with. Why would they want to sell stolen art?"

"I don't know," Paxton admitted. "There was never any mention of art when I was undercover with them. They ran drugs and guns."

"Could they be payment for drugs and guns with other

gangs?" Tinsley asked. "Maurice said they have some buyers already lined up."

"Could be. What about money laundering?" Paxton asked.

Peter nodded. "That could work. They have Tinsley sell the art. She takes the dirty money, and when she wires it from her escrow account, it gets cleaned. I already looked at the account they had Tinsley deposit the money into. It's a front. The company sells artwork. The address is a one-room desk rental space in an office building. Not an art studio, but a respectable address if you have no reason to dig. The money is still sitting there, too. It hasn't moved yet and no one has asked for a withdrawal. Tell me what you know about Maurice and Murray."

Paxton closed his eyes and thought back through all the FBI files he had on the gang. "Curtis Engle is the leader of the Myriad. I never had enough to take him down, but I was getting close. Maurice and Murray were street lackeys. They sold heroin laced with fentanyl on the street. They must have been moved up in the organization.

"The night I was shot, I was closing in on Engle. He had a meeting that he said would change the gang forever. He handpicked the members to go with him and I wasn't on the list so I followed them to an abandoned warehouse. That's when things went to hell. I was spotted by one of them. I called for backup when the alarm was sounded. My team was supposed to move in, but they didn't. My coms had gone down without me knowing it so I walked in with no backup. Engle waved off the meeting before I could see who it was with and the gang converged on me. It was like the shootout at the O.K. Corral. I took most of the members down with me, including the second-in-command and half the security team before taking three shots to the chest. The brothers were probably moved up after that." Paxton didn't like remembering that night—the shouts, the gunfire, the fear he was going to die.

"How did you get out of there?" Tinsley asked quietly.

"In a body bag. My team only moved in once the shooting started, but they were blocks away, waiting for my signal. The last thing I remember was Engle standing above me. He said, "It's a good thing you're dead or I'd kill you myself." Then he took off running when my team appeared. My boss was there and said I was dead loudly enough that anyone nearby would hear him. I was put in a body bag and loaded into an ambulance in case Engle was watching. The doctors managed to save me. A week later, my boss retired and moved to a beach house in Central America. He told me in the hospital right before he caught the plane out of town that he and his wife had been saving for decades. Then he handed me my transfer papers as his last act as my boss." Paxton still felt the punch in the gut at being handed the transfer. He was the number two man in the office, and instead of his team being there to support him, they'd abandoned him.

Peter crossed his arms over his chest and narrowed his eyes in thought. "You said once you thought something was off. I shoved it aside, but you're right. I've led my fair share of raids and that's not how it was done. The timing of your boss retiring is also interesting. I was going to see if someone from your team could look into Maurice and Murray, but I don't think so. I want to keep this away from them."

"Someone has their hand in the money pot," Miss Tibbie said with a nod as if it were a done thing.

Paxton had to smile at seeing this elegant old lady talking about drugs and gangs. "I think you're right, Miss Tibbie."

"I don't know anything about this, but I have a confession," Tinsley said as she played nervously with her fingers. "My cousin looked into you. He said your report was filled with citations for insubordination. You weren't listening to your superior. Do you think that's the reason for the transfer when in reality it had nothing to do with the night you were shot?"

Paxton felt so surprised he almost fell from the chair. "You looked into me?"

"My cousin did. I told him not to, but you can't tell Ryker anything."

"We know about that. The new head of the department, Mark Trevino, had it changed," Peter told them. "There're no disciplinary actions in his original record. Instead, there are plenty of commendations. Luckily, I had printed it off when Paxton transferred to my office. We thought Mark was the issue, but was your old boss in on it, too?"

"Of course he was," Tibbie said with a roll of her eyes. "The man left the country a week after Paxton was shot. And you call yourselves agents. David Thrumble was a donor to the Historical Society with us. He just took off for Ecuador one day after he sold his company, a company the buyer didn't know the IRS was investigating for tens of millions in unpaid taxes. He even left his wife, Mary Lewis, at their home wondering what was going on when it was seized by the IRS. She had no idea he'd emptied their bank accounts, not paid taxes, and skipped town. Bless her heart. You," Miss Tibbie said, pointing to Paxton, "are Mary Lewis."

Damn. He was.

"It was all a setup. But why?" Peter asked.

"I swear you two wouldn't last one second in Charleston society," Miss Tibbie said as she rolled her eyes. Again. "You're the sacrificial lamb. The question is who hung you out to dry so they could advance?"

"Mark Trevino," Peter and Paxton said at the same time.

It was weird feeling relieved, but that's what Paxton felt. Relief. It all made sense now.

"You know, Mark didn't realize you were still an agent," Peter told him.

"He didn't?" Paxton asked.

Peter shook his head. "He thought you were on medical leave."

"Wait, I don't understand. Why would this Mark guy offer you up to Engle?" Tinsley asked, stopping Paxton from asking more questions.

"Mark never plays by the rules. I always thought Engle had to have an inside man on the team. There were too many times I got so close to busting Engle but when I tried to nail down the evidence, all of a sudden, it was gone. Now it makes sense. Engle was meeting someone big that night. I had just cut Mark out of the case. Instead, I was reporting to my boss, and my boss only. I have no doubt my boss had been saving for that retirement house, but he was only fifty-three. There's no way he'd saved enough while putting two kids through college. Mark had to have paid him off. Keep Mark in the loop and he'd make sure my boss could retire early. My coms were cut on purpose. I bet Mark did it and then tipped Engle off that I was there as proof of his loyalty. Engle would kill me and Mark would be in."

Tibbie nodded and Paxton sat back in his chair and let out a long, slow breath.

"But what does this all have to do with stolen art? And why are they in Shadows Landing?" Tinsley asked.

"That's what we need to find out." Paxton didn't like where his mind was going. Pieces were clicking into place and they all pointed back to Mark Trevino.

14

"There's our screamer," Ridge called out as Tinsley and Paxton walked into the bar for dinner.

Tinsley stumbled over her own feet as she shot a horrified look at Paxton. "You told my brother?" she hissed as Paxton reached out to steady her. The proud smile on his face made her want to roll her eyes.

"As much as I'd love for you to praise my sexual prowess publicly, I believe Ridge is talking about the alligator and me."

Tinsley snorted and slapped her hand over her mouth to keep from laughing out loud.

"Who's screaming?" Peter asked, and Tinsley smothered another laugh.

"You will be later," Paxton whispered as he held out a chair for her.

Peter joined them at the table. "Sorry to interrupt dinner and the rightful merciless teasing Paxton is about to receive, but I need to talk to him."

"Do you have an address?" Paxton asked as he turned away from the table.

Tinsley leaned back in her chair to eavesdrop, but then the door opened and Granger and Kord entered. They took one look at Paxton and slapped both hands on their cheeks and screamed.

Ridge and Tinsley's family lost it. They were cracking up and tossing out jokes as the lawmen joined the table.

"At least they aren't telling you to break up with him," Edie said from where she sat next to Tinsley. "It also shows he can take some ribbing. If he couldn't, your family would run him out of town faster than grass goes through a goose."

"Ignore them," Savannah said from across the table. She leaned forward so they could hear each other better. "How are things going between you two?"

Tinsley smile was automatic and the women shared a look that said they knew exactly what that smile meant.

"That well, huh?" Darcy asked with a wink.

Harper handed out drinks before sitting down next to Ellery. "Don't worry, you're not the only one. Gavin threatened Dare, too."

"He did?" Ellery asked. "My sweet Gavin?"

"Um, you should know better than anyone that Gavin is not sweet and kind when someone he loves is in danger," Harper said before taking a sip of her drink.

Tinsley looked over her shoulder and saw that the men were gathered behind them now. They were leaning forward, their heads bent down as they tried to talk quietly. "Paxton! If you're talking about the case, you do it here with all of us."

Tinsley saw all the women's eyes zero in on their husbands. If looks could kill, they'd be dead. The men shuffled their feet and all returned to the table.

"Peter told us the address Maurice and Murray returned

to. It's the Myriad's headquarters in Atlanta," Paxton told her before having to explain who the Myriad were to the rest of the table.

"I read an article on how gangs are expanding," Ryker told the table. "They work together across state lines. Like a local chapter to a national organization."

"The Myriad have expanded into Charleston recently," Peter said.

Tinsley watched as Paxton nodded. "I wouldn't be surprised by it. Gangs have changed over the years," Paxton explained. "There're the low-level street gangs who distribute the drugs or weapons. Then there're wholesale gangs where the street gangs get their supplies. At the top of the pyramid is the supplier. The street gangs have a loose relationship with the national organization and use it to work together and get supplies across state lines. What I saw in Atlanta were outside gangs trying to get a foothold in the city. I'd expect the same is happening here as well. A gang from L.A. or Chicago may want to expand and Charleston, Atlanta, and Nashville are all prime places for expansion."

"Not only that, but in Charleston we're seeing local gangs reaching out to the larger national ones," Peter added. "The locals want the infrastructure they can supply. The ability to get better deals on drugs and weapons from the suppliers and backup if they need it in a fight against another gang."

"The question is, was Myriad moving into Charleston before I got transferred here and they had no idea I was here until I asked to be transferred, or have they been here longer?" Paxton asked.

"I'll have to ask Agent Whitlock with gangs."

"You are being transferred?" Ridge asked.

Peter shook his head and answered for Paxton. "When Agent Mark Trevino in Atlanta got the transfer request, he didn't know Paxton was still an agent. After he got the request, he went in and changed Paxton's record and then denied the request," Peter explained. "Those disciplinary actions now in his file—they're not real. They never happened. I have Paxton's real file if you need to see it." Peter aimed that at Ryker and Ridge.

Ridge had the grace to look a little embarrassed. Ryker didn't bat an eye. "You can send me a copy. Thank you."

"Ryker!" Tinsley yelled at her cousin.

"I look after my family. Get over it."

"Why don't we get this over with now," Paxton said. "What do you want to know?"

"Everything from whether you ate paste in preschool to the results of your last blood test," Ryker said calmly but with steel in his voice.

"I didn't eat paste," Paxton began, "although I did like the smell of Play-Doh. I graduated from high school with honors. I graduated from college magnum cum laude. I respect my elders and am close to my grandmother. I don't kick puppies or hit women. I'd love a dog at some point. I don't have a green thumb. I can cook enough to impress a date, but not well enough to impress her over time. I haven't dated anyone in a while because I was undercover. I flirted with the women around the gang but never dated them. I bought and sold drugs, but only with prior superior approval. I also think Tinsley is amazing and you all underestimate her strength. There, does that answer enough for you, Ryker?"

Ryker narrowed his eyes.

"Should we talk about you now?" Paxton asked. "I have

my own file with your name on it. Should we start that night when you were a senior and—"

Tinsley reached out and grabbed Paxton's arm. "Don't." It was all she said but it was enough. Paxton saw the concern in her eyes before turning back to a now rigid Ryker. "Unlike you, I'm an open book. Ask anything you want."

"I have a question," Ridge said, breaking up the staring contest that had developed between Paxton and Ryker. Tinsley didn't know whether to be relieved or worried.

"Have things changed between you and my sister from the last time we talked?" Ridge asked.

Well, crap. This wasn't going to end well. Tinsley braced for Ridge to leap across the table.

"Yes. We're together now. That's all I'll tell you. If Tinsley wants to tell you more, she can. I defer to her on how much privacy she wishes to maintain." Paxton looked over at her and smiled. His hand reached for her thigh and he gave it a little squeeze. "I will say I realize I'm one lucky man."

Tinsley sighed along with the rest of the women at the table.

"Is the interrogation finished? I do have a case that needs to be solved." Paxton looked around the table. Ridge and Ryker grumbled but didn't ask anything else.

"So, there's no one on the FBI task force you can talk to?" Peter asked.

Paxton shook his head before making a funny face at baby Chase.

"What about local law enforcement?" Granger asked. "Every city has a Street Crimes Unit. Atlanta probably has a huge one."

"I never worked with them. It would be hard to know who to trust, but it's a decent place to start," Paxton said.

"Tinsley?" Granger said, turning toward her. "Could you

ask your family in Kentucky if they know anyone we could
trust there?"

"How would they know?" Paxton asked.

Tinsley smiled as she thought of them. "They know
everyone. My uncles run a military and law enforcement
training facility. They're all former military and law
enforcement, including FBI. I also have several cousins in
law enforcement."

"Then ask them. Let's see if I can get a local contact.
Maybe I can have them pay off an informant for
information. That's how we get most of our tips," Paxton
told her.

"You know," Granger said, "you're known in Atlanta, but
we're not," he said, motioning toward himself and Kord. "We
don't have jurisdiction, but we don't need it to pay off some
informants."

"I could help," Dare said. "After all, ATF does go after
firearms and most gangs are involved in weapons dealings. I
could see if my ATF buddies in Atlanta have any
information on Myriad or if they have heard any rumblings
about corrupt FBI agents."

Peter and Paxton shared a look. "Looks like we're going
on a road trip."

Paxton turned to Tinsley then and took her hand into
his. "I hate leaving you. Do you think you can close your
gallery for a couple of days? I don't want to leave you
unprotected while I am gone."

"She can stay with me," Ryker said. "My house is well
guarded and the men staying for the meetings all have
bodyguards."

"I know when to be cautious. I'll stay with Ryker. But
what happens if I close the gallery and Maurice and Murray
become suspicious?" Tinsley asked.

"I have to bring my team back to Charleston. They weren't equipped for surveillance." Peter said. "I could have one of them stay at your gallery with you during the day."

"It's not necessary," Ryker said calmly. "I've just ordered private security for her. She'll be here tomorrow morning."

Harper looked over at Tinsley and grinned. "Paxton, Peter, Dare, Granger, and Kord on a guys' trip to the sunny and welcoming Myriad territory in Atlanta. Who'd have thought? I wonder if they'll have a pillow fight?"

Tinsley laughed as she pulled out her phone and sent a text to Walker Greene. He was Edie's brother and had grown up in Shadows Landing before joining the Navy SEALs. He was then recruited up to DEVGRU, which was the old SEAL Team Six. He was the elite of the elite. He'd been injured in the same act of treason that left Edie's husband dead. It had been a long road to get to Shadows Landing and have Gavin fix him up medically, but that's how they met their Keeneston cousins.

Tinsley's great-grandmother had been a piece of work and not the good kind. She'd treated her daughter, Marcy, horribly. She'd wanted a servant, not a daughter. When her great-grandmother moved to South Carolina from Keeneston for Tinsley and her cousins' grandfathers to join the Air Force, Marcy had stayed in Keeneston with the love of her life. Tinsley's great-grandmother had disowned her and told Tinsley's grandparents lies about her that caused a long-standing rift.

But then Walker needed help and Gavin had sucked it up and asked Dr. Layne Davies, their cousin and expert physical therapist, for help. Walker and Layne fell in love, and the Davies and Faulkner families had healed old wounds to become one big happy family.

Tinsley's phone rang a second later. She excused herself

and headed for a quieter spot in the bar to talk to Walker. "Hey!"

"Hey? You're asking me about dangerous gangs and trusted police officers and you say 'hey' like we're going to chat about the fam?" Walker asked, sounding all big brotherly even though he was only a cousin by marriage. Tinsley filled him in and Walker grumbled. "I don't like this. Should I come for a visit? I can bring an army."

"No kidding. I'm fine here. Ryker said he's hiring a private bodyguard for me while Paxton goes to Atlanta."

"I thought you didn't like that guy?" Walker asked.

"I didn't get him. I thought he was making fun of me, but he wasn't. He's quite wonderful and if you or any of the cousins or uncles ruin this for me, I will have my vengeance."

"I make no promises," Walker said. "But I can get the guys some support. I'm sure one of the uncles will know someone who can help. How's my sister? I talked to her a couple of days ago. She sounds good, but I could tell it was for show."

"She's getting better every day. I know it's been a little while since she lost her husband, but she's just not ready to move on yet. However, she's getting out more now. She's involved in the community and we have plenty of girl time together. She's taking self-defense at the church with me, too. I think that's helped more than anything. She's truly skilled with a blade."

"Gotta love Shadows Landing. Send me Paxton's number, and I'll let him know what I find out."

"Are you going to threaten him?" Tinsley asked, knowing darn well Walker would do so.

"Of course I am. Talk to you soon. Call if you need anything. I can catch the next flight there if you need me."

"Thanks, Walker."

Tinsley hung up and sent the contact. A second later, she saw Paxton look down at his phone and frown. Walker moved fast with his threats. He was never one to sit back and wait. Unfortunately, that was all Tinsley could do now. Sit back and wait for Paxton to solve his case.

15

Paxton had made contact with Walker Greene, who promised to have someone on the ground in Atlanta by lunchtime. The guys were meeting at seven and driving down in an FBI SUV that was used for undercover work. That left tonight with Tinsley. He didn't like leaving her but the faster he could put the case to bed, the faster he could take Tinsley to bed and not worry about leaving it ever again.

He had it bad. So bad he was packing up their things and loading the suitcases into their cars to go off and spend the night at Ryker's house. He wasn't sure how it would be any safer until they pulled up. Then it all made sense. Ryker Faulkner was a crazy protective super-rich guy with a dark past and a chip on his shoulder. Of course he went overboard to keep his private life private.

Paxton followed Tinsley through the iron gate and counted the number of cameras and motion detectors he saw, guessing there were three times that number of hidden ones.

Paxton parked and got out to help Tinsley carry in her

bag. She didn't blink at the large house or the armed guards at the door to the guest house. Instead she talked about how sweet Ryker was. Paxton wasn't buying it. There was nothing sweet about Ryker. He was a stone-cold businessman who was known to take no prisoners during negotiations or takeovers. He ran his shipping company with a ruthlessness that would make mob bosses seem cuddly. The garden door at the back of the house opened for them and Ryker glared at him.

"Thanks for letting me stay here, Ryker." Tinsley leaned up and placed a kiss on his cheek before brushing past him and walking inside.

Paxton wasn't so lucky. Ryker crossed his arms and narrowed his eyes.

"Yes, thank you for keeping Tinsley safe while I'm away," Paxton told him, but Ryker didn't move. He didn't even blink. So Paxton leaned forward and placed a quick kiss on Ryker's cheek. Ryker was so stunned he let Paxton walk by him and into the house.

"Should we take the guest room at the top of the stairs or the end of the hall?" Tinsley called out from somewhere in the house. Paxton hurried forward and found her halfway up the stairs.

"Tinsley, you're in the room next to mine. Paxton's staying in the guest room down here," Ryker said with steel to his voice.

Tinsley just laughed and motioned for Paxton to follow her. Ryker's hand clamped onto Paxton's shoulder. "My house, my rules. Your room is around the corner and down that hall. It affords a good view of the front drive."

Paxton dropped Tinsley's bag at Ryker's feet and smiled. "Thank you. I'm sure it'll be perfect."

Paxton walked over to Tinsley who looked ready to

explode and kissed her slowly on the lips. "Goodnight, Tinsley. Sweet dreams." He headed for the room and smiled to himself as Tinsley read Ryker the riot act. Paxton had to give it to the man. He didn't give in, even when Tinsley stomped on his foot.

Paxton closed his bedroom door and headed for the window. It was a good security location. An hour later there was a soft tap on the door. He knew who it was before he opened it.

"Do you need another kiss?"

"Bite me, Kendry."

"Ooh, I should have guessed the powerful Ryker Faulkner is into the kinky stuff. But hey, I don't kinkshame."

Ryker rolled his eyes and Paxton stopped joking as he saw the strain on the man's face. Ryker pushed past him and dropped into one of the lounge chairs in the large room.

"Did something happen?" Paxton asked as he took the seat next to Ryker.

"Something is always happening, Kendry. Only this time it's Tinsley. Look, I know she has an older brother, but you don't understand what she means to us. Harper is Harper. Hell, I think she's tougher than all of us cousins. Tinsley is the complete opposite of Harper. She's all happy colors, rescuing butterflies, and finding the good in everyone. I don't know how you got it, but I guess I saw what happened to me. Tinsley is the reason I'm still here. She was a little slip of a teen when it happened. As you can imagine, I was in a very dark place. Everyone wanted to help. I know that now. However, it was Tinsley who saved me. It was her pure heart, her goodness, her faith in humanity that saved me. Well, as much as I ever could be saved after what happened."

"You were found innocent," Paxton said. As much as he

wanted to give Ryker crap, it was clear the man loved his family and Paxton would never give him crap for that.

"Doesn't mean I am innocent." Ryker took a deep breath. "Did she tell you about the assault?"

"Assault?"

"Walker, the guy who texted you from Keeneston, was in trouble. Someone was looking to kill him. His sister, Edie, had just lost her husband who was a part of Walker's DEVGRU team. She was staying at Tinsley's house. The man who killed her husband and was after Walker broke in, beat up Tinsley, and kidnapped Edie. I will never, in a million years, forget seeing Tinsley bruised and battered. Tinsley is special to me. You hurt her, you hurt me. You break her heart and I'll break you. So, do what you need to in order to make Tinsley safe. If you can't, because your hands are tied by being an agent, call me. I'll handle it. But I swear, you put her in harm's way and she gets hurt, I'll kill you. You know I'm capable of it."

"I would never let harm come to Tinsley. I swear on my life. It's yours to take if I fail." Paxton had to calm himself. He hadn't known about the assault or the kidnapping. Just thinking about it made him sick to his stomach.

Ryker stared at him and then shoved himself up. "You're not who I pictured for her, but she's happy. She's confident now. I noticed the change even if Ridge is pretending she's still a little kid and burying his head in the sand."

"Does that mean I have your approval to be with her?"

"Do you need it?" Ryker asked.

"No, but family is important to her. It's important to me, too. It's not easy to admit. You did a search on me. You know what the past years have been like for me. I care for her, Ryker. More than anything. I will do everything I can to make her happy, and having her family's approval will make her happy."

"I don't *don't* like you," Ryker admitted.

Paxton chuckled. "I'll take it."

"That's a good-looking man," Paxton heard a woman whisper.

"Not my thing, but even I can appreciate a torso like that. There's just something about the way his ab muscles seem cut from stone," a second female voice said.

Paxton pretended to stretch in his sleep and then he was sitting up with a gun pointed at the early morning intruders. One was a tall woman with long, blonde hair pulled up in a high ponytail. She had on a form-fitting white cotton tank with a lightweight, short-sleeved blazer over it. Her lips were red, her dark-wash jeans were skin-tight, and her heels were high. The other woman was a petite brunette with stunning eyes and an impeccably fitted suit. Both women had bulges on their hips indicating they were armed. Neither seemed fazed at having a gun pointed at them.

"Darlin', I'm everyone's thing," Paxton said with a slow Southern drawl.

"You're my thing if I weren't an unspecified number of years older than you or married," the blonde said with a smile.

"She's more my thing. Think your delicate male ego can handle that? Do you need a tissue?" the brunette asked.

"Who are you two and why are you in my bedroom?" Paxton asked, still not lowering his weapon.

"Ryker hired me to look after your probationary girlfriend. I'm Mallory Westin-Simpson. I own Westin

Security in Atlanta. By the way, here's a police contact for you." She tossed him a business card, but he didn't look to see where it landed.

"Probationary?" Paxton questioned.

"I hear you're the one on probation until your ability to keep Tinsley safe has been determined," the brunette answered. "I'm Blythe Kencroft of Creed Security. Walker sent me to keep an eye on Tinsley. I've met her at some Keeneston weddings. Walker told me I could castrate you if you stepped out of line or if you proved unworthy. Just one sec." Blythe pulled out her phone and snapped a picture. "Marcy Davies should see this."

"I sent your fingerprints to Ahmed while you were sleeping. I'll know everything about you in the next ten seconds. Or less," Mallory smirked as her phone pinged. "Ouch. I'm looking at your medical records from when you were shot."

"Don't worry, the scars are sexy," Blythe said with a wink.

"Look at this, Blythe, he got a B- in high school chemistry. Let's hope he has better chemistry with Tinsley," Mallory said as she showed the phone to Blythe.

"Who the hell is Ahmed and how does he have access to this information?" Paxton demanded as he leaped from bed. The flash went off again on Blythe's phone. "I'm starting to think I am your thing."

"Nope. Totally not my thing. However, Marcy asked for it and if Miss Marcy asks for something, you get it or you don't get any apple pie. I would kill someone for that pie."

"Then you'll have to try Miss Ruby and Miss Winnie's apple pies," Tinsley said from the doorway. "Blythe, what are you doing here? Is Veronica with you?"

Blythe, still ignoring the gun aimed at her, turned and

hurried to hug Tinsley. "No Veronica on this trip. I'm here on business."

"Business?" Tinsley asked, and then her whole face changed. It went from wondering, to realization, to unfettered delight. "You're here to look after me?"

"We both are. Hi, I'm Mallory Westin-Simpson."

Paxton lowered his gun as he was completely forgotten. As the women chatted, he grabbed his phone and headed for the shower. While the water heated up, he searched out the two women. They were exactly who they said they were, but Mallory was way more than just the owner of one of the region's largest private security firms. Her father had been a senator and she'd married into the powerful, Atlanta-based Simpson family that ran a large international corporate conglomerate. The fact that Mallory was here and not one of her employees spoke volumes to what kind of relationship she had with Ryker.

"Paxton?" Tinsley called from the other side of the door. "Can I come in?"

"Of course," he called out from the shower. He saw the door open through the fogged glass.

"When do you leave?" she asked as she leaned against the granite counter in the bathroom.

"In twenty minutes." Paxton turned off the shower, and when he opened the glass door he found Tinsley leaning against the counter with the towel in her hand.

"I thought you were going to come to my room last night," Tinsley confessed as she handed him the towel.

"Ryker and I had a talk. Then I had to plan for Atlanta. I'm sorry. I wish I had more time with you. But the faster this case is solved, the faster I can come home to you," Paxton told her as he wrapped the towel around his waist.

"You'd better come home to me. Don't do anything

stupid like getting yourself shot." Tinsley reached out and pressed her hand over the cluster of scars on his chest.

"I won't. As much as it kills me, I'm going to be the one in the van. We can't risk anyone recognizing me. Tinsley, call me immediately if anything happens or if you get any weird gut feeling. I've learned to listen to my gut over the years. Promise?"

"I promise. Paxton, be safe. I—" Paxton kissed her then. She looked so worried for him he couldn't stand it. Whatever she was going to say was lost on his lips.

Tinsley became wild in his arms as she ripped off his towel. Her lips were just as demanding as her hips. Paxton smiled against her neck. She was assertive and went after what she wanted and he was happy to comply with her demands.

"Normally I love to hear you scream, but I might get shot if you do it today," Paxton told her as he rested his forehead against hers.

Tinsley pulled a condom from her pocket and shrugged. "Eh, you've been shot before. You'll live."

"You're perfect for me, Tinsley. I think you were made for me to love."

Paxton saw her eyes shoot up at his. Love. He hadn't meant to go there yet. He hadn't even gone there in his mind yet, but when he lifted her onto the counter and she wrapped her legs around him, he admitted he was wrong. She wasn't just made for him. He was meant for her, too. They were made for each other.

16

Atlanta, Georgia

Paxton looked down at the text message from Walker. "Next right. We're going to meet his contact and then go meet with Mallory's contact."

Peter maneuvered the SUV down the street lined with hotels. A man in jeans, cowboy boots, a worn T-shirt, and mirrored sunglasses stood looking in their direction. His head was shaved, and as they drove closer Paxton noticed the man was a little older than Paxton had first thought. In fact, he looked to be old enough to be his father. Though Paxton didn't know any fathers who looked like this scary-ass dude.

Dare snorted in the seat behind him. "I know our contact. You all thought we were badasses? That's Harper's Uncle Cy Davies."

"That guy scares me," Kord told them as they drove closer.

"I'm man enough to admit he scares me, too," Granger

said.

"Who is he?" Peter asked.

"A former spy. That's all I've gotten from the few family things we've been to. He's retired now and runs a farm, as well as training people at their military training center. I know his sons, Parker and Porter, better. Parker is a new US marshal and Porter is a top-ranked professional rodeo rider," Dare told them as they approached.

"What does he know about gangs?" Paxton asked.

Dare shrugged. "I've stopped asking questions when it comes to the Davies uncles."

Peter stopped the SUV and the man yanked open the front door and stared at Paxton. "You're in my seat."

Paxton instantly leaped from the SUV. The man's voice demanded obedience. "Yes, sir."

"I'm Cy. I'm here to help." He dropped a duffle bag and his hands whipped out lightning fast as they grabbed Paxton's shirt. "I know how to make a body disappear. You hurt Tinsley and you'll never be found."

"Yes, sir." Those were the only words Paxton could get out. This man may be in his early sixties, but there was no question he could do everything he'd just threatened.

Cy let go and climbed into the front seat. "So, you have a gang problem. Just tell me where to go and what information you need."

Paxton blinked. "You want to go undercover? That's what Granger, Kord, and Dare are doing."

Cy turned and looked them all over, but all Paxton could see was their reflections in Cy's mirrored aviator sunglasses. "They'll do, but you need someone a little more seasoned to do the talking. Also, you need someone not bound by the law. Dare, you're my muscle. Kord, you're my top seller.

Granger, you're my supplier. If any dirty work needs to be done, I'll do it. Got it?"

"Yes, sir," rang out through the SUV.

"We checked out Mallory's police contact and he's good to go. He's gotten us permission to operate in his jurisdiction. Well, you all have permission to be here with him to run this operation. I'm not here. Got it?" Cy told them.

"Yes, sir," they chorused.

"If we need off-the-books backup, they're forty-five minutes away by plane. So if you think things are going to be FUBAR, let me know. My brothers are looking forward to another guy's trip," Cy said.

"Guys' trip?" Paxton asked. "To take down a gang?"

Cy turned in his seat and Paxton found himself looking into the mirrored glasses as a slow smirk appeared on the older man's lips. "We do this shit for fun."

Cy turned back around and they all rode in silence to the meeting location. Who the heck was Tinsley's Kentucky family?

Paxton got out of the SUV at the hole-in-the-wall diner on the outskirts of Atlanta. They walked into the diner as a large group. The glass door slammed shut behind them and they had to let their eyes adjust to the dim light for a moment. A man in a worn but clean suit waved them over from where two tables had been pushed together. His cool umber face was shaved clean and the tightness around his brown eyes showed the amount of evil he'd seen in his life.

"You must be the guys from South Carolina that Mallory told me about. I'm Sergeant Connor Gibbs of the Targeted Enforcement Unit. We are the umbrella unit for the Gang

Unit and Gun Reduction Task Force, and we work with the ATF. We all work together, so, Dare Reigns, I got you federal permission to operate with my team. Everyone should be covered." Connor's eyes moved to Cy. "Except you. I don't know you."

Cy just smirked but didn't say anything.

"I'm Paxton Kendry, FBI. This is my boss, Peter Castle. Then that's Dare with ATF. This is Granger Fox, sheriff of Shadows Landing and his deputy, Kordell King."

Connor nodded and motioned with his head for everyone to sit. "Mallory filled me in a little. She didn't know what she was allowed to share, but she asked that nothing went to the FBI gang unit or anyone friendly with them, yet here sit two FBI agents. One of whom is a white-collar guy in art crimes. I'm a little confused."

"I was part of the gang unit here until I was shot three times. I believe I was double-crossed by the new unit leader," Paxton told Connor who was seasoned enough not to look shocked, but instead saddened.

"I see you don't look surprised," Granger said to Connor.

Connor shook his head. "No. I was hoping it wasn't true, but it's been too many coincidences to pretend they have a clean house over there. My captain has noticed, too. We're separating ourselves from them. We've stopped sharing information and, lo and behold, we started getting major busts again. We knew there was a rat. We just didn't know who it was."

"I think it's Mark Trevino leading it. I don't know who else is dirty," Paxton told him before laying out his history with the unit and subsequent transfer and art case.

Connor sat back and pursed his lips in thought. "You think the art could be used to clean dirty money or a payoff?"

"I couldn't see the payoff," Paxton told him. "Usually art is used by gangs to trade. A painting for a case of guns or a kilo of drugs. That kind of trade."

Connor nodded but leaned forward as if he knew something Paxton didn't. "I think it was a payment to the Myriad and now they're cleaning it to get the cash to expand. I have no proof of this, but it's a hunch."

"You never discount a hunch," Cy said seriously.

Connor looked over at him in confusion. "Who are you?"

Cy didn't answer.

"The night I was shot," Paxton said, ignoring Cy, "Curtis Engle was supposed to meet with someone about a big deal that could change everything for them. What are you hearing?"

"Nothing concrete. I know Curtis has expanded into Florida. To do that, you have to have the gun power and top quality and quantity of drugs to claim a section of the market," Connor answered.

"We're thinking they're making a play in Charleston, too," Peter told him.

"I'm sure Kendry can tell you," Connor started to say, "that something had to happen for Myriad to be able to make this move. They didn't have the resources to do so two years ago."

Paxton agreed. "Curtis Engle took over the Myriad two years ago. That's when I joined undercover. As soon as he took control, he began to push for more power, more control, and worked to actively expand their area. Which means this art has something to do with those goals. Otherwise, he wouldn't bother with it."

"Are any of your CIs intact or did Trevino know of them?" Connor asked him.

"I have a couple who no one knows about. What about you all?"

"I have one we can talk to," Connor answered.

"You two work those angles. When we have all we need from CIs, I'll put together the next phase of the plan." Cy crossed his arms over his chest. It wasn't a question up for debate. That was his plan and he was going to do it.

"Who are you again?" Connor asked Cy.

Tinsley kept looking at her phone all day. She hadn't heard a thing from Paxton since they left that morning. Luckily, the gallery had been busy when a tour from a cruise ship came to Shadows Landing. They only allowed one guide to bring in these large tours once a week during the summer. It benefited everyone, but it also prevented them from becoming overrun with tourists. Shadows Landing was just too small to handle that large an influx of visitors.

Mallory and Blythe were naturals at selling art they knew nothing about. Tinsley was going to have to muck out the gallery after all the BS they spewed, but the sales made it worthwhile.

"You do know that wasn't a modern art take on the evolution of feminism, right?" Tinsley asked Blythe after checking her phone for the hundredth time.

"Art is open for interpretation," Blythe said with a shrug. "And I did sell it for twice the price."

"Can't argue with you on that, but feminism?"

"It looked like a vagina, didn't it?" Blythe asked, looking to Mallory for backup.

"I thought it was a butterfly," Mallory told them.

"It was an abstract rose garden," Tinsley said with a roll of her eyes. "The artist is into abstract flowers."

"You mean she painted her dewy folds?" Blythe asked as seriously as she could.

"It's her flower," Mallory said with a nod of agreement.

"It's literally her rose garden," Blythe said with a smirk.

Mallory cocked her head as she looked at the painting they needed to wrap up for delivery to the ship. "It's her pink petals as her bud is about to blossom."

"Oh, that's a good one," Blythe agreed.

The door opened and Harper strode in wearing workout clothes. She stopped and looked at the painting. "It's a vagina that needs a good wax."

"The garden does need trimming," Mallory agreed.

Tinsley rolled her eyes as she finished the wrapping and labeled it. A separate van would take all the purchases the tourists made to the ship before they left the dock in Charleston. "Have you heard from Dare?"

"Nope. I usually don't when he's undercover. Hence, why I'm taking you to the church. I need to work out some pent-up energy," Harper told her. Tinsley couldn't agree more.

"At church? Is there a fun little aerobics class taught by senior citizens?" Blythe joked.

"Something like that," Harper said with a smirk for Tinsley who smiled at the thought of what the church held.

"That sounds perfect. Just let me load this up and we'll change and meet you there."

"Mallory, can you run back to Ryker's and get us all workout clothes while Blythe and I get all the paintings loaded into Skeeter's van for him to transport to Charleston?" Tinsley asked.

· · ·

The next half hour was hectic but soon the four of them were heading into the back of the church. Tinsley and Harper just smiled as Mallory and Blythe joked about even needing to change clothes for the hardcore workout.

"Mitzi, not like that," Tinsley heard Miss Ruby say.

"Fiddlesticks. I'm better at knitting," Miss Mitzi said as they approached the door.

"Darn, it sounds exhausting. I should have brought some more water," Mallory joked.

"No, Mitzi. Like this." Tinsley and Harper hurried into the room just as Mitzi fired the crossbow. The arrow zoomed through the air and lodged in the door right next to Blythe's head.

"What the hell?" Blythe cursed as she pulled her gun.

"Can you move a little to the right, dear?" Miss Ruby asked Blythe. "And stand very still. I want to show Mitzi how to line up the sights on the crossbow. Don't worry, I probably won't shoot you."

Mallory didn't risk standing next to Blythe and leaped into the room doing an action movie-worthy tuck and roll as Miss Ruby fired off the crossbow. The arrow lodged an inch above Blythe's head.

"I can't shoot an old lady," Blythe said standing frozen. "What do I do?"

"You any good with that?" Miss Ruby asked her as she motioned toward the gun.

"Yes. Very."

"Then come try the crossbow. Mitzi's much better with a boarding pike anyway," Miss Ruby told her and motioned for her to join her.

Tinsley went to the armory door and entered a code. The lock slid free and she opened the metal doors wide.

"Your church has an armory filled with swords. I'm at a loss for words," Mallory muttered in amazement.

"The town and church were founded by pirates. These are what they left the women to defend the town with," Miss Winnie said as she shuffled toward them with a dagger in her hand. She reached in and handed a cutlass to Harper and then one to Tinsley. "You look like a boarding ax kind of girl. You think you can handle the weight?" Miss Winnie asked Mallory.

"Yes! Rapiers, cutlasses, axes, this is amazing," Mallory said reverently while Blythe squealed with excitement as she hit the bullseye with the crossbow.

"This is the best class ever!" Blythe yelled out.

Tinsley laughed as she began the introductions. Soon they were all covered in sweat as they practiced their sword work. Time passed and Tinsley found herself feeling better as she worked out her anxiety for Paxton's safety. So that's why Harper was in such good shape. She worked out to take her mind off the danger the man she loved was in.

Somewhere between throwing knives and fencing with the rapier, Tinsley had felt the knowledge settle into her heart. My, how things had changed. She took aim and with the flick of her wrist sent the knife flying. The knife landed in the bullseye with a satisfying *thunk*. She'd been wrong about her first impression of Paxton. It gave her pause as she pulled the knife free from the wood target. Now that she knew the depth of her feelings, what did she do about it?

17

Paxton looked up at the rusted, old plumbers box van. He had never been in the van, and this time he would be exclusively in the van. Opening the back doors, though, didn't bring him face to face with a dirty interior. No, the interior was shining and full of monitors, computers, and other surveillance devices.

Paxton went to get in when Cy put a hand on his arm and stopped him. "If you see me touching my thumb to my middle finger, cut the surveillance."

"Got it, but Cy, Peewee isn't dangerous. He'll tell you anything for the right price," Paxton said of the criminal informant both he and Connor had used in the past.

"You never know. This is for now and anytime in the future. Understood?"

"Yes, sir."

Cy flipped up the hood of his black sweatshirt. Nighttime in Atlanta was still hot, so Paxton had no idea how Cy was surviving the heat, but the man didn't seem bothered by it—or the massive number of weapons he was carrying under his sweatshirt. Including a weapon Paxton had never seen before.

"Ready to roll?" Connor asked from the back of the van.

"Let's go." Paxton stepped up into the back of the van to join Connor and Peter as Cy shut the doors. The van took off as Cy and his crew got ready to walk to the corner where Peewee was known for selling drugs.

The van parked a short distance from the corner, but they still had visual and audio on Peewee. He'd earned the nickname because he was tiny—not just short, but scrawny as well.

Kord was the first to approach Peewee with Dare a short distance behind him. Granger and Cy took up positions on each side of the group, effectively surrounding him, but kept their eyes roving the streets behind them.

"Hey, man. I heard you were who we should talk to for information," Kord said with his patented easygoing smile.

Peewee looked nervous. "What kind of information?"

"Don't worry, it's the kind we pay for," Kord said easily as he pulled a hundred dollar bill from his back pocket.

Peewee took it but Paxton could see the indecision on his face. "What do I have to do for it?"

"We need to know what's going on with the Myriads," Kord said. "Can you tell us about them?"

Peewee nodded. "I can, but they're dangerous. I ain't putting my life on the line for a hundred bucks."

Dare peeled off another hundred-dollar bill and handed it to him. "No more negotiating. We've paid fairly. I want to know all about their expansion."

Peewee leaned forward and dropped his voice. "You didn't hear it from me, but they took over six more blocks here in Atlanta. They expanded to Jacksonville, Florida;

Chattanooga, Tennessee, and Charleston in the last six months."

"That takes money. Where did they get it?" Dare asked.

"That's the thing. Nobody really knows," Peewee admitted. "There's talk of a merger with someone from out of town."

"A national gang?" Dare asked.

"No one knows. I'd tell ya if I did. Word is something big is going down. Lots of money involved and only the inner circle knows. Us street guys are being kept in the dark, which tells you something right there."

"Anyone new to town?" Cy asked, his voice deep and barely audible.

"How'd you know that?" Peewee asked. Cy didn't answer. "There have been some new faces. Real fancy like. Speak with an accent."

"What kind of accent?" Dare asked.

"I'm not entirely sure. Spanish I think, but it sounded different. They showed up right after that FBI raid that killed a bunch of Myriads." Peewee was talking about the night Paxton got shot. "Word on the street is they have Engle's full attention."

"We got company," Granger said with a nod of his head down the street. Paxton saw Cy tap his fingers and Paxton "accidentally" stopped recording as a group of Myriad members stalked toward them.

"This doesn't look good," Connor said, getting ready to call for backup.

"Wait," Paxton said, covering the radio. "Let them handle this. You may want to turn around so you don't see anything you'd feel obligated to report."

The leader of the pack flicked a blade open. "No talking.

Only buying. If not, you need to move along or we'll make you move along," he said as he approached Cy.

Cy leveled him with one punch. Then it was chaos. Peewee did what he did best—he ran. Dare was battling one of the gang members over a gun. Granger and Kord were each fighting with someone but it was Cy who cleaned up the mess.

"Who *is* that man?" Connor asked as Cy added two more bodies to the heap of moaning men at his feet.

The last man standing went to run, but Cy grabbed him by the neck and lifted him until only his big toe touched the ground. "Tell Engle there's a new man on the block, and I'm taking this area for my own. He could fight, but as you can see, it won't go well. I'm better financed and better armed than he is. He has one week to clear out or I'll bring my boys in to toss him out. Got it?"

The Myriad member made a strangled gurgling sound that Cy took for a yes. He dropped him hard to the ground and then watched as he scurried away.

"Well, that drew some attention," Connor muttered as he pointed to the monitors. Curtains on the residential street had been pulled back as faces filled the windows.

"Yoohoo!"

Paxton along with everyone on the street turned to find the source of the voice calling out. "Oh, crap. It's the knitting club."

Cy, Dare, Granger, and Kord turned toward the voice. Three elderly women with salt and pepper hair sat on rocking chairs on the porch of a small brick house. One had a silk scarf partially covering her hair. The other had her short hair in braids, and the third woman's natural curls were styled to perfection.

"Would you boys care for some lemonade?" the leader of

the elderly trio called out as she set down her knitting needles.

"That would be lovely, ma'am," Cy responded for the group as he headed toward the patio lined with colorful flowers.

"What is he doing? Doesn't he know they're dangerous?" Connor asked.

"It's a knitting club," Peter scoffed.

"Shadows Landing doesn't have a knitting club? Everyone knows they're more dangerous than the CIA," Connor answered as Paxton nodded.

"Could you say no to Miss Winnie or Miss Ruby?" Paxton asked Peter.

"Oh, crap. I've got to rescue them," Peter answered frantically as Cy climbed the stairs to the patio with Dare right behind him. Granger and Kord stood at the bottom of the steps and smiled up at the ladies as they passed out lemonade.

"Why don't you have the boys in the van join us?" the knitting club leader asked, although it wasn't a question. It was a demand and Paxton found himself already reaching for the door before catching himself.

"What boys in what van?" Cy asked. The ladies stopped knitting and stared at Cy, ready to give him a scolding.

"Bless your heart, you're not a good liar," the leader said as she wagged her finger at Cy.

"Why does everyone say that? I'm an excellent liar," Cy huffed as he tossed his hands up in the air.

"No one likes a fibber," one of the other ladies told him.

"Sorry, ma'am." Cy motioned for the men to come out of the van. Their cover was already blown, but now it was going to be blown to smithereens, set on fire, then stomped on.

One of the ladies in the rocking chair narrowed her eyes at Paxton. "I know you. I thought you were killed. It does my heart good to know you're still alive."

"Hello, Miss Ethel. It's nice to see you again," Paxton said to her as she set down her knitting and waved him forward. She lifted her face and waited for Paxton to buss her cheek. "Miss Josie," he said, kissing the other cheek of the third woman sitting on the patio before stepping forward to the leader. "Miss Trudie. It's good to see you again."

Miss Trudie huffed. "We were very upset when we thought you were dead. Then you saunter onto our street without even a 'how do you do?'"

"I'm not supposed to be here. I don't want to put you in danger," Paxton told them.

"Those useless men won't bother us. I'd stab them with my needles. Now you," Miss Trudie said, turning to Cy, "you're welcome to sit a spell with us and tell us about why you're here."

"Thank you, ma'am. Call me Cy." He took Miss Trudie's hand and kissed it.

"Wow, they're good. I've been with you all day and he's never told me his name," Connor whispered.

"There's no whispering, Sergeant Gibbs. That's just bad manners," Miss Josie snapped.

"How do you know who I am?" Connor asked with horror.

"You've had six stakeouts on this street in the past year, and you've never introduced yourself. Really, were you raised in a barn?" Miss Ethel and her friends shook their heads in disappointment and clucked unhappily at him.

"Now, young man," Miss Trudie said to Cy as she handed him a tray filled with cookies. "Why are you here tonight and bringing the dead with you?" she asked as she looked toward Paxton.

"Two Myriad members going by the names Maurice and Murray," Cy started to say before turning to Paxton. "Show them the pictures."

Paxton held out his phone to display images of Maurice and Murray. The three women nodded with recognition.

"They're trying to sell stolen art and my niece, the sweetest darlin' you've ever met, has been put in the position as the art broker. We traced them back here and are trying to find out what the Myriad is up to and what it has to do with art." Cy cracked faster than an egg ready for an omelet.

Paxton noted the women didn't look surprised, but they also weren't sharing. The dangers of the knitting club. They gathered information but rarely parted with it.

"Do you think you can help us?" Paxton asked.

Miss Trudie looked up innocently from where she was knitting. "Oh, we don't know anything. We're just three old ladies."

Cy's lips twitched up in a smile. Kord busted out laughing.

"Ladies, we all know that's an even bigger fib," Kord said with a smooth smile on his lips. He gave the women a wink and they all smiled back at him, proving you were never too old to flirt.

"How about an exchange? You give us information and I'll help you out," Dare suggested.

"We do not need payoffs like low-life drug dealers," Miss Josie said with a sniff of displeasure.

"Oh, I wasn't going to trade money for information," Dare said, looking down at Miss Josie's knitting. "I was going to show you how to clean up your stranded floats. Then I could show Miss Ethel why she's having trouble attaching the I-cord, and then help Miss Trudie with that intarsia technique."

The women all looked down at their knitting and back up at Dare. He'd surprised them so much they forgot to mask it on their faces.

"You knit?" Miss Josie sputtered.

"I do. I'm part of my town's knitting club. So, do we have a deal?" Dare asked as Paxton and Connor glanced at each other, clearly holding their breath.

"Sit a spell and let's chat. My, what a fine group of men you have with you, Paxton," Miss Trudie said. Cy walked back to the van and pulled out two folding chairs. Granger and Kord sat down on the steps. Cy and Dare sat in the chairs on each side of the knitting club. Peter leaned against the white iron railing and kept lookout while Connor did the same on the other side of the steps. Paxton walked up the four cement steps and took a seat on a porch swing.

"See, there have been new men in town. They arrived the day you were killed," Miss Ethel told them as she nodded to Paxton. "They've been strutting around like they own the place ever since. Never once stopped to introduce themselves. To anyone. Peewee is a thorn in our side, but he has good manners at least. He never sells to kids and he even takes out our trash cans for us."

"But these new men don't. They aren't from here either. They're from Argentina. We heard that no-good Curtis Engle talking the other week. Stopped right in front of our house where we were knitting in the living room with the window open," Miss Josie said, picking up the story. "He said the Argentinians are demanding they fence the paintings and get them their cash by the end of summer or they'll pull their support of the Myriad's expansion."

"That's right," Miss Trudie said, nodding with a sour

look on her face. "That no-good Curtis was talking to Maurice and Murray, or rather, the Spiller brothers, as everyone knows them. The Spiller brothers are almost always together. They slithered into Curtis's favor after all that shooting went down and Curtis lost most of his inner circle. Was that you?"

"Yes, ma'am. Before I took three shots to the chest and was run out of the gang unit," Paxton told them.

"Run out, you say?" Miss Ethel asked.

"That's right. I was transferred out of state and my subordinate was promoted." Paxton pulled up a photo of Mark on his phone and showed it to the ladies. "Mark Trevino."

"We haven't seen him, but I think we've heard talk about him," Miss Trudie confirmed. "See, when Curtis was talking to the Spillers, he said they needed the sell the paintings immediately and said the Argentinians wanted half the sales price in cash for them. The Spillers said they had a fence in Shadows Landing, South Carolina. Curtis said, 'Be careful, our man inside said an enemy came back from the dead in Charleston.'"

"I should never have applied for that transfer back here," Paxton cursed. Peter gave him a sympathetic look. They'd unknowingly stirred the hornets' nest.

"Anything else useful we should know? Guns? Drugs? Anything you'd like to see stopped that we can help with?" Dare asked.

"They're selling drugs to kids down at the basketball courts in the park. Someone tried to sell my grandson a dime bag. He's thirteen," Miss Josie told them as the others shook their heads with disgust.

"I'll take care of it. You have my word," Connor swore to them.

"There's also a van with this license plate," Miss Ethel said, handing her phone to Connor. "They sell guns out of the back of it. Here's video."

Dare leaned over and watched the video. "I can take care of that for you, ladies."

"I have no doubt. Now, those two are clearly cops," Miss Trudie said, pointing to Granger and Kord. "And our back from the dead boy is FBI and that fella looks like FBI, too," Miss Trudie said, pointing to Paxton and Peter. "You, I don't know. But you probably wouldn't tell us anyway," she said to Cy who gave her a wink. "But you don't fit," she said to Dare.

"ATF, ma'am. Now let me show you how to fix your knitting." Dare emailed the video to himself and handed the phone back to Miss Ethel. "Let's knit, ladies."

Tinsley didn't think protective service would be so much fun. However, she'd had a blast with Mallory and Blythe. Now they were curled up in Ryker's home theater watching a movie and eating popcorn.

"So, you and Paxton. I heard it's an opposites attract type thing," Mallory said with a wink.

"I thought he didn't like me when we first met. I thought he was an arrogant know-it-all," Tinsley said, laughing at how badly their first meetings had gone. "I was very wrong."

"I understand that. It wasn't all roses for my husband and me either," Mallory said. "But now we've been married forever, have our kids, and couldn't be happier. What about you, Blythe?"

"My girlfriend's name is Veronica. I think I fell for her while I was hitting this guy with a stun gun and Veronica calmly called the police. She even winked at me while she was talking. It was like ten thousand volts of electricity hitting my heart. Well, except it was fifty thousand volts I was shooting into a very bad man."

"You scare me a little. Want a job?" Ryker asked Blythe from the doorway of his home theater.

"Thanks, Ryk. That's nice of you, but I'm happy in Keeneston," Blythe called out from her recliner.

"Are you joining us?" Tinsley asked. They used to do movie and game nights as kids right up until Ryker's incident. Then he had shut them out. Gone was the happy-go-lucky boy he'd been. When he dug and buried himself, it was Tinsley who had pulled him from the black hole he was stuck in. He wasn't the type to ever sit back and laugh anymore. No more board games. No more movie nights. No more laughter.

"What are you watching?" Ryker asked.

"To Catch a Thief," Mallory answered.

"How appropriate," Ryker said dryly as he walked through the darkened theater and took the recliner next to Tinsley on the far side of the room.

Tinsley reached out and placed her hand gently over his on the armrest and gave it a little squeeze.

"You ever shot anyone with fifty thousand volts, Ryk?" Blythe asked, using the nickname no one else was brave enough to use.

"Can't say I have, Miss Kencroft," Ryker answered. Tinsley looked over at him. His face was partially in shadows, but she saw the twitch of a lip.

"You want to?" Blythe asked. "I bet if you just smile at that young assistant who is walking around here like she's your girlfriend, she'd let you stun her."

"She totally would let you do it," Mallory added with a snort of amusement. "Heck, I almost got her today."

"What did Bianca do?" Ryker asked them, looking confused. Ryker probably didn't pay attention to lowly assistants.

"I guess her name is Bianca," Tinsley said slowly. "Well, Bianca doesn't realize I'm your cousin. She cornered me in my room and told me, quote 'Ryker will tire of your sluttish ways by the end of the week so you better not unpack.'"

Ryker growled deep in his chest and his hands fisted. "Did you tell her you were my cousin?"

"No. I just slammed the door in her face. I figured she'd find out soon enough. Sorry, Ryker. I know you have a lot on your plate right now. That's why I wasn't going to bother you with it."

"You're family, Tinsley. You never bother me. I'm here to protect you and that includes harassment from out-of-line assistants."

"Actually, we're here to protect her," Mallory reminded him with a grin. "However, Tinsley wouldn't let us stun that Bianca chick."

"What are you three doing in here? This is off limits to your kind," Bianca interrupted, with her hands on her shapely hips in the dark doorway.

"Speak of the devilette," Blythe muttered.

"Kind? What kind are we?" Mallory asked innocently as she leaned forward to block any view Bianca might have of Ryker.

"You're after Ryker, but you're too late. He's mine."

Tinsley almost felt sorry for Bianca. Almost. Mallory leaned back in her chair as Ryker leaned forward so that Tinsley, Mallory, and Blythe no longer hid him from view. "Bianca, I take it you haven't met Tinsley Faulkner, my cousin, who is closer to me than any sister could be?"

Tinsley waved. She even gave a big smile, hopeful the dim light in the theater room would let Bianca see it.

Bianca's face fell as she realized Ryker had heard everything. "These are her bodyguards, Blythe Kencroft and

Mallory Westin-Simpson. Yes, *that* Simpson family. Marge will have your final check ready in the morning. You can pick it up at the Charleston office when you turn in all business-related items in your possession. Your services are no longer required."

Ryker leaned back into his recliner and took a deep breath. "Blythe, pass the popcorn, please."

"Sure thing, Ryk."

Blythe passed the popcorn and Bianca stomped her foot. With a little cry of disappointment over losing out on any possibility to bag Ryker, she stormed from the room. Tinsley smiled at her cousin. He might not notice the small changes, but she did. Ryker was finally starting to peek out of the bunker he'd been hiding in since that night so long ago now.

Paxton had staked out the Myriad headquarters for two days, but he hadn't seen the Spiller brothers once. He had seen men moving drugs and guns for Myriad, though. It had felt good to go on a bust again. Kord and Granger were having a grand old time working undercover. Kord bought some drugs and Granger got a gun at their separate takedowns. Connor arrested the drug dealers and a basket of homemade muffins was brought to the surveillance van by Miss Josie's grandson. That afternoon, Granger had approached the gun dealer and bought some weapons before the team went in and busted him. Dare handed him off to a local ATF agent. Miss Trudie and Miss Ethel sent their grandkids to the van with seven matching knitted caps for next winter and a plate of brownies.

They'd been in Atlanta for three days, slowly taking

down sections of the Myriad and gathering intelligence. What he hadn't done was call Tinsley. As they watched Cy set up the gun dealer's now empty van to ram into Myriad's headquarters, he asked Dare about it. "Do you call Harper when you're undercover?"

"Nope. But if you're wondering if you should call Tinsley, then maybe you should reach out to see how she is so you can focus back on the case. Look at that creative engineering. I swear you can do anything with duct tape and bungee cords."

Paxton looked to where Cy finished rigging the van and set a brick on the gas pedal before leaping back. The van tore off down the street. It jumped the curb, raced up the wooden steps, and slammed into the house that served as the Myriad

headquarters. Cy stood out in the open, and as the first men started pouring out of the house, he gave them the middle finger.

"Tell Engle I'm coming for him!" Cy yelled before getting in the SUV and taking off.

"He's crazy," Connor muttered, shaking his head as they took pictures of everyone running out of the house. "But it worked. There are lots of guys we haven't seen before. I'll run all the pictures through our database."

"I'm not seeing the Spillers, though," Paxton said with a sigh, before he perked up again. "Hey, there's Curtis."

Paxton watched as the head of the Myriad strode out of the house in a towering rage. He was on the phone and yelling orders to everyone around him, including whoever was on the other end of the phone call. "Let's see who shows up and where Curtis goes. He must have another location where the drugs, weapons, and art are stored. If we want to put Curtis away, we need those items in his possession when we bust him."

Dare and Connor worked on getting the photos uploaded to their various departments, but it was the SUV pulling up that drew Paxton's attention. "Get that SUV and anyone who comes out of it on camera."

"Who do you think it is?" Peter asked.

"I think it's Trevino. It has F-E-D practically stamped on it."

Paxton leaned forward and zoomed in the telephoto lens. Unfortunately, the driver's window never rolled down. However, he snapped a picture of the plate as the SUV tore away from the house and in the direction Cy had driven.

The back door to their van opened and Cy jumped in. "So, did I stir up the hornet's nest enough? You think they'll move forward quickly now?"

"I do. The license plate for the SUV is registered to the federal government," Connor said.

"There goes Curtis." Paxton pointed as the man jumped into the passenger seat of a massive pickup truck. "Go. Kord and Granger, gunmetal gray truck," Paxton said into his coms. Kord and Granger were in two different undercover vehicles on various side streets, waiting for Curtis to pass them.

Cy picked up his phone and dialed a number. "Hello, Miss Trudie. Do you know anyone who wants to report a van running into a house at 555 Peachtree? Yes, ma'am that is the Myriad's headquarters." Paxton could hear Miss Trudie's laughter from across the van.

A minute later, Connor's police scanner went off reporting the accident. "Looks like I'm up. Dare, do you want to come in with me to investigate any guns we might find?"

Dare and Connor jumped from the van and headed for Connor's cruiser parked a few blocks away.

"You and Peter follow Granger and Kord. See if Curtis leads you to the art," Cy ordered. "I'll stay here and monitor it all."

Paxton hopped from the van with Peter and raced toward their undercover SUV. In minutes they were following Curtis per Granger's and Kord's locations. Paxton drove, his hands tight on the wheel. He wanted this over so badly it hurt. He wanted Tinsley safe and the only way to do that was to find the paintings.

Paxton pulled to a stop in front of the warehouse where he'd been shot. Dark and painful memories fought to be freed, but he pushed them back. Now wasn't the time.

"Where is Curtis?" Paxton asked into the coms.

"Inside. The driver is still in the car," Granger replied.

"An extended SUV is pulling into the back," Kord told them. "Two men are getting out and knocking at the back door. The door is opening and they're going inside."

There was no movement out front, and as Paxton scanned the warehouse, he couldn't see any movement in the front rooms either.

"Wait, they're coming back out carrying large suitcases," Kord told them.

"Big enough for paintings?" Paxton asked.

"Aw, crap," Kord cursed over his coms. "It's not the paintings. One of the guys knocked a suitcase over and white powder seemed to explode inside it. I just see puffs of cocaine floating in the air now. No paintings."

Peter was already calling it in to Connor, who immediately sent a unit. The SUV wouldn't get far and Curtis was going to be pissed when a lot of his coke was confiscated.

"That'll push Curtis over the edge," Peter said as if reading Paxton's mind.

"I was thinking the same thing. If he owes money to some South American gang and loses all of his product, he's going to have to sell the paintings ASAP."

"Paxton, Peter," Connor's voice sounded hushed over the coms. "Agent Trevino just appeared on scene and is demanding to take over. We were able to go into the house to check out the car and saw weapons and guns in plain sight. We were able to confiscate, but Trevino wants them all. No paintings, though, sorry."

Paxton clenched his hand into a fist. "You can't let Trevino take over. All that evidence will go missing and no charges will be brought."

"I had my team move fast. I already arrested and transported fourteen Myriad members who had either outstanding warrants, possession of drugs they had on them, or unregistered firearms. I got them out of here the second their rights were read. Trevino wants them, but I'm not going to give them to him without a fight," Connor said.

"I'll take care of it," Cy's calm voice said over the coms. "I've already made a call."

"Curtis is leaving, and he's not carrying a thing," Paxton sighed. "We're coming back to the van."

Paxton fought not to feel defeated as they all drove back to the van. Police sirens drew close to them and sped past them on the way to arrest anyone in the SUV filled with drugs.

When they reached the van, Connor was missing from inside, but the rest of the crew were waiting for Paxton and Peter.

"We've got nothing," Paxton said between his gritted teeth.

"We've gotten a lot, Kendry," Cy's hard voice said. "We'll be able to take down Curtis's inner circle and cause him to panic. He'll be making his move to sell those paintings soon. You need to get back to Shadows Landing now. I'll clean things up here. Now go. Go home and protect my niece or I'll be the one you'll have to worry about, not Curtis."

"We should get to Tinsley. Curtis is out of options. He'll be moving those paintings any day now," Peter told him.

The urge to get to Tinsley was almost overwhelming. "Thank you, Cy," Paxton said, holding out his hand to Tinsley's scary uncle.

"It's been fun. I'm protective of what's mine, but you'll do nicely for Tins. I'll see you at the wedding. September is a lovely time to get married on the beach there." Cy smiled at him as Paxton's mouth just seemed to hang open. Then Cy picked up his cell phone and they were all dismissed. "Marshall, get the guys together. It's a guys' trip to Atlanta to take down a gang and a corrupt FBI agent."

"*Yes!*" was heard through the entire van.

Tinsley had said her family was interesting, and he'd learned firsthand that was true. They made him smile and gave him the courage to do what was needed to protect Tinsley. He knew he had backup.

19

Tinsley was curled up in bed at Ryker's when a soft knock at her door had her looking up from the book she was reading on her phone.

"Come in," she called out.

The doorknob turned and Ryker entered. He strode into the room and sat down with a sigh in one of the chairs. "How are you holding up?" he asked her.

"I'm fine, but something tells me you're not."

Ryker waved the question away. "Just some work stuff. Nothing to worry about. I wanted to let you know that Granger called me. They're on their way home. Should be here in the next thirty minutes."

Tinsley's heart started beating fast as she sat up in bed. "Did they find the paintings?"

"No. But they got the whole organization desperate to sell them. I'm sure Paxton can fill you in when he gets here."

Tinsley fell back against the mountain of decorative pillows Ryker's interior designer had picked out. "So, it's not over yet."

"It's not but, Tinsley, I can take over. I can claim to own

the gallery. Ridge and I were talking and we don't want you in any kind of danger. I know enough about art to get by. Plus, I don't have a family. Ridge didn't like it but he understands. I don't have someone who loves me waiting for me at home. That makes me the best choice for a dangerous job. Let me take on Myriad and keep you safe."

Tinsley's heart broke for Ryker. "That's not true. You have a family who loves you and I refuse to put you in danger. I don't have someone waiting for me either. I appreciate your concern. But Ryker, I can do this. I have to do this."

"I know you can. I just don't want you to. And you do have someone waiting for you—someone that Granger told me was driving over a hundred miles per hour to get back home to you. Someone who screamed into a SUV full of men that he wasn't sleeping in the guest room anymore." Ryker placed his hands on the arms of the chair and pushed himself up to standing. "He might not have said it yet, but that man loves you, Tinsley. It's clear as day you love him, too."

"What?" Tinsley asked, stunned. No one had noticed her slow change of feelings. At least she thought no one had. She shouldn't be surprised Ryker saw what no one else did. He had a way of sitting back and observing. It served him well in business, but it's also what kept him from having a personal life. There were too many Biancas in the world out to land his money, not his love. It would take someone very special to break through the reinforced walls of his heart.

Ryker gave her a small smile. "I've seen your paintings, Tinsley. They're a testament to your love for him. You have your chance to be happy. Don't pass it up. Let me fill in for you. I can bullshit my way through anything, even with some guys who know nothing about valuable art."

Tinsley was sure both Ridge and Ryker thought she would happily step down, but she wasn't going to. "No. Thank you for the offer, but I refuse to step down. Ryker, this is my life. This is what I'm good at and I can help. I want to help. I don't come into the middle of one of your negotiations and tell you that I'll take over. Don't come into mine and do the same."

Ryker was silent for a moment and then a sad smile crossed his face. "I knew you were the strong one. Everyone always looked out for you, but I saw you. I saw you looking out for everyone else. They thought they were taking care of you, the youngest of us, but it was always the other way around. You saved me. You protected Edie with everything you had. You made sure everyone always had what was needed. You always said yes to any favor asked." Ryker stood at the foot of the bed and his small smile turned downward into a frown. "I know what it's like to feel compelled to do more. I won't get in the way, but I'd feel better if I were close by."

"You can visit Savannah upstairs all you want," Tinsley said with a smile. "I'll even carry Tina if it makes you feel better."

"That would make me feel better," Ryker said, reaching behind him and pulling Tina from his waistband. "Where you go, Tina goes. Got it?"

"Yes, cousin. I got it."

Ryker looked down at the phone in his hand. "Paxton is here. I'll see you tomorrow and we'll all go to church together."

"Thank you for looking out for me, Ryk."

Ryker nodded and then left her room. Moments later she heard the pounding of footsteps running up the stairs and then he was there. Paxton looked frazzled. He'd raked his fingers through his hair so often, it was practically standing up. But his eyes said it all. They were dark with passion and his breathing was heavy. She opened her arms and he raced to her.

Paxton's arms tightened around her. He buried his face in her neck and only then took a deep breath. His hand ran over her hair as he sat on the bed, just holding her. "I missed you."

Tinsley smiled against his head as she gently threaded her fingers into his hair. "I missed you, too."

"I'm sorry, Tinsley. I failed you. I didn't shut the whole operation down."

"You hurt them, though."

"Yes, but now they're like a wounded animal and even more dangerous. They're coming here next. I don't know when. I just know they will come for you to sell the paintings. They need them sold," Paxton told her. He finally released his tight grip on her and leaned back enough to cup her cheeks with his large hands.

"They're not coming tonight," Tinsley said gently. "Tonight we can just love each other."

A sly smile formed on Paxton's lips. "Are you telling me you love me, Miss Faulkner?"

Tinsley laughed before leaning forward to kiss him. "You know I love you, Agent Kendry."

Tinsley placed her lips on his, but then it was all Paxton. He angled her mouth to kiss her deep, long, and hard. Only when she was breathing heavily and lost in a pleasured daze did he break the kiss. "I love you, too, Tinsley. You've been the only one for me since I first saw you."

Tinsley knew when there was a time for words and when actions spoke larger than words. Now was a time for action. "Make love to me, Paxton." Tinsley scooted into the middle of the bed and pulled off the tank top she was wearing. She shimmied out of the matching sleep shorts and drank in the sight of Paxton undressing.

Their eyes never left each other as he grabbed a condom and crawled up her body. Tonight was different. It was deeper. It was slower. It was intense as every touch and every kiss painted the story of their love upon their bodies and hearts.

"Get ready," Tinsley whispered the next morning.

"Did I really just put down a donation for barbecue? We are in a church, right?" Paxton asked as he surveyed the packed church led by Reverend Winston.

Reverend Winston had given a sermon about never underestimating the smallest of the flock. Paxton had looked repeatedly at Tinsley, but she didn't act singled out. The littlest of Lydia's kids came up to collect the donations. Tinsley had instructed Paxton to place the donation in either container one or container two after eating a sampling of the two different barbeques. This was the most surreal church service he'd ever seen.

"Yes, and as soon as Reverend Winston announces a winner, we run for that restaurant. Since I'm small, I can dart around the crowd easier and I'm usually the first from the family there. If you get there first, get a table for all of us. Darn!" Tinsley cursed as she looked around at the congregation.

"What?" Paxton still had to be dreaming after a night of the most amazing sex of his life.

"Quad Clemmons is here. He has a full scholarship on

the top basketball team in the country. He's fast. Really fast. Okay, here we go."

Tinsley already had one foot into the aisle as Reverend Winston spoke. "We conclude today's service with the winner of the barbeque. It's close, but the winner this week is Low—"

Paxton couldn't even hear the full name of the restaurant because people were suddenly going crazy. "Go!" Ridge yelled, shoving Paxton into the aisle. Paxton followed the crowd outside where he heard engines gunning, tires squealing, and two old men on motorized chairs racing off down the street.

Even the knitting club ran past him. That was enough to get him into action. "Tinsley!" he yelled, seeing her sprinting up ahead of him. Next to her was a young man with hair cut short on the sides and back, but long curls on top of his head. He had to be Quad Clemmons because he was at least six foot seven and was sprinting past people with ease. Tinsley tried to cut him off, but he practically hurdled her.

"Go, Tinsley!" Ridge yelled from somewhere up ahead of them.

Ellery ran past with the baby strapped into the stroller. "If you want to be in this family, you need to condition better!" she yelled over her shoulder.

Okay, Paxton was done. This might be the most bizarre event he'd ever witnessed, but Miss Mitzi the cat lady was not going to beat him to the restaurant. Paxton ran as hard and fast as he could. He'd caught up to Ridge as the line of people slid to a stop. Tinsley and Ryker were up front behind Quad.

"Up here!" Tinsley waved and the slowpokes of the Faulkner family moved up in line.

"That's my boy," an older version of Quad said, slapping his son on the shoulder. "You shaved a whole three seconds off from spring."

"Wait, doesn't he play for—" Paxton began to ask, but Tinsley just nodded.

"With the best conditioning coaches in the country. That's cheating, Quad," Tinsley teased the college-aged young man who towered over her.

"Sorry, Miss T, but a man's gotta do what a man's gotta do for the fam." He rested a hand on her shoulder and Paxton almost laughed at how it engulfed Tinsley's small frame.

"You're going to owe your old babysitter tickets to the championship game to make up for it," Tinsley grinned up at him.

"From your lips to God's ears. We were so close this March."

Then the line moved and the restaurant filled in seconds. Paxton noted that as soon as the race was over, the competition faded and a jovial family-like atmosphere took over. Lydia and all her kids came over to say hello. Ellery and Gavin made rounds with their baby to talk to each table. People cruised from table to table until the first round of food came out. Then everyone was seated and ready to eat.

They were halfway through their meal when Tinsley's brow furrowed. She picked up her phone and answered. "I'm sorry, I'm at family lunch. Can I call you back?"

Paxton and Ryker leaned forward to hear better, but everyone else was too busy talking to notice the way Tinsley had paled.

"You're here now? I'm sorry, we're closed Sundays."

That got Ridge's attention and he leaned closer, too.

"Of course, Maurice. I'll be right there," Tinsley said,

hanging up. The table was completely quiet. "They're here with the paintings."

"It's the smart move. They saw the whole town running to the restaurants. They'll know the police station is empty and the chance of someone walking off the street to come see what you have is slim to none," Paxton told her as they both stood up. "I'm coming with you. They'll need help bringing it into the gallery, after all."

"I'm coming too," Ridge said, standing up.

"No, it'd be too obvious. Tell Granger and Kord that Paxton will be in contact with them. Have them check for people surrounding the gallery. You can all walk down after lunch if Paxton texts that it's okay. We can't blow his case now." Paxton looked at Tinsley and saw the command in her. Gone was the woman who'd smile and do anything to please her family and in her place was a warrior. "Let's go."

"Yes, ma'am," Paxton said with a smirk. He saw her touch the small of her back and then relax a little. He wondered what was hidden under the little pink cardigan sweater.

They didn't talk as they walked toward the gallery. Tinsley kept her eyes on the large van out front and Paxton tried to nonchalantly look around to see if Maurice and Murray had company with them.

"Hello, gentlemen. I'm sorry for the delay. On Sundays, everyone eats together after church. I had to hunt down my helper to carry in all the paintings you said you brought." Tinsley smiled as if nothing was wrong. Paxton tried to keep his head down in case someone recognized him. Who knew if Trevino had handed the Myriad's a new photo of him?

"We're sorry to intrude on your personal time," Maurice said smoothly. "Our grandmother has taken a turn for the worse and requires an expensive surgery that insurance won't cover. Our older brother has asked us to sell these as quickly as possible."

Tinsley looked at the two men sympathetically. She reached out with both hands and squeezed their hands. "Your grandmother is blessed with such good grandsons. I'll pray for her and her surgery."

"Thank you, Tinsley," Murray responded. His eyes kept traveling back to Paxton. "We got this. You can go back to your lunch if you'd like."

"Whatever is fine with me. I don't mind helping. I know Tinsley is very concerned about damaging the art. Did you know the value of even the most famous masterpiece can fall ninety percent if it's damaged just a tiny bit?" Paxton bullshitted. He had no idea if it were true or not, but it had the desired effect.

"Murray, why don't you help him with the art," Maurice suggested, looking nervously at the truck.

Tinsley unlocked the door, turned off the alarm system, and then moved to prop the front door open. "Well now, let's see what your grandmother's art collection is like."

20

Tinsley's heart was beating a mile a minute as painting after painting was brought into the gallery. They were wrapped in moving blankets and lined the far back wall three paintings deep. Some were quite large while some were no bigger than a photograph.

She took a small painting the size of a page of notebook paper and carefully laid it on the desk. She used her fingernail to peel up the edge of the plastic wrap holding the blanket around the artwork in place. Tinsley slowly unwrapped the art and then held her breath as she looked down at the two hundred-year-old painting. This wasn't stolen from someone's home. This artwork had a long story. One Tinsley swore she'd discover.

"This is a Vermeer," Tinsley said with awe. "How long has it been in your family?"

"My great-grandparents bought this collection in Argentina after World War II, and it was passed down to my grandmother after their deaths in the seventies," Maurice said, handing her a thick envelope of papers. "How much do you think it's worth? The small Vermeer?"

Tinsley didn't know what to say. Vermeer paintings were among the rarest pieces. Most sold for tens of millions of dollars.

"If this is the quality of work you have under the blankets, we should have no trouble getting well above any amount you require for your dear grandmother," Tinsley said, wrapping the painting back up. "Now, let's go over the paperwork and then I'll get to selling."

"We'd like this to be a private sale. My family would appreciate it if you could keep the art in the back and not out for display. This is very personal for us and very hard for us to part with. I'd hate to have people gawking over my grandmother's paintings," Maurice said so sincerely Tinsley almost forgot these were most likely stolen.

"Of course, Maurice." Tinsley put her hand to her heart as if she were touched by his love for his grandmother. "Now, this will take me at least a week to go through and get ready for sale, but then I should be good to go. Is that timeline acceptable for your family?"

"Yes, but if you get done even quicker, we won't complain." Maurice signed the papers and handed them all over to her. "These paintings mean everything to our family. I need to know they will be kept safe."

"I have a large vault in the back and a very good security system. Also, the police department is just right down there," Tinsley said as she pointed down the street. She enjoyed the slightly uncomfortable look on Maurice's face.

"This is the last one," Murray said, interrupting them as he led Paxton to the back of the room. Paxton was carrying a large painting at least four feet tall. She couldn't wait to get a look at it.

"Thank you for entrusting me with your family's art. I

will do right by the collection. I'll call as soon as I'm ready to start selling them." Tinsley stood and shook Maurice's hand.

"We have some private buyers as well. The ones we told you about. Get a list of the art and text me with the painting names and how much each is worth. I'll see if I can send some sales your way. When it comes to buyers I send you, I'll tell you the price I will accept. No negotiating is necessary."

"Whatever you want, Maurice. I'll get that to you as soon as I catalog everything," Tinsley promised. She would say anything at this point to get them out of the building so she could uncover each painting.

Tinsley walked them to the gallery door and waved goodbye as they got into the van. She smiled, waved, and wished they'd get out of there. As soon as they were heading down the street, she locked the front door and ran toward the back of the gallery.

Paxton had kept quiet and as soon as he was no longer needed, he'd slipped into the back of the building. Out of sight, out of mind.

"Paxton! There's a Vermeer!"

Paxton strode from the back rooms with a look of disbelief. "A Vermeer? I don't think so."

Tinsley put her hands on her hips and rolled her eyes at him. "Are you doubting my ability to identify a Vermeer?" She gestured for Paxton to open the painting on the desk as she pulled out the paperwork Maurice had brought her.

"Holy crap! It is a Vermeer. How would they end up with a Vermeer?" Paxton looked up at her with wonder.

"I'm not the expert here on forged papers, but these look a little new for being receipts from the 1940s." Tinsley handed them over to Paxton to examine.

"This is current printer ink, but the paper has been

tumbled in a dryer for a bit to make it appear older. They're from Argentina. That's it. I knew I was right," Paxton said excitedly.

"Right about what?" Tinsley asked.

"The Myriad gang is working with the Argentinian mob. The Myriad want to expand their gang and their illegal businesses, but they can't do that without muscle and money, which the Argentinians are giving them. I bet they teamed up. The Argentinians will become a silent partner for the Myriad, so to speak. They'll supply the drugs and guns, and the Myriad will sell them. With a partnership like that, the Myriad will be able to corner a larger part of the illegal markets, and the Argentinians will just sit back and rake in the money. Plus they can take their illegal activities out of Argentina and then receive laundered money in return. They can look legit."

"That makes sense to me, but not the art. Where does this all fit in?" Tinsley gestured to all the art.

"This is the expansion money. Half of the sale price goes to the Argentinians, and then the other half goes to Curtis for a fencing fee. There's danger attached with fencing a lot of valuable art that a lot of people must be looking for. If he's successful, then Curtis has the income to buy the best drug runners, dealers, chemists . . ." Paxton paused and then smiled. "They're going to bring in some buyers, right? This is how they're going to clean their money—pay the Argentinians and use the art to get the guns and drugs they need. Say you need a million dollars worth of guns and have a two million dollar painting. You sell the painting for one million to the gun dealer, so he's not out two million. However, the gun dealer can go sell it for two million and bam, you're both square and it's all clean money. Or he can trade it for something else with another criminal."

"I guess we'll find out when I see how much they authorize the sale for," Tinsley said, looking down at the Vermeer. "You won't actually make me sell this, will you? This is history. It shouldn't be used in black market dealings."

"I don't know what we'll do. We might be able to sell a forgery or go forward with the sale and then immediately arrest the buyer. However," Paxton said with a grimace, "we need to prove these are stolen. Then I need to link them to Curtis. After I have that evidence I can start taking down the people who come in to buy the paintings."

"We need to get to work. I'll call Ellery to see if she can come help, too." Tinsley pulled out her phone and called her cousin-in-law while Paxton began moving the paintings to the back rooms. They would fill every inch of space, but they'd be safe from prying eyes.

"Ellery will be here in twenty minutes," Tinsley told Paxton as she set up three easels in the back room. She lifted a wrapped painting onto each of them and then helped Paxton move paintings until Ellery showed up. It didn't take long to fill her in on what was going on and then she was rushing past them to the storage area.

"A Vermeer? Are you sure?"

Paxton snickered at Ellery's comment and Tinsley shot him the finger.

"Why does everyone think I suddenly don't know Vermeer?"

Tinsley followed Ellery into the back room that was filled with paintings wrapped up for safekeeping. They were at least spread out now. "Didn't Maurice say there were eighty paintings in the collection?" Tinsley asked as she looked around the room.

"Yes. There are only forty here. It's smart. They are not putting all their eggs in one basket," Paxton told her.

"Or they're testing the basket's strength before adding more to it," Ellery said with a frown. "If there are more, we have to find them."

Tinsley was already reaching for the first wrapped painting. "First we need to see what we're dealing with. Let's unwrap them."

An hour later, Tinsley was sure she'd stopped breathing. She, Paxton, and Ellery stood shoulder to shoulder with their mouths hanging open, eyes wide, unable to say a word.

A tear ran down Tinsley's cheek and then she finally sucked in a long deep breath. "I never thought I'd have my hands on art like this. Vermeer, Rembrandt, Renoir, drawings by da Vinci..."

"Picasso, Matisse, Degas..." Ellery muttered.

"Manet. Or is it Monet?" Paxton teased and then they were all laughing.

"Manet, definitely Manet," Tinsley laughed as tears flowed down her face.

"This alone is worth hundreds of millions of dollars," Ellery said into the silence after they stopped laughing.

"And it's sitting in my little gallery in Shadows Landing, South Carolina," Tinsley said with amazement.

She heard Paxton's phone ring but didn't watch as he stepped away to answer it. She couldn't take her eyes off the paintings and drawings. It was an incredible collection and sadly, it was stolen.

"You don't think it's from the Isabella Stewart Gardner

Museum, do you?" Ellery asked about one of the largest unsolved art heists of all time.

"I don't know. I need to catalog it all and run them through the stolen-art database. See if anyone has reported any missing. Maybe ask the insurance companies, too. I can't imagine not having insurance on these," Tinsley said.

Paxton stormed back into the room as Tinsley was getting her laptop ready to start cataloging. "I have to go. Charleston police just called. My apartment was just broken into. I've called Granger and Kord. They'll be here any minute."

Tinsley's hand went to her back and she breathed a little easier when she felt Tina.

Paxton hurried over to her, leaned down, and kissed her lips. "I'll be back as soon as I can. Don't go anywhere without Granger or Kord."

"I won't. Be safe," she whispered up to him.

Ellery looked away to give them some privacy.

"I'm more worried about you. I love you. I'll be home as soon as I can."

"I love you, too, Paxton."

Tinsley watched as Paxton hurried out the door. A second later, Granger stood in her back room letting out a low whistle. "Even I know some of these names."

"What do you think of the break-in at Paxton's?" Tinsley asked Granger. They hadn't talked much about what had happened in Atlanta, but when they'd returned, they'd all had a new respect for each other.

"I think there are no coincidences. We just got back from Atlanta where we took out a big chunk of Myriad's men, drugs, and guns. For his apartment to be broken into, they have to have thought he was a part of it. News reports from Atlanta are nuts. Your Uncle Cy is nuts but whatever he's doing on his guys' trip is working. It's breaking the gang. Unfortunately, it might be sending them our way," Granger told her.

"Oh goodness. I didn't know they sent Uncle Cy. He must like Paxton if he didn't kill him. That's a good sign, right?" Tinsley asked Ellery.

"Very good sign. I would also expect a call from Great Aunt Marcy soon, asking about a wedding date."

Tinsley smiled, but the smile fell as she looked around. "Granger, are you telling me this art, worth hundreds of millions of dollars, is all the assets the Myriad's have left?"

"That's exactly what I'm telling you."

"I can't let them take this again. These are priceless pieces of history. Granger, call Reverend Winston. Ellery, call the family. The second a painting gets logged I want it hidden at the church."

"On it," they both said as they picked up their phones.

Tinsley took a deep breath, grabbed her laptop, and got to work methodically taking pictures, writing down notes, and identifying the artist of each piece. As soon as she moved away from one painting, it was re-wrapped by Ellery and taken away by Ridge, Gavin, Wade, Trent, or Ryker to the church via the back entrances. There they were handed off to Harper, Darcy, and Savannah. They worked with Reverend Winston to store them and even diagram exactly where each painting was set down. Meanwhile, Skye and her best friend, Karri, staged an accident next to the sheriff's station to prevent any out-of-town traffic from coming into Shadows Landing.

When Tinsley was done, she sat back and let out a deep breath. "The history, Ellery. I'm shaken that this history was stolen. It was taken from a museum or a collector or multiple museums and collectors and used to trade for guns and drugs. It's a sacrilege. Now, how do I run this through the stolen-art system without tipping anyone off?"

"We need to find someone who can do the research on the quiet. The quietest possible," Ellery said stretching her back. "But first, I need a drink. A big one."

"I agree with that wholeheartedly," Granger said from where he'd been standing with a view of both the front and back door.

"Before I have that drink, I need to make my vault look full," Tinsley said, looking around at the pile of blank canvases prepped but yet to be painted. "Let's move them into the back of the vault and then I can put my originals that aren't on display in there, too. When I send the catalog to Maurice, I'll tell him that I have everything locked up so he'll give me advance notice so I can pull the right painting and not keep anyone waiting. That way I can get it from the church and not put the others at risk."

Ten minutes later Tinsley locked the vault, turned on the alarm, and joined the rest of her family at Harper's bar. No one seemed to talk. They all stared at their drinks until Darcy spoke. "This is so different from when I discovered the sunken treasure."

Wade nodded. "It had been sunken for protection from bad people who were long gone. This art was most likely stolen from good people and bad people are still using it for their own gains. It's just sad. Sad that there's a chance all this artwork could once again disappear, never to been seen again."

"I won't let that happen," Tinsley said with determination. "Ryker, do you know anyone powerful enough inside the art world who could run these paintings through the database of lost and stolen artworks and keep it off the books?"

Ryker raised an eyebrow as if to look insulted, but it was Georgina the bartender who answered. "I do."

Tinsley and the whole table of Faulkners turned to look at the young bartender. She'd applied for a bartender's job and had been incredibly overqualified with her education, but had zero work experience. Harper had seen someone who needed help, and despite her tough-as-nails attitude, Harper was all about helping women in need. So, she hired Georgina Grey, a cute young woman with sophisticated manners, a pronounced New England accent, and so soft-spoken it had taken a week for Tinsley to learn she was from Martha's Vineyard and was an expert equestrian.

To this day, no one knew what brought the twenty-five-year-old to Shadows Landing, who her parents or family were, or why she was still hanging around after a year. They all thought she'd be gone in a month. Instead, she'd turned her posh New England accent into a butchered Southern one with help from Gator, Skeeter, and Turtle. She'd bought an old pickup truck with three hundred thousand miles on it and was so proud of it she had driven everyone she knew up and down Main Street in it. She even babysat for Lydia. The woman was a saint.

"You know someone who could pull this off without anyone knowing about it?" Tinsley asked skeptically. Ryker just sat back and watched as if he knew something they all didn't.

"Is it very important?" Georgina asked as she nibbled on her bottom lip.

Kord stood up and walked over to her. He was gentle as he put his hand on her back. "It is. I think you know about art, so you know the names Vermeer, Rembrandt, Renoir, Manet, Degas . . . Now, I'm not as smart about that type of thing as I think you are. We think very bad people stole them and are trading these beautiful paintings, some that have moved me unlike anything I've ever experienced before, for drugs and weapons. They'll disappear again, lost to the dark underworld. We can prevent that if we can prove they're stolen."

Georgina was white as a sheet, her lips turning bluish in color as she pressed them tightly together. Her hands were visibly shaking but she nodded her head. "Get me a list and it'll be done."

"No, Georgie," Harper said, stepping in. "Ryker can get it done. This clearly upsets you, and I won't have that." Harper turned to Ryker. "You can do it, right?"

"Of course," Ryker said, his eyes never leaving Georgina. "Lady's choice."

Kord pulled Georgina close to him. While she was taller than Tinsley—heck, everyone was—she seemed so small curled into Kord's side. But then she straightened her shoulders and lifted her chin. "If you can't do it, call me and I will get it done," she said to Ryker.

No one had wanted to pry into Georgina's past. It was clear she hadn't wanted to speak up, but Tinsley saw the worry on not only Harper's face, but everyone else's. She had a feeling tonight everyone would be searching the Internet for Georgina Grey.

Tinsley had other problems to focus on. She pulled out her phone and forwarded the email she'd sent herself with the catalog of paintings to Ryker. A minute later he looked up from his phone and nodded. "It's done. I'll let you know when I have answers. It shouldn't take too long."

"Miss Georgie?" Gator asked slowly as he, Skeeter, and Turtle came in through the door and caught sight of her still in Kord's embrace. "Are you okay?"

"Did Anne Bonny's ghost scare you again?" Skeeter asked. "I told her to stop doing that."

Georgina took a deep breath and pasted on a smile. "No, Anne and I have come to an understanding. Nothing's wrong, just sorry Tinsley is in the middle of some wicked nasty business. Now, let's get you gentlemen some drinks."

In a split second, Tinsley saw the old Georgina reappear only to realize it had never been the real Georgina at all.

21

Paxton surveyed the wreckage of his apartment and felt his hand flex at the snake spray-painted on the entire back living room wall. The snake's head was cut off, red spray paint showing the dripping blood. It was a clear message. The Myriad was after him.

"Damn. This isn't good," Peter said as he stepped into the apartment. "Did you have any work files here? Anything relating to Tinsley or Shadows Landing?"

Paxton took a deep breath and shook his head. "No, thank goodness. My computer is in Shadows Landing and I have my phone on me. Nothing else is written down. I hadn't even fully unpacked since I thought I'd be going back to Atlanta soon."

"But the apartment does tell the Myriad that you're alive. Agent Whitlock, what does Gangs have to say?" Peter asked the agent in charge of gang activity in Charleston.

The agent stepped over to them along with a local police officer. "The Myriads began expanding into Charleston before Agent Kendry arrived. They came in with a bang, a violent takeover of a prime real estate area. They assassinated the leadership of the old local gang and took in the old members who wanted to join, but promised to kill anyone who didn't. It gave the Myriad had a sizable territory and a whole network of members practically overnight," Agent Whitlock explained.

The local officer nodded along with Whitlock's explanation. "I'm Boyd with Charleston Street Crimes Unit. I'm assigned to the Myriad. They've been dealing in high-quality cocaine. We're not sure where it's coming from, but we know it's not local. Their market is big and growing rapidly. They're targeting high-end clients with one brand of cocaine, and they have an economy grade, too. It's cut with cheaper, less stable ingredients. That mark on your wall is the tag for the Charleston Myriad. You've been made a target and they're coming for you."

"I guessed that," Paxton said, looking at the snake. "But is it locals or from Atlanta? I need to know who is after me."

"Locals. See in the blood drips," Boyd said, pointing at them. "You see CHS. That's the Charleston chapter. ATL would be if it were the Atlanta chapter."

"Thank you, Boyd," Peter told him before turning to Whitlock. "Do you have agents outside keeping an eye on the place?"

"We do. There's a lot of curiosity. We even did a couple of stop-and-frisks on suspicious people. They were clean, but they also didn't leave. They're watching the building."

"Thank you, Whitlock," Peter said, dismissing him and Boyd.

"Shit," Paxton cursed as soon as they had privacy. "What about Tinsley? I can't leave her unprotected like this, but I also know I can't blow the art deal."

"We need to sneak you out of here," Peter told him.

"Actually," Paxton said, stopping him. "We need them to think I'm somewhere else. They need to see me to put a name with my face now that I'm not undercover."

"You can't walk out like that. They'll recognize you if any of them share a picture with Maurice and Murray."

"I'm not going to look like me," Paxton said with a smile. "Think Miss Tibbie would let me borrow a wig?"

Thirty minutes later Peter returned with a wig and some makeup after sneaking out of the building and back in via the fire escape. Paxton held it up and grimaced. "It's a mullet."

"It's the Florence Henderson Brady Bunch wig," Peter announced with a smile.

"You're enjoying this too much," Paxton said as he pulled on the wig. "Hey, this isn't that bad." Paxton grabbed a rubber band and put the mullet flip part of the hair into a low ponytail. He used the makeup to darken his face where his beard would be if he had grown it out. Up close it looked ridiculous but from far enough away it would pass for a closely groomed beard.

"I'll make sure everyone is back across the street and I'll meet you down there. Do you have a plan?" Peter asked as Paxton picked up his phone.

"I do. Just make sure you call my name real loud and ask me where I'm going," Paxton told him.

Five minutes later, Paxton walked outside the apartment with a bulletproof vest underneath an oversized sweatshirt. Best of all, Ryker Faulkner's helicopter was ready and waiting for him at the airport.

"Hey, Kendry!" Peter yelled loud enough for half the block to hear. "Get back to the office. We need a report on this."

Paxton turned to face Peter who was across the street,

pretending to talk to Whitlock. "No can do, boss. I'm going to Atlanta and taking care of this once and for all," Paxton yelled back.

He got into his car and noticed two men break away from the crowd and head toward their own vehicles. Paxton didn't wait for them, but he also didn't make it hard for them to follow him.

Paxton kept an eye on them in his rearview mirror as he navigated the narrow downtown streets. They kept their distance within the city, but as soon as Paxton was on the highway heading toward the airport, they changed tactics.

They were no longer trying to stay hidden. Instead, they were trying to catch him. Good. It was exactly what Paxton wanted. He needed them to chase him and see him arrive at the airport. They all needed to think he was on his way to Atlanta. Paxton sped up as he cut in and out of traffic. Horns blared and his pulse raced as his speed increased to over a hundred miles per hour.

Paxton kept his gaze in the mirror as he used every defensive driving technique he knew to get to Ryker's helicopter. The *ping* of the first bullet hitting the back of his SUV as he tore down the off-ramp toward the airport had him radioing ahead for airport police to be waiting for him.

The second shot shattered the back window. Glass cracked, and the *pffft* of the bullet whizzing by him and out the front window had Paxton ducking in his seat. He began to swerve to make it harder for the gang members to shoot at him, but Paxton didn't have much farther to go. He heard sirens up ahead, but a second later a flurry of shots rang out. The bullets came through the back window and slammed into the front dash and into the headrests.

Paxton grabbed his gun with his left hand and drove

with his right. He reached across his body, aimed his gun through the destroyed rear window, and blindly fired off some rounds. They must have hit because the car chasing him swerved. Finally, he saw police lights ahead of him. Paxton fired off a few more rounds and then gave them the middle finger as the gate to the private airfield came into view.

The car behind him slammed on the brakes and spun in the street. They were already taking off in the opposite direction before the airport police had made it out of the parking lot.

The second Paxton stopped his car a man opened the door. "Agent Kendry, I'm your pilot. Shall we depart for Shadows Landing?"

So this was how Ryker rolled. Paxton wondered at the fact the pilot didn't blink at the gunshot car or the gun Paxton holstered as he got out of the driver's seat.

"That would be great, thank you." If the pilot could act as if a high-speed shootout were normal, so could Paxton.

Tinsley was going to ask Ryker how he was going to get the information on the stolen art when his phone rang and he stepped outside. No one at the table spoke. Instead, they looked over at the bar to where Georgina smiled and joked with Gator, Skeeter, and Turtle.

"What happened to her?" Tinsley asked Harper.

"I don't know. She'll tell us when she's ready. Don't anyone push her or I'll kick their ass," Harper threatened.

Ryker pushed open the door and strode back to his seat at the table. "What's happened?" Tinsley asked.

"Paxton called and needs a lift," Ryker said as he shrugged out of his suit coat before taking his seat. "Georgina, I'll take a bourbon, please," he called out to her.

Georgina poured the drink and brought it to him. Tinsley smiled at her as Georgina placed it in front of Ryker. "Someday you'll have to tell them who you really are, Miss Grey*son*," Ryker murmured, his voice barely a thread of sound. Tinsley's eyes widened as Georgina's face lost all color for the second time that night. Georgina looked around to see if anyone overheard and Tinsley looked away, pretending not to hear. It was clear Georgina had a past she didn't want anyone to know about and Tinsley wasn't going to pry. Harper had been correct. She would tell them when she was ready.

"Ryker, what's going on with Paxton?" Tinsley asked once Georgina was back behind the bar.

"Gang members were watching his apartment. Miss Tibbie gave him a wig and he staged a race to Atlanta to confront the leader. He's trying to keep his cover here intact. He's hoping the members staking out his apartment took pictures of him in his costume and are sharing that look among the gang. He's probably going to have to lie low once he's here, too. He just doesn't want to leave you. Want me to call Mallory and Blythe back?" Ryker asked.

"Let me talk to Paxton first. Thanks, Ryker."

Tinsley and her family hadn't taken a bite of dinner before the door opened and Paxton came in. He tossed a wig on the table and sat down next to Ryker.

"Thanks for the loan of your helicopter. The back of my vehicle is now shot to shit, but I got into the private airfield before they could gain too much on me. Happily, the airport police were waiting to chase them off." Paxton leaned over and kissed Tinsley. She saw the dark brown makeup on his face and wanted to ask him what happened when Ryker cursed.

"What is it?" Tinsley asked, her whole body on edge. Paxton reached over and took her hand in his as they waited for the bad news.

"The Vermeer has been traced to the last owner before the Smith family got it." The table fell silent as Ryker handed his phone to Tinsley. Her eyes raced over the report and she had to read it again because her brain didn't compute it.

"Is it the Isabella Stewart Gardner Museum?" Ellery asked when Tinsley wasn't quick to respond.

"No," Tinsley said, feeling her hands begin to shake. She took a deep breath and handed the phone back to Ryker. "Ryker's contact found the art dealer the fake Smith family supposedly bought the art from in the late 1940s."

"That's good, right? So it wasn't really stolen or was it stolen from that art dealer?" Ellery asked.

"It was most definitely stolen, but it wasn't stolen by the Smith family. It was given to them by the Argentinians to be fenced would be my guess," Tinsley said as she imagined the timeline of the provenance of the art.

"I don't understand," Ellery said slowly.

"I know Smith is a fake name. I know the last provenance from the 1940s is fake. What wasn't fake was the name of the art dealer in Buenos Aires. When dealing with stolen art, the more truth you keep to the provenance and story of the paintings, the harder it is to find out it's stolen. Like any good lie, you keep to the truth as much as possible.

There was an art dealer in 1949 Buenos Aires who got this painting from a Señor Roberto Fernandez. However, in 1964, Roberto Fernandez was kidnapped from his middle-class suburban home in Buenos Aires because his real name was Mannes Reuter, a close associate of Adolf Eichmann, one of Adolf Hitler's most trusted men who had killed tens of thousands of innocent people in Budapest during 1944 and countless people before that.

"The dealer who sold the art in 1949 was one of Eichmann's soldiers. Eichmann and Reuter escaped Hungary and made their way to Italy. The leader of Argentina, which at that time was allied with Hitler, gave them fake papers and passage from Italy to Buenos Aires. There they hid in plain sight, selling off artwork they'd stolen from Jewish families until they were tracked down by a group of Nazi hunters who smuggled them both out of the country and brought them to justice for their war crimes."

Tinsley sat back in her chair. Her eyes filled with unshed tears as they processed what this meant. She swallowed hard, the lump in her throat making it difficult to do so. "That painting, most likely all those paintings, were stolen from innocent Jewish families by Nazis during the war. Those families may not have survived the war but some may have. I have to find out. I have to get them back to their families. I have to, Paxton." Tears broke free as Tinsley grabbed Paxton's hand. She tried to slow their flow but couldn't. How there could be such pain and suffering attached to such beautiful art, she couldn't fathom.

"It's estimated that over a hundred thousand pieces of such art are still missing from the Second World War," Paxton told the group. "If we can get eighty of them back to their families, we will. Sometimes these pieces of art are literally all people have left to remember their families who were murdered during the war."

"I'll call Cy and let him know," Dare said quietly before stepping away from the table.

"Yes, we have to find the rest. I have half. We need the other half," Tinsley said, drying her tears. "Now, what do I need to do to find the owners of this stolen Nazi artwork?"

22

"Miss Tinsley, I won't ask what's going on, but I will offer my help," Gator said as he, Skeeter, and Turtle approached the table.

"Me too. Anne said she would also help," Skeeter told her. "She said those paintings have seen more death than she has."

"That right there gives me the heebie-jeebies," Turtle said as he reached for the large knife at his waist. "I'll help, too. It's the right thing to do."

"I couldn't help but overhear," Maggie Bell said, coming from the back of the bar with her brother, Gage. "We want to help, too. We can store the paintings if you need. Or if you need a place to stay, we have rooms open now."

"Thank you all," Tinsley said, touched that she had so many people ready to help her. "I'll let you know as soon as we have a plan."

Everyone nodded, knowing she would call on them if she needed help. The noise level rose in the bar again, but Tinsley's table was still quiet.

"We can't look into the real owners until this is over," Ellery finally said.

"Agreed," Paxton said as they watched Dare come back inside.

"What did Uncle Cy say?" Tinsley asked Dare.

"He grunted a couple of times, said he'd take care of it, and hung up on me," Dare told them. "But," he said, stopping Tinsley as she got ready to ask a question. "Then Aunt Annie called me and said she and Bridget were taking a girls' trip and wanted to stop by Shadows Landing because Bridget is training the dogs to hit on artwork. She's training them on the scent of old paint and canvases painters used many years ago. There are some agents in customs that are already using dogs to search for stolen art and cultural antiquities that are being trafficked. She asked that you lay a polyester cloth and some cotton balls over some of the stolen art for a couple of days. They'll be here Friday."

"Um, okay," Tinsley said, looking to Paxton to see if she was the only one slightly confused.

"Oh," Dare said suddenly, "and you can't tell the uncles that Annie and Bridget are here or in Atlanta."

"Why not?" Tinsley asked.

Dare shrugged and held up his hands to say he had no idea.

"No, that couldn't be it," Paxton muttered, but it was too late. Everyone was already looking at him.

"What?" Tinsley said with annoyance. She felt as if she were missing something and didn't like it.

"Well, Cy called his brothers in for a guys' trip to take on the gang. Now your aunt called it a girls' trip and it just made me wonder if they were coming to do the same thing but didn't want the guys to know. No, that's silly. Your aunt isn't former military."

"No, she's former DEA, but Bridget is former military," Tinsley said with a slow smile. "Go girls!"

"Nah, the uncles will have it wrapped up before Bridget and Annie even get to town," Ridge said.

"Care to bet on that?" Tinsley asked.

"I'm in," Harper said, slamming a twenty on the table. "Aunts, all the way."

A flurry of bets rang out and ended as Gator added a twenty to the pile. "Sorry, men, but I've seen Annie Davies wrestle Bubba. The ladies got it."

Paxton had laughed when the bets were made but now it felt like a lifetime ago, not just a couple of hours. Long gone was the laughter. It was now replaced with worry. He knew this feeling. It was the feeling of being on the cusp of cracking a case. Go one way and you solve it. Go the other way and you end up dead. There was no middle ground anymore.

"We need to buy time," Paxton told Tinsley at the end of the night as they lay in bed in her house.

"I think I need to stay in constant contact with Maurice. It's when I don't reach out to him that he randomly shows up. I wouldn't be surprised if he shows up to check on the art," Tinsley told him as she snuggled up against him. She rested her head on his shoulder and absently ran her fingers along his bare chest.

"What if you tell him you have to travel to some archives? That could buy you a couple of days where you're not here so he wouldn't stop by." Paxton ran his fingers absently over her arm as they brainstormed a plan.

"I'll call him every day. I think that's a good idea. Tell him what I'm working on and the prices I have so far. Then when he starts to get itchy about sending buyers, I will need to make the trip to the archives. What archives? I don't know, but I'll figure out something. Hopefully, that gives Cy time to find the other half of the paintings and even time for Bridget and Annie to do their thing, too."

Paxton snuggled Tinsley closer to him. He couldn't wait for this to be over. They needed to move on with their lives as a couple. It was one thing to accept the risks in being an agent himself, but it was a completely different thing having Tinsley involved. If anything happened to her because of him, he wouldn't be able to live with himself.

"We have a plan. I don't want to worry about it for the rest of the night," Tinsley told him before placing her lips on his chest and kissing her way across his muscles.

"That's the best plan I've heard all night." Paxton ran his fingers through her long hair and tightened his fingers to a fist so he could gently tug her wandering lips up his chest, over his neck, and to his mouth. "I love you," he told her a second before taking her lips with his.

Tonight was about them. About their love. About their future. About their passion. Curtis, stolen art, the Myriad, everything else could all wait until morning. Paxton needed Tinsley to know how much she meant to him. He'd told her he loved her, but those words didn't seem to be enough. So, instead of telling her, he showed her.

Paxton flipped Tinsley so he was on top. He stretched her arms toward the headboard and then took his time kissing, licking, and nibbling every inch of her smooth skin.

Tinsley's words started coherently, but by the time he reached her center, they were just passionate murmurs. She was lost in the feeling of their bodies becoming one. When Paxton joined with her, his own words failed him. Instead, the two of them fell headfirst into their shared climax.

Tinsley picked up the phone and took a deep breath. It was Thursday. She'd kept Maurice at bay, but she knew her time was up. He was getting itchy to have some paintings sold. Today was the day she needed to tell him she was on her way to the archives for research. She'd been setting it up in previous conversations with Maurice and hoped she could buy herself the weekend.

Cy and her uncles were cleaning house in Atlanta. They were busting all the street-level dealers and working their way up the chain of command. Curtis had been missing in action for the past week. Even Maurice and Murray hadn't been seen. Unfortunately, the art hadn't been seen either.

The phone rang, but it didn't get picked up. The FBI had been trying to trace the calls, but it was no good. Maurice would let the phone ring, then call back using a burner phone. Tinsley hung up and waited. It only took a minute for Maurice to call her back on an unknown number.

"I hope you have good news," Maurice said, his voice tight and lacking the fake gentlemanly manners he'd used before.

"I do," Tinsley said, adding a little extra sweetness to her voice. "We can start selling the paintings on Monday. I'm leaving today to visit an art library to get the final estimates needed on some of these exquisite pieces with no online sales records."

"Monday? Why so long?" Maurice asked.

"I have a plan to get you the most money possible. I'm preparing a catalog with a picture of each painting or drawing. It includes the sales price and the history of the painting. I'm giving everyone one week to make their bids. By next Friday, the entire collection will be sold and your family will be able to afford any surgery your grandmother will ever need. We're talking generational wealth here, Maurice. Your grandparents might be cash strapped, but this collection is her ultimate gift to you."

"That much?" Maurice asked. Tinsley had fed him one painting a day, not the whole lot. She was saving it for just this time.

"You said that this is half of her collection, correct?"

"Yes, that's right," Maurice said eagerly. "We were hoping to get five million for half of it."

"Five million," Tinsley laughed. "Just the half I have is valued at over a hundred million, Maurice."

Tinsley heard muffled conversation over the phone. Maurice was not alone.

"Would you and your family like to come see it one last time Monday morning before I start meeting with your private buyers?" Tinsley asked.

"That's nice of you, Tinsley. I'll check with everyone and text you later. We do want the pieces we're privately selling pulled from the catalog. The public doesn't need to see them since they are already sold," Maurice instructed.

"Of course. I'll send you a complete list now. You can send me an email with the pieces and purchase prices you want me to aim for with your buyers and I'll pull them from the catalog. I can also start setting up sales appointments."

"I'll set them all up. It'll be in the email I send you. I'll be in touch. Thank you." Maurice hung up and Tinsley remembered to start breathing again.

Paxton looked down at his phone and shook his head. "They still weren't able to get a location on Maurice. You executed the plan perfectly, though. We'll have undercover agents all through town and arrest every buyer as they come in. We will then quickly whisk them away before the next person comes."

Tinsley nodded. Paxton had come up with the plan and Ryker's contact had worked hard trying to identify all the art. Unfortunately, they weren't listed in the Stolen Art Database of the United States. They had all come from Argentina, stolen from who knows where. Now they were in a holding pattern until the thieves were arrested and the other half of the art was found. Only then could they risk digging deeper into the true owners of the artwork. Until then, everyone would be arrested for the fraudulent provenances.

Paxton's phone rang and Tinsley went back to work on the catalog as he went to answer it. When he came back into her office, he had a smile on his face.

"What happened?" she asked.

"The money was finally moved from the shell account. My guys were able to dig into the account and found it belonged to an art dealer, but the owner of the account is dead. They have him set up as a real person, but he died forty years ago. After the money left the dead art dealer's account, it was transferred multiple times. Once through another shell company to make it look legit and then it was divided. Half went to a bank account in Buenos Aires and the other half to a company in Atlanta." Paxton smiled wider and she knew he wasn't done. "We are requesting CIA operatives to look into the bank account in Buenos Aires. But the account here in Atlanta is for a money services business, a cash-for-paychecks type place. When we dug into the company and through all the protective layers to hide the owner, we discovered that Curtis Engle owns the company."

"That's enough to get him on the stolen Castille, right?" Tinsley asked.

"It's a good start. He could still claim he didn't know it was stolen and this was a repayment of a loan or they were just wiring it for a customer. My agents are still digging into it, but it'll be a slam-dunk case if we can link Engle to the dead dealer's account."

Tinsley's email alert sounded and she pulled up an email that looked like spam. However, the subject line was *Art Buyers*. The email listed ten works of art. Next to the title of each painting listed was a time, not a name.

Vermeer. Monday 9:00

Degas. Monday 10:00

And so on until ten paintings with ten appointments were listed.

"Paxton, look." Tinsley pointed to her computer.

Paxton came over and read the email and clenched his jaw. "He was smart. His name isn't anywhere on the email and neither are the names of the buyers. I'll tell tech and see if they can find out where the email came from. What's your email and password?"

Tinsley gave them to him and then waited as he talked to someone over the phone. She saw a slight smile and Paxton give a small fist pump before hanging up. "It was from a public library in Atlanta. We're working on getting a subpoena for any security cameras, and Connor is going to reach out to traffic to see if we can find out who it was and where they were going."

"So what now?" Tinsley asked.

"We go home and spend the weekend making love when I'm not working."

"What about me?"

"You know the deal I made with Ryker. For us to move

back to your house, you have to be with me at all times. So, do you think you can train Bubba to be your attack gator while I work?" Paxton asked with such a serious face that Tinsley laughed.

"I don't know. Your high-pitched screaming might draw too much attention." Tinsley sent him a wink and walked past him. She heard him chuckling as she began to close down the art gallery.

23

Paxton followed his plan to the letter. He worked, made love to her, and then went back to work. Tinsley had woken up at three in the morning and found Paxton in the kitchen, working on his laptop.

She'd kissed the top of his head before he wordlessly pulled her onto his lap and made slow love to her. Tinsley was still breathing hard when he escorted her back to bed and tucked her in.

When she woke up again at seven, he was gone from bed once again. Tinsley poured a cup of coffee and took a seat on her back patio while Paxton finished a phone call. The smell of the coffee and the hint of hazelnut from the creamer put a smile on her face as she watched the birds fly and the little animals scamper in the woods behind her house.

The screen door opened and Tinsley looked up to see Paxton take the seat next to her. He leaned over and kissed her. "Good morning."

"Good morning. Did you sleep at all?" Tinsley asked.

"I got a couple of hours. They made progress on the art

dealer's account. Cy called too and said last night they had a huge drug bust with Connor. Curtis is going to be livid. What's interesting is Mark Trevino showed up on the scene and cursed out Connor for not including them in the plans. He claimed they had surveillance on the warehouse and were getting ready for their own bust. All lies, but now we know he has some skin in this game. Connor is trying to get a search warrant for Mark's financials."

"So Curtis is going to be very anxious for Monday?"

"Definitely. Lucky for us, anxious and desperate people do stupid things. We're hoping he slips up and we can put the final nail in his coffin."

Tinsley's phone buzzed and she looked down at it. "It's a message from my Aunt Annie. They caught a military flight and just landed at the Charleston Air Force Base. They're already on their way here."

"I don't know what to expect after meeting Cy."

They both paused as they heard a knock at the front door. Paxton had a gun in his hand and was moving back into the house before Tinsley could stand up. She followed behind him and saw him tuck the gun away before opening the door.

"Good morning, Miss Ruby, Miss Winnie," Paxton said, stepping back to let the two ladies inside.

"I told you we should have come earlier," Miss Winnie scolded Miss Ruby.

"You're right, Win. Maybe if we ask, he'll take his shirt off and just pretend we caught him getting dressed for the day."

Tinsley smiled and hid her laughter as Paxton winked at the ladies. "I could make that happen if you tell me what smells so good."

"Backup plan for the win," Miss Ruby said, digging into her basket and pulling out a fresh-baked apple pie.

"I have a feeling you're not going to just give that to me, are you?" Paxton asked skeptically.

"You're a smart one," Miss Winnie said with mischief in her eyes as she patted his cheek.

"You see, Trent's poster with our pie got us a lot of attention the other week. The fall festival is up next. We can't just reuse the same sign," Miss Ruby said matter-of-factly. "That would be bad branding."

Tinsley clamped her mouth shut to stop the laugh from escaping as Paxton raised an eyebrow and tried to appear intimidating.

Miss Winnie rolled her eyes at him. "Don't bother with that look, young man. We could stare the devil in the face and still not hand over our apple pie until he stripped for it."

"If I'm reading this situation correctly, you want me to strip for the next banner and in return I'd get this apple pie?" Paxton asked.

"You'd get this one, and one pie a month for one year. That's what we're doing for Trent," Miss Ruby said with a look that implied she knew she had Paxton hook, line, and sinker. To seal the deal, she moved the pie slowly under Paxton's nose. Tinsley couldn't be sure, but she thought Paxton was drooling.

"Deal," Paxton said, yanking his T-shirt off as he reached for the pie.

"You got the camera, Win?" Ruby asked, walking by Paxton as she held the pie up.

"Sure do. You're thinking nature shots?" Winnie asked as Paxton followed as if he were tethered to the pie.

"Yes. I think he'd look real nice leaning against a tree."

Tinsley just shook her head as she followed the group outside. Paxton had stripped along the way. There were shoes, socks, and a pair of pants strewn about on the way out the back door.

Tinsley followed behind, letting Miss Ruby and Miss Winnie instruct Paxton on how to lean against the tree.

"Now lose your drawers," Miss Winnie instructed and Tinsley saw Paxton pause.

"What? Can't I just hold the pie down here?" Paxton asked.

Miss Ruby replied by sticking the pie under Paxton's nose again. Paxton stepped behind the tree and shucked his boxers. Then he leaned out and held out his hands for the pie.

"Sneaky devil," Miss Winnie muttered.

Miss Ruby handed the pie over and Tinsley was treated to the show of a lifetime. She didn't know if it were funnier to watch Paxton trying to keep the pie in front of him or Miss Ruby and Miss Winnie trying to get the pie to slip to the side a bit so they could sneak a peek.

Tinsley was still snickering when three blurs of color shot by. One was tan, one black, and the other one was red. They streaked past her and right toward Paxton. Paxton jumped back behind the tree, but it was too late. The three dogs had zeroed in on the pie.

"No!" Paxton yelled as he ran around and around the tree with the three dogs chasing him. The red dog made a leap for the pie and Paxton was forced to hold it up over his head.

Miss Winnie gasped and then turned to Tinsley with a smile. "Lucky girl."

"I know," Tinsley said with a wink.

"Well, this is certainly a different kind of welcome than I expected. Can't say I'm disappointed, though."

"Aunt Annie! Miss Bridget!" Tinsley jumped out of her

chair and hurried off the porch. The two ladies watched as Paxton reached up with one hand and began to pull himself up into the tree while still holding the pie with his other hand. They got a nice clear view of Paxton and his not-so-little Paxton.

"Does he regularly climb trees naked?" Annie asked.

"No. He got naked to get twelve apple pies from Miss Winnie and Miss Ruby."

"Heck, I'd get naked for that," Annie said, and Bridget nodded her agreement.

"You think I should tell him Robyn can climb trees?" Bridget asked Annie.

"Nah, let him experience that surprise on his own," Annie said before turning back to Tinsley. "So, this is the guy?"

"That's him. All of him."

Bridget leaned forward and lifted up her hand for a high five.

"Help!" Paxton yelled from where he now sat halfway down the first branch in the tree. "I will not lose this pie after stripping down for it. And you two better delete any picture of me being chased by these dogs!" The last word was yelled in surprise as the red Vizsla ran straight for the tree, leaped up, bounced off the trunk and up onto the thick branch Paxton currently occupied. "Oh no. I don't care how cool that was. You're not getting my pie!" he yelled at Robyn.

"He's braver than your husband," Annie said to Bridget who nodded.

"Ahmed gets nightmares if he sees Robyn in trees. He loves her to death, but he says it's just not natural for a dog to be able to climb a tree. Robyn's father, Bob, did that and it freaked him out."

"He has a good point. It's a strange sight," Tinsley said as she watched the dog walk carefully forward and then sit. She cocked her head to the side and reached out with her paw to place it on Paxton's arm.

"Ahmed can't resist that. Paxton's a goner," Bridget whispered to them as Miss Winnie snapped pictures.

"One bite and that's it," Paxton tried to say sternly as Robyn's short tail thumped with victory.

Paxton fed her a bit with his fork and then Robyn licked him and Paxton was lost forever to the rust-colored dog.

"Tinsley, you think you could help this sweetie down? I don't want her hurt," Paxton called out.

"Told you. Point for Robyn. Though your guy also gets a point for treating her well," Bridget said before she walked over to the tree. She patted her chest and Robyn leaped instantly from the branch and into Bridget's arms. She caught the forty-plus-pound dog and set her down before looking up at Paxton. "Do you need help down?"

"Are you going to catch me, too?" Paxton asked.

"I was going to offer to take the pie," Bridget said with a grin.

"No thanks. I feel as if I've fought a battle for this and I'm not letting it out of my grasp until the pie tin is empty and licked clean."

Bridget gave a command and all three dogs raced to her to side and sat perfectly in a row. "You're good. They won't move until I tell them to."

Bridget turned around and left the three dogs staring up at Paxton. Sure enough, they didn't move even as he climbed down and got dressed.

"Now, where are these paintings?" Annie asked Tinsley as Paxton collected his clothes.

"They're at the church," Tinsley told her. "Do you really think the dogs will be able to track them in Atlanta?"

"I'd like to know that, too," Paxton said as he joined them, finally fully clothed.

"We got the addresses for all of the properties used by Curtis Engle. We plan to search them all," Bridget said.

"And beat my husband and his brothers to the punch," Annie said with a smirk.

"They think you wives don't know what they do on their guys' trips, do they?" Tinsley asked.

"That's right. They think we actually believe the texts Pierce sends of them fishing," Annie said with amusement.

"My husband joined them last night. He tried to play it off as the Davies brothers were having so much fun fishing, he just had to join them. Fishing for drug dealers, that is." Bridget rolled her eyes.

"Where did you get that list of properties?" Paxton asked Bridget.

"My son." That was all she said. Tinsley could tell Paxton wanted to know more, but that was all he was going to get.

"Now that we're all dressed and you have your pie, let's take Annie and Bridget to see the paintings." Tinsley turned to her aunt and friend. "I've stored them with cotton balls and the polyester strips just like you asked."

"Great. That will help the girls with their tracking." Bridget whistled and three dogs raced to her side. "This is Robyn. She's a Vizsla who belongs to a family friend but has one heck of a nose on her," Bridget said, introducing the red dog that had climbed the tree. Bridget then pointed to the tan lithe dog. "This is Susi the Malinois. The last dog is obviously a Bloodhound." Bridget smiled at the dog with the large floppy ears, big black nose, wrinkly face, and oversized jowls. She was black along her body and then tan on her legs and head, and Tinsley just wanted to snuggle her. "This is Buttercup," Bridget told them as she rubbed the Bloodhound's head, sending her big ears flapping. Buttercup's tongue lolled happily to the side as she leaned against Bridget's legs.

"I didn't think Bloodhounds were used to track anything besides people," Paxton said, smiling at the happy dog.

"We brought a diverse team. Susi is great for tracking hot trails. If someone or something was recently in an area, she would find it. Plus she's a patrol dog and can take a criminal down faster than any dog I have trained. Think of Susi as an all-around dog. Robyn is good for scent work, too, but is a little more specialized. Plus she's smart—scarily smart. She can find a trail and won't freak out if she loses it. She'll work the area until she finds it again. And then there's our scent specialist, Buttercup. Bloodhounds are amazing at working cold trails. Scent work is all Buttercup does. She'll take the scent from the scent article and will be off. She can even sniff the air for the scent. Buttercup had gone to a crime scene before where a woman's body was found laid out in a city park. It was obvious the murder hadn't been committed there. Buttercup backtracked the woman's scent out of the park, down an alley, into the back door of an apartment, into a stairwell, up three flights, down the hall, to a specific apartment, and then straight to the bathtub. Police found the woman's blood in the drain and arrested the apartment owner for her murder. That's what Buttercup can do. She's the tortoise, where Susi is the hare."

"What is Robyn in that scenario?" Paxton asked.

"Robyn would have called an Uber and met the others there," Bridget said with an affectionate smile.

Tinsley felt hope bloom as her aunt and Miss B said hello to Miss Winnie and Miss Ruby before they headed out to look at their paintings. Energy surged through her body and she suddenly couldn't wait to get Annie and Bridget the scent items and have them on their way to Atlanta.

Paxton absently rubbed Robyn's head as Annie and Bridget stared in wonder at the paintings.

"First, this is the coolest church ever," Annie said. "Second, these paintings are . . . just wow."

Paxton watch Bridget put each scent item into its own plastic evidence bag. She labeled them and put them in her backpack. The dogs sniffed around and Bridget smiled at Buttercup. "Want to see how she works?"

"I'd love to see," Paxton answered.

"How long ago were these paintings put in here?" Bridget asked.

"Sunday, so five days," Tinsley answered.

"Bring me something with scent on it from one person who carried a painting in," Bridget instructed.

"My brother, Ridge, sat in the pew on Sunday. Can Buttercup use that?" Tinsley asked.

Bridget pulled out a small package containing a sterile gauze. "Show me."

Annie and Reverend Winston stayed with the dogs, but Paxton followed to see how this worked. Bridget took the gauze and rubbed it over the pew where Ridge had touched the wood. They walked back down to where the dogs were. Bridget held the gauze out for Buttercup. "Scent."

Buttercup took in a big snorting breath and then stuck her nose up in the air. She sniffed the air with deep breaths that made her jowls jiggle. Then her nose turned to one of the paintings. She sniffed the painting and bayed, the soulful song of a Bloodhound.

"Good girl. Scent," Bridget told her.

Buttercup's big nose went to the dirt floor. Instead of heading out the way they had come into the storage area— through the front door of the church and behind the altar— Buttercup led them out the back door, down a long, dark dirty hallway, and out a back door of sorts that led them to the cemetery. Her nose never left the ground as she walked behind the buildings and turned left at the art gallery. She headed straight for the gate to the small courtyard, through Tinsley's back door, and through the gallery to the front door. Tinsley opened it and Buttercup shot through the door, crossed the street, and pawed at the front door to Harper's bar. Paxton opened it and Buttercup trotted through the bar to where Ridge was leaning against the kitchen door talking to Harper. Buttercup sat down and bayed again.

"What the hell?" Ridge yelled as he jumped in surprise at finding a Bloodhound sitting directly behind him.

"Good girl!" Bridget said, tossing Buttercup a treat.

Paxton was impressed, but it also gave him an idea.

"Can you wipe down what our suspects have touched in the gallery and use Buttercup to track them in Atlanta? They had to pick up the artwork so their scent should also be there," he asked Bridget as Tinsley told Harper what was going on.

"Of course. You've seen what she can do."

"Let me show you where Maurice touched the most." Paxton led Bridget back across the street while Harper and Ridge talked to their aunt and played with the dogs.

An hour later they'd collected all the samples, had an early lunch with the Faulkners, and then Annie, Bridget, and the dogs were on their way to Atlanta.

Paxton's phone rang and he answered it as Tinsley drove him back to her house. "Connor, is there any news?"

"Cy is one scary-ass dude. But then I met Ahmed last night and almost crapped my pants. Your girlfriend has some very scary friends. You should remember that if you're serious about her. These guys could make you disappear in a second. Cy and Ahmed are having a contest to see who can make the gang members cry the fastest. I'm simultaneously petrified and encouraged. We're getting leads left and right now."

"Bridget, Ahmed's wife is on her way with Cade's wife, Annie. They have scent-tracking dogs with them. They have your number but you have to swear you don't tell the men the women are in town. They've decided they're going to find the art before their husbands do," Paxton told Connor, feeling as if he were living in an alternate universe even as he said it.

"You're kidding, right? This is nuts. They're having *fun*. They brought in a military helicopter so they could fast-rope into a warehouse last night. They raced down the ropes. Then there's this guy named Pierce who keeps using our computers to doctor pictures of the guys to make it look like they're fishing. I'm at a loss for words, but there's no way in hell I'll send them away. I want to keep them forever. They've taken down more gang members, confiscated more guns and drugs, and destroyed more meth labs in one week than we did in the past eighteen months."

"I guess that's good, right?" Paxton said, not knowing what else to say since Connor sounded dazed.

"Yeah, I guess so. I just thought you should know if I disappear for some reason, it was probably this Ahmed guy. I'll be on the lookout for the wives. They're nice, right? They won't dismember me for fun?"

"Annie might," Tinsley whispered with a huge smile on her face.

"Nope, great ladies. Oh, and Connor, get the dogs some pie and they'll love you. Call me if they get anything." Paxton hung up the phone and stared out the car window, taking it all in. "I really don't know what to say."

Tinsley pulled into her driveway and parked her car. "Good, what I'm thinking of doesn't involve words."

She got out of the car and stepped out of her shoes the second she hit her patio. Her shirt followed and then Paxton was running after her. Paxton didn't know what to make of her Keeneston family, but when Tinsley's bra was tossed onto the couch, all thoughts of her family fled and he knew exactly what to do.

24

Neither Maurice nor Murray called Tinsley over the weekend. They had lain low Thursday, Friday, and Saturday. On Saturday, Tinsley's family had come over for dinner and game night. Somehow Paxton had ended up with baby Chase for most of the charade game. His finger was chewed on, there was drool down his shirt, and Paxton had to admit he loved it.

Tinsley, marriage, babies, and family—those thoughts were consuming him even as Connor and Annie kept him up to date on the case. The days he and Tinsley were able to spend together only made his feelings for her to grow and deepen. He felt as if roots were being laid deep in his heart for both Tinsley and Shadows Landing. Which was what had him wide awake at four o'clock Sunday morning.

Paxton had wanted that promotion in the FBI. He wanted to rise in the ranks and while he was technically now a higher rank as the head of art crimes than when he was in gangs, it had felt like a punishment. Until now.

Paxton lay in the bed with his arm around Tinsley and punishment was the complete opposite of what he was feeling. He needed to sit down with Peter and talk about his career. He needed to pull the transfer he'd had Peter put in for New York and Chicago the day before this case had started. Instead, he was determined to grow in the agency, only this time he was going to expand the art crimes division here in Charleston so he could stay with Tinsley. It felt right.

The screen to his cell phone lit up and Paxton had to untangle himself from Tinsley to answer it. "Hello?" he whispered into the phone.

"It's Annie. Buttercup hit on Maurice's scent. We're going in. I thought you'd like to watch."

"Yes," Paxton said, swinging his feet over the side of the bed and not trying to be quiet. "Put it on video. Did you call Connor?"

"Yes, but he's tied up with our husbands. He'll get here as soon as he can. We're moving in because we just saw a light turn on in a bedroom," Annie whispered. "We can't chance them leaving. Here we go."

"What's going on?" Tinsley asked sleepily.

"Buttercup is on a scent," Paxton told her as he turned on the video call and began to record it.

That woke Tinsley right up and she moved to sit next to him as they stared at the video feed of a home in a middle-class neighborhood. "That's Maurice's car," Tinsley whispered.

Paxton nodded. His heart beat wildly in his chest as if he were on the raid with them. Where was Connor? Two women shouldn't go into the house alone. They would be outnumbered. He should be there with them.

Buttercup led them right to the car, then up the walkway, and to the front door. Instead of baying, she sat and rested her nose against the closed door.

"Annie, take Robyn around back and put her on a sit-stay," Bridget whispered. The video then showed Annie and Robyn running silently around the house to the back patio. Annie put Robyn on a sit-stay hidden in the shadows between two patio chairs before running back to the front of the house. Bridget came back into view. Buttercup was on a long tracking leash that Bridget held in her left hand. On her right, Susi was on a short leash, obviously amped up and ready to go. Bridget opened a package and told Susi, "Scent."

"Open it," Bridget whispered as Annie moved to place the phone in a backpack strap on her chest.

With two free hands, Annie picked the front door lock and then pulled out her weapon. Bridget handed her Buttercup's leash and then reached out with her free hand and slowly opened the door. "Scent," Bridget whispered to her dogs.

Paxton saw a gun appear in Bridget's hand as Susi took the lead and strode inside with her nose to the ground. The house was a ranch style and Susi headed straight for the side of the house where all the bedrooms were located. Maurice must be sleeping. However, Buttercup took a detour. She headed straight for a door off the kitchen.

Annie opened it slowly and flipped on the tactical flashlight attachment to her Glock. She made her way down the stairs into a basement that couldn't be seen from the street. Buttercup pulled her through the dark, and Paxton held his breath as he watched the scan of the light while Annie cleared the area. Buttercup had something. She was pulling hard as she led Annie away from the stairs.

He saw what Buttercup had scented at the same time Tinsley did. He heard her gasp next to him. "I think we found your paintings," Annie whispered as she used her flashlight to scan the area. At least forty wrapped items were leaning against the far wall.

They couldn't celebrate, though. Suddenly there was shouting from upstairs. Annie was running with Buttercup beside her. She took the basement stairs two at a time to find the front door open and the back of Curtis Engle running out of the house.

"*Stellen!*" Bridget yelled from deep inside the house. Susi shot past Annie and out the open front door.

Annie raced after her and Paxton watched as Susi leaped onto the car. She was snarling and barking on the hood of the car as she used her paws to try to claw at Curtis through the windshield. It was too late, though. Curtis threw the car into reverse. Annie called for Susi who leaped from the moving car and into the front yard. Annie was about to go after Curtis, but then they all heard Bridget.

"You asshole!" Bridget yelled.

"Susi!" Annie yelled but didn't need to. The Mal was already bolting back into the house to rescue her handler.

The sound of glass breaking had Annie turning from the hallway to the back door. There were the simultaneous sounds of men screaming. One from a bedroom and the other from the backyard.

"Bridget?" Annie called out.

"I'm good. Get the one who went out back!" Bridget yelled, but Annie was already running that way.

Paxton chuckled as Annie opened the back door. "That's my girl," Paxton called out to where Robyn had Maurice by the balls—literally. Maurice was frozen in place with tears running down his face.

"Get him off me," he pleaded.

Paxton had muted the phone and covered the camera.

"We don't want Maurice hearing or recognizing us," he told Tinsley.

"Only a girl would bring a man down by the balls, dimwit. Hold him, Robyn," Annie ordered as she placed cuffs on Maurice.

The sounds of sirens could be heard in the distance as Annie and Bridget hauled the men to the front porch. Connor was the first to arrive. The second vehicle was an SUV filled with Davies brothers.

"What are you two doing here?" a man sputtered at Annie, who looked completely unconcerned.

"That's her husband, Cade," Tinsley told him.

"Weren't you were going to a spa or something?" a very scary-looking man asked Bridget in an aggrieved voice.

"That's Ahmed," Tinsley filled in. "And there're Cy, Miles, and Marshall."

"Oh, we did. It was great. Had a mud bath and a facial. Then we found a hundred million dollars worth of stolen art and captured these two men," Annie said with a smirk.

"How's your fishing trip going? Catch anything?" Bridget asked sweetly and Paxton lost it. He was glad he was on mute because he was laughing so hard Tinsley had to take the phone from him.

"Yup, that's my family," she said, laughing.

"I can't wait to join this family," Paxton admitted and liked seeing the radiant smile Tinsley gave him in return.

"Really?"

"Sweetheart, I love you even more because of your family. Maybe I didn't make it clear enough when I told you that I love you, but I'm in this forever. Not just right now."

The Keeneston contingent was forgotten as Tinsley dropped the phone and vaulted into his arms. She knocked him back onto the bed and kissed him deep enough to rock his world. They probably would have continued if Cy weren't suddenly yelling Paxton's name over the phone.

When Paxton picked up the phone from the floor, he saw that Maurice and Murray were gone and everyone was down in the basement with the stolen art.

"Kendry, you knew they were here and didn't tell us?" Cy demanded.

"You are not welcome on any guy trips," Miles pouted.

"Don't worry, Paxton. You can come to the spa with us," Annie said with a smirk.

"Sorry, guys. A gentleman is only as good as his word and they made us promise not to say anything. And I'd be happy to go to a spa with you ladies anytime."

Robyn suddenly appeared and then disappeared from the screen as she jumped up and down like she was on a pogo stick. "Aw, there's my good girl. I'll give you some more apple pie next time I see you," Paxton said, fully aware he was baby-talking over the phone to a dog who was now happily yipping and wagging her tail in response.

"I'm surrounded by traitors," Ahmed grumbled as he glared at Robyn. However, Robyn knew just what to do. She went to Ahmed, sat down, cocked her head, and placed her paw on his leg.

"There's my baby girl," Ahmed said in matching baby-talk. He patted his chest and Robyn leaped into his arms. "I should have brought Nemi. Mother and daughter were working together. I'll have Mo fly her here in his plane so we can catch that bad Curtis together. Would you like that?" he asked Robyn who licked his face in return.

Suddenly all heads turned toward the camera. "Is there an engagement?" Cy asked.

"No, Uncle Cy," Tinsley said patiently.

"Yet," Paxton added with a wink to him.

A wall of Davies brothers filled the screen. "We'll come to Shadows Landing soon and we'll decide if you can marry our niece."

Tinsley groaned. "You're worse than Ridge."

"We're older and have more experience at chasing off undeserving men," Miles said, crossing his arms over his chest.

"Couples' trip?" Cade asked the group as he slung his arm around his wife.

"Great idea," Marshall said with a grin. "Let's see how he does with our wives. They're even more protective of Tinsley."

Annie rolled her eyes. "Tinsley is perfectly capable of taking care of herself."

"No, she's not," Cy said.

"She's too sweet," Cade added.

"Way too nice," Miles said.

"I'm surprised she isn't constantly being taken advantage of," Marshall said to his brothers.

Then they all turned to glare at Paxton.

"I'm not taking advantage of her," Paxton swore.

"If you saw him naked, you'd know who was taking advantage of whom," Bridget said and then gave Annie a high five. Tinsley groaned and covered her face in embarrassment. However, Cade and Ahmed looked at Paxton with such a glare that Paxton was afraid they'd reach through the camera and kill him.

"Anyway," Connor said, getting everyone's attention back to the case. "Tinsley, I'm going to have the art transferred to you and Paxton after we log it into evidence. I want you to identify it and Paxton can trace it along with the other art. "

"It looks like we're headed to Shadows Landing. We can take it with us," Cy said.

"You tried to take my wife, you tried to take my dog, and you tried to take my friends' niece," Ahmed said into the camera. "And now I know your name. It's never good when I know your name."

Bridget rolled her eyes. "He didn't try to take me. He was doing a naked photoshoot with those sweet old ladies who make apple pie."

The men snickered.

"Hey, I'm getting a pie every month for a year for that photo," Paxton defended, and suddenly the snickering stopped.

"Are you talking about Miss Ruby and Miss Winnie's apple pies? *Twelve* of them?" Miles asked.

"That's right," Paxton told them.

"Heck, I'd get naked for that," Cade said.

"Absolutely," his brothers agreed.

"Okay, so maybe I won't kill you . . . yet," Ahmed said slowly before he ended the video call.

"Well, today has already been interesting," Paxton said, setting down his phone.

"And we haven't had the church barbeque run yet." Tinsley pushed him back onto the bed. "It's almost over, isn't it?" she asked as she climbed on top of him.

Paxton rested his hands on her hips and looked up at her. "They've taken down the Myriad and recovered the artwork. All that is missing is Curtis Engle. As soon as the bust is done on whoever shows up tomorrow to get their paintings, you're done. You're out so I can breathe again."

"Hmm," Tinsley said, shifting her hips against his. "I think we should celebrate. I wonder—"

"Wonder what?" Paxton asked.

"If I can make you scream," Tinsley said before bending down and capturing his lips with hers.

25

Tinsley sat at the end of the pew as the donations were counted in the Lowcountry Smokehouse and Pink Pig donations jars. Reverend Winston gave a stirring talk on loving your neighbor, but even he knew by this point in the service it was all about the barbeque.

The choir sang and Reverend Winston grabbed a candlestick from the altar. He approached Tinsley with a smile on his face as the congregation grew restless. "I heard you have a big day tomorrow. Take this for your office desk, just in case."

Tinsley smiled and took the candlestick that had been part of the church since its founding. "Thank you, Reverend Winston."

"Why did he give you a candlestick?" Paxton asked as Reverend Winston went back up to the altar.

"Because it has a dagger hidden in it."

Paxton snorted. "What do you know about using a dagger?"

"Just hope you never find out," Tinsley replied calmly.

The volunteers compared counts as Reverend Winston blessed the congregation. The card was handed over to him and everyone stood, ready to make the mad dash to lunch.

"Peace be with y'all and today's Sunday Special is at the Pink—" Reverend Winston probably finished his sentence, but Tinsley was already off at a dead run.

Tinsley leaped over Miss Winnie and bolted around Terry Clemmons only to have his son, Quad, catch up to her.

"It's cute when my babysitter thinks she can outrun me," he shot over his shoulder as he sprinted past her.

Tinsley pumped her arms and stretched out her legs. She might be short, but she was quick. The church was a blur as she ran past the property and approached her gallery. All that stood between her and victory was Quad, her art gallery, and the historical society.

Behind her, she heard the rumble of Mr. Gann and Mr. Knoll's electric scooters. Both elderly men had been competitors on the dirt track racing circuit and had modified their electric scooters with large motors to compete in the weekly dash to lunch. If they weren't ramming into each other, cursing at each other, and adding more and more modifications to their scooters, they weren't really living.

Tinsley smiled at herself when Quad looked over his shoulder at the old men racing down Main Street and stumbled. She could overtake Quad at the historical society.

Tinsley pushed herself hard only to be yanked to the side so hard it felt as if her arm was dislocated. She gave a yelp of surprise that had Quad looking back again.

"You're a hard woman to get in touch with. You're in deep trouble and I'm your only way out of it."

Tinsley looked up at the man holding her tightly. He

wrenched her arm behind her and slapped on handcuffs faster than she could scream. But scream she did.

"Hey, man. Take your damn hands off my babysitter." Quad towered over them, looking ready to knock the man in the suit out.

He reached into his pocket and pulled out a badge. "FBI. Get lost, kid. Or do you want to be arrested, too?"

"Screw you. You can't take my babysitter. Tinsley has never done anything wrong a day in her life."

Tinsley fought against the handcuffs, but the man just wrenched her arm to the point she was afraid it was going to snap.

"She's stolen a hundred million dollars worth of art. She's under arrest and you will be too if you don't back off." The man claiming to be FBI pulled a gun and Quad backed off.

"What? Who are you? Let go of me!" Tinsley renewed her fight as the man dragged her toward a car.

"It's okay, Tinsley," Quad said gently as the man shoved her into a running car that certainly looked like an FBI vehicle. "Sheriff!" Quad yelled. "He's taking Tinsley!"

"Let go of her!" Mr. Gann yelled as he grabbed his cane like he was going to joust the agent.

"Trevino!" Tinsley heard Paxton yell, but it was too late. Mark Trevino sped away from the curb with Tinsley locked in the back of his FBI vehicle. Tinsley glanced behind her to see Mr. Gann and Mr. Knoll gaining on them in their motorized scooters. No longer were they competing against each other, but they were working together to try to save her. Tears sprang to her eyes as Paxton's worried face faded until all she could see was the distant image of the two old men racing after her.

"You're not arresting me, are you?" Tinsley asked, gathering her wits.

"Sure I am. You are in possession of stolen property and you'll be arrested unless you hand it over."

Tinsley took in the FBI agent most likely responsible for shooting Paxton and working with Curtis Engle. He was around five foot nine, lean, and had coloring that spoke of Mediterranean heritage. His dark brown hair was slicked back and he wore a ring on his pinky.

"The paintings are in my gallery," Tinsley lied, trying to get him to turn around.

"No, they aren't. I searched your gallery, broke into your vault, and also searched your home. You're a very talented artist, Miss Faulkner. I bet the prices of your art will skyrocket once you're dead," Mark said as if he hadn't just threatened her life.

Tinsley was quiet for a moment as she watched them head toward Charleston. She knew the whole town would be in hot pursuit by now. Paxton would be leading the charge. Granger, Kord, Ridge, and Ryker would be right behind him. She almost felt sorry for Mark if Harper got to him first.

All of this meant she needed to buy time. The best way to buy time was to be quiet except for the little sniffles and tears she deployed, observe everything, and then make her move. All her life, people had underestimated her at every turn. This man would be no different. He hadn't even checked her for weapons. Tina was on her thigh under her dress. It was a fitted tank top that went down into a flowing maxi skirt. The dagger was hidden in the candlestick in her purse, now strapped to her by the handcuffs. All she needed to do was sit quietly, look fearful, and then talk them into taking off the handcuffs. She didn't need her family, friends, or even Paxton to rescue her. Tinsley was perfectly capable of rescuing herself and she was sick and tired of being scared. Tired of being overlooked. Tired of being taken advantage of because she was the nice one. No, she was going to take Mark Trevino down and Curtis Engle with him because she'd bet anything that was where Mark was taking her.

Paxton's mind was in chaos. He wanted to race after her on foot and did until Granger's police SUV skidded to a stop next to him. "Get in," Granger yelled. "Who was that?" Granger asked as he sped off in the direction Mark had driven.

"FBI Agent Mark Trevino," Paxton said, his mind going in a million directions at once as he worked to get himself under control.

"Dammit," Granger cursed.

"Exactly. He's taking her to Curtis. I know it. I failed her." Paxton wasn't the only one who had failed her. Quad was so upset he was in tears. Ryker was so livid he couldn't even talk. He simply shot off a text and took off on his own. Harper broke a potted plant in anger. Ridge smashed the other potted plant and now Paxton looked in the side mirror to find multiple cars following them.

"What's that?" Granger muttered as he leaned forward in his seat.

Paxton looked out the window and saw two dots on the horizon. "It's the old guys in the scooters," he said with wonder. They'd made it miles but were now sitting by the side of the road up ahead.

Granger picked up the police radio and called in for

someone to pick up both the men and their scooters as he slowed down and stopped next to them. Like a train, so did the line of cars behind them.

Paxton rolled down the window. "Thanks for trying to save her. Granger has someone coming to pick y'all up."

"We'd do anything for Tinsley," Mr. Gann told them.

"We were able to follow long enough to see which direction they were going once they got out of town. They took her onto Interstate 26 toward Charleston," Mr. Knoll told them.

"Where would they take her?" Granger asked Paxton.

"It has to be the Myriad headquarters in Charleston. I have an idea. Thank you," Paxton called out to the men as Granger took off the way Mark had gone. Paxton called into the office and waited for the secretary to answer. "It's Kendry. Put me through to Agent Whitlock immediately."

"Can you trust this Whitlock guy?" Granger asked.

"We'll find out," Paxton said as he tried to remember to breathe. He put the phone on speaker and waiting to be connected.

"This is Whitlock."

"It's Kendry. Mark Trevino of the FBI Atlanta gang unit just kidnapped my girlfriend from Shadows Landing. He's dirty and working with Curtis Engle."

"Shit," Whitlock cursed. "What the hell is going on? Does this have something to do with your case and why your apartment was tagged?"

"I'll fill you in, but I need to know where they'd take her in Charleston. They got on I-26 heading that way," Paxton told him.

"Myriad headquarters is in North Charleston," Whitlock answered immediately before giving the address.

"On it," Granger said as he radioed in the address so Kord, and probably everyone else behind them, would know where they were going within seconds.

"Give the summary," Whitlock ordered. It was a leap of faith as Paxton told Whitlock everything. Peter trusted him and that would have to be enough.

"I wish you'd have told me this sooner," Whitlock told him as Paxton heard the unmistakable sound of him running through the office yelling at his team.

"There was already one FBI agent under Curtis's pay. I didn't know who I could trust. I'm sorry, Whitlock."

"I didn't say that I don't understand why you didn't tell me. My team will meet you at the old chemical warehouse. It's abandoned, in the industrial district, and about three miles from the Myriad headquarters . Do you know the one?"

"This is Sheriff Granger Fox," Granger answered for Paxton. "I know the plant, but I know a better, more secure place to meet. Tinsley Faulkner's cousin is Ryker Faulkner. Let's meet at his shipping company. We'll be there in ten minutes."

"Ryker Faulkner? Damn, this just got worse," Whitlock cursed again before hanging up.

Paxton sent off a flurry of texts. First to the entire Faulkner family, then to Peter, and finally to Cy Davies.

We're already on our way.

It was hard. Paxton wanted to run straight to the headquarters in the house that they knew was a Myriad hangout and find Tinsley. Even in his anger, in his grief, and in his guilt he knew that was the wrong move. Curtis would shoot her before they even breached the property. He had to be smart about this, which is why he'd texted Cy.

"Breathe, Paxton. We'll get her back," Granger told him, but Paxton wouldn't breathe easily again until he made sure that Tinsley was safe or he'd died trying.

26

Tinsley watched the North Charleston landscape as they drove down the main road that traversed North Charleston. North Charleston's crime rate was the highest for the area. It was a mix of hard-working people and people like Curtis Engle who came in with their drugs and guns, flashing money around. In turn, it kept some of the neighborhoods literally in the line of fire.

Tinsley knew they planned to kill her. Mark hadn't hidden his identity. He hadn't blindfolded her either. She was going to die the second she was no longer of value to them. She had to find a way to appear to cooperate in order to get free and then take her chances with escaping.

Thanks to her family, Curtis's Atlanta empire was crumbling. He'd lost his drugs, his guns, and half of his stolen paintings. She was his only chance of surviving. If he lost all of the paintings, it wouldn't only be the FBI and police after him. It would also be the Argentinian mafia who had hired him to fence the art. Tinsley knew Mark was also hanging by a thread, but something told her Curtis might be her shot at escaping. She just had to walk the balance of being cooperative yet still indispensable.

Mark turned left before they reached I-526. They crossed over Bloom Drive and headed for the marsh that lined the Ashley River. She didn't ask Mark where they were going as the landscape turned from residential to industrial. Mark finally slowed as he turned onto a gravel drive leading to a metal box of a building up on stilts that jutted out over the marsh.

Mark honked and the metal sheeting serving as a garage door was pushed open. Mark drove under the building and the sheeting was lowered back down. Two armed men approached as Mark got out of the car.

"Grab her," Mark ordered one of the men.

Tinsley shrunk back into the seat and tried to scamper to the other side of the car, but it was no use. The door was opened and she was roughly grabbed and dragged out. Her arms hurt where he'd yanked her out of the backseat and also from where her purse dangled from the handcuffs, causing them to dig into her skin. No matter how scared she was, she had to focus.

Tinsley needed to stay calm so that she could read the room and take in every chance for escape. It was easy to get the tears to roll down her cheeks. She didn't need to fake the fear she was feeling. She just had to control it so it wouldn't overtake her.

"Please," she begged the man pulling her up the stairs behind Mark. "I haven't done anything wrong. What do you want with me?"

The man ignored her as he roughly hauled her up the stairs. He shoved her through the door and into a giant open area. It looked as if the place had been a biker bar at one point. It was decorated with motorcycle accessories and there was a square bar in the center of the room with at least forty mismatched stools around it. Most of them were occupied by men, including a guy who was behind the bar handing out mugs of beer. Old square tables filled the room. Some had been knocked over and some were filled with more men. Dartboards with unfinished games hung along a wall, unlit neon signs covered some of the windows.

A big-screen television played in the far corner. Chairs had been lined up as men watched a baseball game. She counted at least fifty men in the building. As Tinsley looked around, one of the men stood up. At about six foot three, he was much taller than Mark. There was a giant tattoo of a snake that started with its opened mouth on his neck and coiled down the length of his arm.

"This must be my art dealer," he said as her captor let go of her arm and headed back downstairs to his post. Mark shoved her into a chair off the side of the table and went to stand by the man who appeared to be Curtis Engle.

Tinsley let the fear show on her face. Tears tracked down her cheeks as she looked up at him with wide eyes. "I don't understand what I've done wrong. Who are you and what do you want with me?"

Curtis grabbed a chair, dragged it close to her, straddled it, and crossed his arms on the chair's back. He looked at her as if he could read her inner thoughts. "We have a mutual friend, Miss Faulkner. What's his real name?" Curtis looked to Mark.

"Paxton Kendry," Mark answered. "FBI Agent Paxton Kendry."

Tinsley wrinkled her brow. "I don't know any FBI agents by that name. I know one named Peter. He dates one of my friends, but the only Paxton I know is my art handler. He helps me transport art, hang it, and fixes stuff in my gallery. But his last name is Johnson."

Tinsley had to think fast. They knew about Paxton and she was afraid she was going to have to give him up. However, she needed to keep her cover. If they knew she'd been helping him, she was dead.

"When did this Paxton Johnson start working for you?" Curtis asked. Now was the time to sell her story. She sniffed and looked as if she were thinking. She was, but not about Curtis's question. She needed a solid story to sell. "Not long. About a month." She dropped her voice and leaned forward so her face wasn't far from Curtis's face. "I'm sorry, I don't know the proper terms for any of this, but am I right in thinking you're a criminal?"

Curtis smiled with amusement and Tinsley knew she had him. "You could say that."

"Did this FBI agent, Paxton whatever, try to arrest you and now you think it's the same Paxton who works for me?" Tinsley asked, keeping her voice low so Mark would struggle to hear.

"That's exactly what I think," Curtis told her.

"So you sent one of your guys after me, pretending to be an FBI agent, to . . . well, sir, now I'm lost." Tinsley sighed and looked flustered. "I thought it was to see if it was the same Paxton, but you could have just taken him. What do I have to do with any of this? I've never broken the law. I do charity work. I babysit in my free time." Tinsley let her lips tremble and drew in a shaky breath.

Curtis was clearly amused by her rambling. Good. It was just what she wanted. "You were recently tasked with selling some very valuable art."

Tinsley nodded. "Yes, I'm selling a private collection."

She wrinkled her brow and really played it up. "You kidnapped me because you want to buy some art?"

Curtis chuckled. "Maurice was right about you."

Tinsley looked excited. "You know Maurice? So you *do* want to buy the art. I have a whole day of buyers coming in tomorrow. I can add you to the list."

"Where is that art collection, Miss Faulkner?" Curtis asked. Behind the amusement was danger.

"I told this guy. It's in my vault at my gallery."

Mark shook his head and then struck out. Tinsley hadn't seen the hit coming. Mark's fisted hand smashed her cheekbone. Pain exploded and tears streamed from her eyes. She gasped, trying to catch her breath from the pain. No acting was required for this reaction. It had surprised her and hurt like hell.

"I told you it's not there."

Tinsley let the tears come. She cried hard now, nearly sobbing. "It *has* to be there. It was there last night when I got home from researching some of the paintings."

The men watching baseball were now casting glances at her. Curtis hadn't reacted to the hit, but Mark looked as if he wanted to hit her again.

"Can," *sniff*, "I," *sniff*, "have a tissue?" *sniff*.

Curtis ignored her question but motioned for Mark to step back. "Do you know this man?" Curtis held up his phone. It was Paxton's FBI employee picture. She couldn't deny it. Mark had seen him in Shadows Landing.

Tinsley nodded. "That's Paxton Johnson, my employee."

"That is FBI Agent Paxton Kendry," Curtis told her.

She shook her head. He was watching her closely. "No, that's . . . oh no." Curtis raised his eyebrow, waiting for her to finish her thought. "He has the combination to the vault."

She swallowed hard as Mark cursed. Tinsley flinched and whimpered.

Tinsley didn't need to fake the flinch. Mark looked ready to kill her. Tinsley started to plead with him, but the hit came anyway.

"Enough." Curtis said to Mark, standing up from his chair. "We need to talk."

Tinsley struggled to slow the tears. She waited until they were a few steps away before she spoke again. "Paxton mentioned a place to me. Maybe he moved the paintings there? I was working when he told me about it so I have to admit I wasn't paying close attention. I'll try to remember it," she lied.

Curtis looked her over and gave a little nod. "Thank you, Miss Faulkner. Remembering would be a big help to not only me, but to you as well."

Tinsley let out a shaky breath as the men moved away and left her alone. Now all she had to do was buy more time. She had a couple of ideas that played into her delicate sensibilities to use to get free. Because, she reasoned, if there was ever a time to fake a case of the vapors, this was it.

27

Faulkner Shipping was a sprawling commercial port in its own right. It took up at least two miles of coastline. Massive cargo ships lined the piers as cranes worked to pull the containers from the holds and move them into the shipping yard.

Men and women swarmed the area, working on the unloading, loading, and the mountains of paperwork that went into each shipment. There was a central, stadium-sized parking lot where Granger and the caravan from Shadows Landing parked to wait for everyone else to arrive.

Ryker had told them they could go inside and use one of the conference rooms, but no one wanted to take even one step farther away from the Myriad headquarters than they had to.

Whitlock and his team had arrived five minutes after Granger had pulled into the parking lot. A large map that highlighted known Myriad houses and businesses had been produced and spread out across the hood of a car. Now they were looking at the map and waiting for the Davies family to arrive.

"Which one is the headquarters?" Paxton asked.

"We're not entirely sure," Whitlock answered and Paxton frowned. What he really wanted to do was to hit something but instead he saved his anger for Curtis.

"Then what are we doing here, Whitlock?" Paxton snapped.

"Waiting and preparing. I have informants coming in. This is the area where they'll have Tinsley. We need to get our supplies ready because I can guarantee they'll be heavily armed."

"Peter's on his way with weapons," Paxton answered. More waiting.

"I have some you can use," Ryker said as he shoved his suit coat off and rolled up the sleeves to his fitted button-down dress shirt. "The shipping business is a very dirty business to be in. Lots of ports are run by organized crime or have deals in place for free rein of them. Containers are stolen. Drugs, stolen goods, and people are imported and exported. Intimidation, theft, and embezzlement happen everyday. The mafia hasn't gone away. They're still here. They're just not the new kids on the block anymore. These street gangs are. Where do you think Myriad gets their drugs to sell?"

"South American mafias," Paxton answered.

Ryker nodded. "Who work deals with the mafia groups who have control over the ports in New York and New Jersey. But with more shipping companies using East Coast ports, there are now three more large ports on the coast—Virginia, Savannah, and right here in Charleston. So yeah, I have weapons. I protect what's mine."

A kid on a bike, a twenty-year-old chipped gray sedan, and a newer minivan all pulled into the lot. Right behind them was Peter in an SUV and then two other SUVs Paxton didn't recognize.

"Here are my informants," Whitlock said.

"Here's our boss," Paxton said.

"And our family," Ryker told them, answering the unspoken question of who was in the last two SUVs. "They caught a private flight here from Atlanta."

Cy was the first out and was already shaking hands with Peter. Paxton wanted to demand they hurry up. He wanted to demand they get to work to save Tinsley, but he knew they had to have a plan first. They weren't moving slowly. They were already walking toward him as they all eyed each other, not knowing who the others were.

The Faulkners embraced their uncles and their friends from Keeneston. Before Paxton could tell them to hurry up, Robyn was pawing at his leg. He looked down and swore he saw sympathy in her whiskey-colored eyes.

"That's my dog," a low, gravelly voice said.

"Ahmed, I'm Paxton. Thank you for coming." Paxton looked at the scary man with his own vizsla in a baby sling across his chest. "Who's that?"

"This is my baby, Nemi. She's Robyn's daughter. Robyn is trained in tracking, but I have trained my Nemi for much more than that."

Joining them, Bridget said, "Robyn isn't our dog. She's our friend's dog. So if we're going into a shootout, I have to keep Robyn in the car. It's not what she's signed up to do."

"She's done her tour of duty, haven't you, my sweet girl?" Ahmed baby-talked to Robyn who wagged her tail. Even though she responded to Ahmed, she kept her paw on Paxton's leg and her eyes on his. It was as if she were reading Paxton's thoughts and even his soul.

Cy approached him and Paxton hoped he waited to kill

him until he'd saved Tinsley. "You brought danger to Tinsley."

"I know. I'll accept the consequences of it, but first we have to save her."

"Or die trying?" Cy asked.

"Without hesitation." Cy stared at him for a moment and then nodded. "Let's get to work," Paxton said to the group. "I'm Agent Paxton Kendry. This is Agent in Charge Peter Castle and this is Agent Whitlock of the drug unit. Then we have Granger Fox and Kord King of the Shadows Landing Sheriff's Department. Lastly, we have the Davies family who are related to the Faulkners."

"Y'all are some scary-ass mother—" The teenage boy who'd ridden a bike there got cut off when the woman who had driven the minivan smacked the back of his head.

"I'm Kendis. My son was killed by a drive-by in our neighborhood a while back. We're good people here. We work hard and try to make a better life for our kids, but then the Myriad moved in," she told them.

A fortyish man with perfectly trimmed hair and some faded prison tats spoke next. "I'm LaVaughn. After my arrest for drugs twenty years ago, I turned my life around. I own a barbershop in town and try to help mentor the men who sit in my chair."

"I'm Roshaun," the boy told them. "My brother's part of the Myriad."

Paxton looked at the boy who couldn't be more than fourteen. "You're very brave to help us. You know there's a chance your brother will be arrested today, right?"

Roshaun nodded and LaVaughn clasped his shoulder in support. "He was my hero. Then he started dealing. He sold to my best friend and he died of an overdose. I begged my brother to stop. My mom begged him to stop. He won't. He likes the money and power. Well, I'm taking back that power. If I can get them off the street, I can save lives. I wasn't able to save my best friend, but I'll be damned if I let my brother kill anyone else with these drugs. I have a little sister to look out for. We'll work our way out of the neighborhood so I don't have to worry about sleeping next to her on the floor in case of a drive-by like the one that killed Miss Kendis's son."

Kendis took a deep breath and nodded. "My son wasn't part of the gang. He was at home, watching television. But the Myriads were fighting for a corner and shot up the whole area. So you tell us what you need and we'll help you in any way we can."

"Thank you all. Curtis Engle, the head of the Myriad from Atlanta, has the woman I love. These are her family and friends and we'll do anything to get her back safely. Now, here's what we know." Paxton filled them in on Tinsley, the Myriad, and Agent Mark Trevino. Then he turned to the map of the area. "We know they came this way, but we don't know anything else."

"They're not at Robinson's place," Roshaun told them as he pointed to a house marked on the map. "I live down the street. He's the second-in-command here."

Kendis nodded. "Brown is the leader here and I passed his house on the way here. There were no cars there."

LaVaughn's lips pursed as he looked at the map. "They weren't at any of their normal hangouts when I drove here. There's here," he said, pointing to some of the commercial areas.

"What about the Tin Can?" Roshaun asked and both Kendis and LaVaughn nodded.

"That's where they have to be," LaVaughn said as he pointed to an area right on the river. "It's an old abandoned biker bar.

The gang took it over and no one dares kick them out. It's the largest building to hang out in and it's far away from anyone. It has one long drive into the place so they can see who is coming.

"Do they watch the river?" Paxton asked as he pulled up satellite images of the property.

"Exactly what I was thinking," Miles said as he looked over Paxton's shoulder at the satellite images.

"If they do, it'll only be one person. They'd be able to hear boats," LaVaughn told them.

"There's a long dock that goes over the marsh and up some steps to the first floor of the bar," Wade said. "I've boated by there several times with the Coast Guard."

"Can we swim up?" Paxton asked and looked to Wade for answers.

"Yeah. There's probably some alligators in the marsh, but otherwise the grasses should help hide us, especially if we go during high tide." Wade looked at his watch and nodded to himself. "It's peak tide in two hours. We could go anytime and be able to swim most of it."

"I can cause a distraction," Cy said with grin as he looked to his brother Cade. "Want to blow some stuff up?"

"I always want to blow stuff up," Cade said with a smirk.

"Hey, I'm ATF. I live to blow stuff up," Dare said.

Cy turned to the three informants. "Which three locations would hurt them the most if they got blown up?"

"Won't that hurt their neighbors?" Kendis asked.

"Don't worry, ma'am," Dare said with a big smile. "We're really good at this."

"I believe you. I think you could just look at the building and it would explode from fear," Roshaun said to Cy who grinned in return.

"Here," LaVaughn pointed to a house.

Kendis still looked nervous, but she pointed to a warehouse-looking place. "Here. They store their drugs here."

"My brother always goes here," Roshaun said, pointing to a business front. "I think they sell drugs from there. Can I come with you?"

Cy shook his head but stepped closer to Roshaun so he could talk to him. "I don't want any of you associated with this. You've all been very brave and anytime you need us, we'll come." Cy handed Roshaun a business card that only had a phone number on it. "But I want you with LaVaughn, sitting in his chair in full view of everyone while this goes down."

"Don't worry," Marshall said to them. "We'll clean up the mess we make."

Roshaun tapped Cy on the arm. "Who's the scary motherfu"—he glanced at Kendis and corrected himself— "guy with the dog strapped to his chest like a baby?"

"I am Ahmed. This is Nemi. We take care of problems like the Myriad for fun."

Roshaun stepped closer to Cy, and Paxton couldn't help but smile. They were a strange bunch that had banded together but there wasn't anyone else he'd want having his back, even if it meant the Davies crew would kill him for putting Tinsley in danger.

"You all can go. Don't tell a soul what's going on," Whitlock told his informants.

"I'll make my cookies," Kendis told them. "That'll clear the street of any children. Just give me thirty minutes."

"You got it," Paxton said as they waited for the three to leave before turning back to the group. "Cy, Cade, and Dare will blow things up in forty minutes. Hopefully, that will empty some of the Tin Can. I need a group to round them up."

"I can help with that," Annie said. "Bridget should take the dogs into the building, but I can help round people up. I would think Whitlock, you, and your crew could help with that, too."

Whitlock nodded. "Yeah, we can do that."

"I'll come in via the water," Wade said.

"Cy, Marshall, and I will, too," Miles said, turning to Wade. "Have any equipment with you?"

"I got you covered," Wade told them.

Peter nodded. "We need an agent with every group. I guess I'm water."

"Faulkners, I want you nearby—especially Gavin. I can't have you in the line of fire," Paxton said to the rest of the family. Everyone nodded, even Harper, but not Ryker.

"I'm going with you," Ryker told him.

Paxton looked over Ryker and tightened his jaw. Ryker stood tall and strong with a look of pure determination on his face. Ahmed looked him over, too.

"We're the door-kicker team," Ahmed said, pointing to Paxton and Bridget.

"Us too," Granger said as he and Kord stepped forward.

Ryker didn't look discouraged. Instead, he shook his head. "I have a better idea. One they won't see coming." Ryker pointed to the top of the office building where a helicopter Paxton hadn't even heard was landing.

"Is that—?" Paxton began to ask, but Ryker was already nodding.

"A stealth helicopter," Ahmed said with a big grin. "How did you get one? I've been trying to get one for years."

"We all have our secrets, don't we?" Ryker shrugged and

Paxton knew there was no way Ryker would tell Ahmed where it came from. "But I'll put in a good word for you."

"Honey, if I get one, can we put a big bow on it like they do for new cars?" Ahmed asked Bridget who just rolled her eyes. "I can't wait to see how she works. We can drop onto the rooftop patio at Curtis's and he'll never hear us coming."

Bridget looked down at Susi and smiled. "Want to go for a ride?" The dog barked happily.

"Ryker, that's perfect. With the distraction going off, they'll be on edge. They'll look out but won't see us coming. We'll come from the water and the air," Paxton said as he looked at a picture of the rooftop patio that had clearly been set up for outdoor bar seating.

"Let Kord and me take the front door. You have all the other doors covered," Granger said, and Paxton nodded his agreement.

"And we'll clean up anyone who tries to escape," Whitlock said as his team nodded behind him.

"Let's get into position. Cy, do you need any explosives?" Paxton asked.

"Nope, I always travel with them. You never know when you might need some C-4." Cy turned and gathered his team as they headed to the SUV.

Doors were opened, equipment handed out, and then they were moving into position. Paxton took a deep breath as he pulled on the gloves for fast roping. He closed his eyes and sent up a silent prayer of protection for Tinsley. *I'm coming, sweetheart.*

28

"Please don't hit me!" Tinsley screeched as Mark and Curtis walked toward her again. They'd left her alone for a good while as they talked. "Oh God," Tinsley said, embarrassed as tears started flowing again. She looked up at Curtis with embarrassment all over her face. "I'm sorry."

"For what?" Curtis asked.

"I was so scared of him I had, um, a little accident. Can you take me to the bathroom, please?" Tinsley let her head drop in complete defeat.

"Take off her cuffs," Curtis ordered Mark.

"What? No. Let her sit in her piss for all I care," Mark spat. "Until she tells us where those paintings are, she's not going anywhere."

"Remember who is in charge here," Curtis said, dropping his voice for only Mark to hear. "Do it."

Mark angrily yanked her arms and Tinsley cried out in pain, but he took off the cuffs. Her purse fell to the floor and Mark grabbed it. "Maybe she has something in here."

He dumped the contents on the table next to her as she rubbed her wrists. Curtis called to one of his guys and turned back to look at the items from her purse. "Why do you have a candlestick?"

Curtis reached for it and Tinsley held her breath. It wasn't easy to see, but the bottom came off and a dagger would slide out. "I bought it at the street fair and took it home. I didn't like it on my kitchen table so I put it in my purse and was going to take it to the office after lunch," Tinsley said.

"Is this real gold?" Curtis asked, and Tinsley snorted.

"Sorry, it's just that I bought it for ten dollars so I'm guessing it's not gold." Tinsley held her breath and almost fainted from relief when Curtis set it back down on the table. Why? Because it was made from real gold with a dagger in its center.

A man joined them who made Mark look like a sweetheart. He glared at her with pure hatred and Tinsley wondered if he knew why he hated her or if he just hated everyone. "Take her to the bathroom," Curtis ordered.

Tinsley let herself be grabbed and yanked in the direction of the bathroom. She didn't fight. She only prayed he didn't go in with her and discover Tina strapped to her thigh. The man pushed the door open and shoved Tinsley inside.

"Hurry up," he told her.

The bathroom had two stalls and two sinks. Two cracked mirrors outlined with stickers hung on the wall above each sink, and one window with light streaming through the frosted glass was opposite the door.

The man watched as she went into the far stall and then the door closed. Tinsley finally took a breath. She had a moment alone. She hurried from the stall and went straight for the window. Tinsley surveyed the window made of frosted glass and wire. It was supposed to be shatterproof.

She looked to see if she could open it, but the best she could do was vent a small portion of it. She unlocked it and pulled the small portion of glass inward, then ducked her head under it the best she could. She had to twist her neck to the side to do so. She felt the disappointment like a tidal wave. She wasn't going to be able to escape through the window.

Tinsley was about to pull her head back in when a small movement in the water made the marsh grass sway. It was probably an alligator but her eyes kept starting at the spot.

"Hurry up, woman!" the guard yelled.

"I'm almost done," Tinsley yelled back as she kept her eye on the movement. A head popped up just above the mucky water and looked right at her. "Wade," she whispered in a surprised gasp. She wedged up her hand and waved. Wade froze, his eyes catching the movement.

Tinsley's neck muscles were shooting pain, but she had to warn him. She moved her hand up and wiggled all five fingers before closing her fingers to form a fist. She did it again just in case he didn't catch it. Then she knew her time was up. The man would burst in soon so she angled herself out from the window and closed it before flushing the toilet. She was in the middle of washing her hands when the man kicked the door open with his gun raised.

"I told you to hurry up."

Tinsley wiped her hands on her maxi-length skirt and felt the comfort of Tina holstered to her thigh. If Wade was out there, Paxton was, too. She just needed to buy some more time and distract the men as much as possible. She'd help Paxton, Wade, and whoever else they brought with them every step of the way—from distracting her captors to providing cover shots.

The man shoved her back into her chair but didn't put the cuffs back on. Instead, Curtis and Mark approached and

Curtis handed her a bottle of water. "Now, tell us everything Paxton has told you."

Bless his heart, you *never* ask a Southerner open-ended questions like that. Tinsley took a deep breath and started spinning her tale. Curtis and Mark had better settle in because she was about to talk them right out of their boots.

Paxton pushed open the door to the rooftop and looked at the helicopter known for its muted blades. Most helicopters were noisy, and while this one still produced noise, it sounded as if a giant pillow were being pressed over the loud blades. It was done with the help of a mostly encased tail blade.

"Mr. Faulkner!" Ryker's secretary yelled at Ryker, Paxton, Bridget, and Ahmed. "You have a phone call! They said it was urgent!"

Ryker looked out of place in his fitted slacks and button-down shirt along with Paxton, Ahmed, and Bridget who wore the more traditional tactical gear. At least Ryker had put on steel-toe boots.

Ryker grabbed the phone as Ahmed and Bridget stepped into specialized harnesses. Ahmed even slipped on a little pair of goggles onto his Vizsla, Nemi. Both Nemi and Susi were all business as Ahmed and Bridget checked the vests the dogs were wearing.

"Let's go," Ryker told them, handing the phone back to his secretary.

Ryker climbed into the helicopter first. Then Bridget. Ahmed lifted Susi and Nemi into the helicopter before jumping in himself. Paxton was the last one in since he was going to be the first one out.

Paxton slid the headphones on so he could communicate with the other teams. "We're airborne," he said into his coms.

"Road crew is in position," Annie replied and Paxton had to smile. He was sure Whitlock was wondering how someone from Kentucky was in charge.

"Ready to ring the doorbell," Granger said.

"The fireworks are ready when you are." Paxton heard Cy's voice say.

They waited a moment and then Wade's voice came on the coms. "The water team in is place. Also, I just saw Tinsley in a window. She couldn't get out. All she could do was angle her head to look out. We made eye contact and she stuck her hand out to signal. Five O. Fifty. I'm guessing that's how many people are inside."

"I told y'all you could never have too much C-4," Cy said over the coms. "Does anyone want to borrow some?"

"Don't worry, we have backup right behind us," Ryker said simply.

"I'm in position," an unfamiliar female voice came over the coms.

"Who are you?" Paxton asked.

"Your backup. Let's move it, my girl is in there," the mystery woman said back to him.

"Okay then. We're a go in two minutes," Paxton said. As the coms went quiet, the helicopter's altitude climbed. They went high into the air and only then did they fly the short distance from one side of North Charleston to the other.

"We're a go," Cy said as Paxton looked down at the bar where Tinsley was confirmed to be inside.

A second later, three explosions sounded simultaneously. Paxton used the binoculars to see people pouring into the streets. "What is he doing?" Paxton asked as Cy sped toward the bar. "We don't have time to find out. Get down there now," Paxton said to the pilot who rapidly descended.

Two ropes were tossed out the side of the helicopter. Paxton looked at Ahmed next to him. Nemi's short tail wagged as she waited to go. She was attached to Ahmed's harness and leaned against his leg. Paxton nodded and together they fast-roped down and onto the rooftop. The second they were clear, Bridget and Ryker began down the ropes. Bridget was down just as fast as Paxton, but Ryker was clearly the new guy. Paxton didn't wait, though, and noticed that Ahmed didn't either.

Paxton got his rifle into position as Ahmed unstrapped Nemi and got into position. Together they headed for the stairs as the helicopter was already taking off.

"Curtis, you coward! I came for you in Atlanta and I'll come for you here!" Paxton simultaneously heard Cy scream over the coms and also from the end of the drive.

"Get that asshole!" Paxton heard Curtis yell below them.

Paxton heard boots on the ground as some of the men emptied out of the front of the bar.

"Water is in position," Wade whispered into the coms.

"Road crew is engaging," Annie said.

"Doorbell is in position," the woman's voice said instead of Granger's.

Paxton looked over his shoulder to see the air group stacked up on the steps by the side door. He was in the lead. Ahmed and Nemi were right behind him, then Bridget and Susi, and finally Ryker bringing up the rear. "Air is ready. On the count of three, we go in. One. Two. Three."

29

Tinsley started inching up her skirt as soon as the phones began to go off. Something was going on. She'd only gotten to Paxton's made-up college years in the saga she was weaving for Curtis when they all heard three loud explosions. Curtis bounded up and Mark ran to the window. Then the phones began to ring. And then Curtis began cussing and kicking things.

"Curtis, you coward! I came for you in Atlanta and I'll come for you here!"

Uncle Cy? Tinsley tried to hide her recognition of the voice, but it didn't matter. No one was paying her any attention right now.

"Get that fucker!" Curtis yelled as men armed themselves and ran out the front of the bar.

Tinsley didn't waste any time. She yanked up her skirt, grabbed Tina, and then used the long skirt to cover her hand with the gun in it. She waited, knowing Wade and Paxton were coming. Tinsley had twelve rounds and she was going to make each one count.

Curtis glanced over at her. "Mark, tie her up."

No way was she going to let that happen. Tinsley waited until Mark was standing in front of her, ready to grab her hands. He sneered at her and she sneered back. Then she shot her leg up and connected with his balls. Mark went down at the same time the side and back doors were kicked open. Mark pulled his gun and crawled behind an overturned table to her right and took aim at the intruders.

"Paxton!" Tinsley yelled in a warning and then chaos erupted. She felt as if she were the point of a triangle. Paxton was the bottom left corner and the back door was the bottom right corner. She was closer to the front door at the top point of the triangle but felt a mile away from her rescuers.

The remaining twenty-five or so people in the bar opened fire and the people pouring in from the side and back doors did, too.

Tinsley couldn't wait any more. She flipped the table to her left over, sending her candlestick and everything else scattering. She raised Tina, her hands shaking as adrenaline raced like wildfire through her body. She saw the men taking cover on her side of the bar and firing at Paxton, Ahmed, Bridget, and Ryker.

Tinsley held her breath and pulled the trigger. She moved her aim and pulled again, and again, and again. She didn't wait to see if she'd hit her target before moving on to the next.

"You bitch! You brought them here somehow!" Mark yelled over the gunfire.

Tinsley glanced from where Paxton was fighting alongside her cousin Ryker, Ahmed, and Bridget. She couldn't fathom how they got here from Atlanta so fast, but they couldn't get to her fast enough to save her. Mark had a clear shot at her. Tinsley swung her gun around and fired. *Click.* She was out of bullets.

Paxton heard Mark yell at Tinsley and everything else was forgotten. He knew what he needed to do. He ran. He ran through gunfire to get to the woman he loved. He couldn't see where Mark was behind an overturned table, but he fired as he ran, keeping the man pinned down.

He kept Tinsley in his peripheral vision but focused his gaze on the table where Mark was crouching. Paxton was only steps from Tinsley when Mark's head appeared with the muzzle of a gun. That was all Paxton needed. He fired and Mark went down.

"Tinsley!" Paxton was so relieved to see her alive he almost dropped to his knees to hug her. The bullet that slammed into him stopped any thoughts of hugging the woman he loved as it sent him tumbling to the ground.

Tinsley ducked behind the table as Paxton fired. She looked up and didn't see Mark anymore. "Tinsley!" Paxton called.

Tinsley opened her arms with relief. Paxton was here! Then everything changed. There was so much gunfire she didn't hear the bullet that hit Paxton, but she did see it slam into him. Paxton was flung back and landed hard on the ground out of her reach. When he hit the ground, his gun skittered off beyond the safety of the table she was hiding behind.

"Paxton!" she yelled, hysterics threatening to overtake her.

A horrible feeling of helplessness and being frozen in fear tried to push its way in, but she wouldn't allow it.

Tinsley looked around and saw everyone engaging in their own battles. The front door was kicked in, and a person Tinsley guessed was a woman due to the long hair under her helmet stormed inside with her gun raised and ready to fire. Behind her, Granger and Kord were in position as they provided relief fire for Wade and his team. The sight of the woman in charge spurred Tinsley into action.

She lunged out from the safety of the table and grabbed hold of Paxton's feet, using all her strength to drag him toward her. Tinsley heard him groan and then his eyes opened as he reached to his side, ripped the Velcro from his bulletproof vest off, and took a deep breath.

Relief that he was alive was short-lived. She had to get him to safety.

"Paxton, wake up!"

"Let sleeping agents lie in their graves," Curtis growled as he advanced on them.

"No! Tinsley screamed as Curtis fired.

She closed her eyes, thinking that was it, but the bullet didn't rip into her. Instead, it was Paxton who was yelling in pain. Tinsley opened her eyes and saw blood pouring from his leg.

"I see you two are together. You're a good actor, Tinsley but Paxton is not. Only a man in love would make an unprotected run for you. I've shot you three times in the chest and you just refuse to die." Curtis looked down at Paxton. "Well, four times, but you cheated with the vest. The one in the leg was to wake you up. I want you to know I've wasted enough bullets on you. The bullet after yours is for your woman."

Curtis pointed the gun at Paxton's head, and all thought fled from Tinsley's mind. Driven by instinct, she leaped onto Curtis's back with a wild cry. She clung to him as she clawed his face, bit his ear, and tore at anything she could. He spun her around trying to get her off him while he cursed, but Tinsley refused to let go. She was wild with rage as she moved to shove her thumbs into his eyeballs.

Curtis howled and fell backward as hard as he could. The initial impact of hitting the floor shocked Tinsley, but then having over two hundred pounds of pissed-off, homicidal male land on top of her shoved the air from her lungs.

"You bitch! I'll kill you first then. Let Paxton watch the woman he loves die, knowing he couldn't save her," Curtis growled as he rolled off her and landed a solid punch to her face.

Blackness crept into the edges of her vision, but Tinsley shoved them back while Curtis staggered to his feet. A red blur shot across the room and leaped through the air. The Vizsla latched onto Curtis's arm as Tinsley coughed, trying to drag air into her lungs. She reached out to push herself up and her hand hit someone familiar—the candlestick.

Her heart pounded as she grabbed the candlestick, yanked the base free, and felt the familiar weight of the dagger in her hands. Curtis lifted his gun and placed it on the dog's head and Tinsley threw.

Her aim was as steady and true as if she were practicing in the church. An overwhelming feeling of Anne Bonny guiding the dagger home came over her as it sank into Curtis's heart a second before the gunshot from Ahmed's gun went through his head and a shot from Paxton went through his back.

Blurs of fur were racing past Tinsley as she stood on wobbly legs. There was less gunfire now and more screaming orders to put their hands up. The sound of guns dropping to the floor and zip ties tightening were all around her, but Tinsley only had eyes for Paxton. His leg was bleeding badly. He'd crawled to where his gun had skidded when he was shot the first time and used it to shoot Curtis. A blood trail showed the ten feet he'd dragged himself. He was now sitting up with his legs stretched out straight in front of him.

Tinsley's eyes met his and Paxton blew her a kiss before he fell back to the ground. Tinsley rushed forward at the same time Ahmed did.

"We need Gavin!" Ahmed shouted into his coms as he pulled a tactical tourniquet from his utility vest.

Tinsley grabbed Paxton's hand in hers and began whispering encouraging words to him as Ahmed tightened the tourniquet to the point of Paxton screaming.

Tinsley looked over her shoulder at the sound of movement. Men in FBI jackets were swarming the group of captured Myriad members. "Uncle Cy? Uncle Miles? Uncle Marshall? Uncle Cade? Aunt Annie? What are you all doing here?" Tinsley asked as they all rushed to her side.

"You're our family. Where else would we be?" the person in the full helmet and tactical gear said as she pulled off her helmet.

"Greer! Do your parents know you're here?" Aunt Annie asked Tinsley's Kentucky cousin.

"Do my parents know *you're* here is a better question." Greer bent down next to Tinsley and put her arm around Tinsley's shoulder.

"Um, let's not mention it. I would hate to hurt your dad's feelings. He was all excited about going to some convention with your mom," Uncle Cade said, looking nervously at his brothers, who all nodded their agreement.

Greer looked over at where Ryker stood next to Wade.

"Thanks for the plane. My team is outside assisting with the arrests."

"As much as I love all of our uncles, I thought the country's top FBI Hostage Team would be useful," Ryker said in response to everyone's questioning looks.

"Thank you all," Paxton said between gritted teeth to the growing family around him.

Gavin pushed in and examined the leg. "He needs surgery. Let's get him to the ambulance."

"On it," Greer said, picking up her coms. "Agent down. I repeat, agent down. We need a stretcher now."

Greer helped Tinsley stand as the stretcher was raced inside. It seemed to be over quickly yet took forever as Paxton was loaded into the ambulance. Tinsley wanted to ride with him, but Gavin was with them and working hard to stop the bleeding. She didn't need him to tell her it was serious. She'd seen the amount of blood Paxton had left behind.

"Come on, Tins. Let's get to the hospital. I want someone to check out your face, too," Ryker told her as he slipped his arm around her waist. With Greer on one side and Ryker on the other, she stepped out into the daylight.

The bright sun made her squint until she could adjust to it. All around her were police, FBI, DEA, and ATF vehicles. Myriad members were being arrested and moved to buses while others were taken away by ambulance.

Outside, armies of people were working to secure the scene, but they all stopped to look over their shoulders at her when she reached the bottom of the steps. They nodded at her and Tinsley nodded back. Then the hive of activity went on. At the end of the driveway, Ridge shoved a police officer to the side and ran by the wall of officers roping the area off. The poor guy didn't even have time to yell at Ridge before the whole Faulkner family was running past him.

"Tins!" Her brother's embrace broke her. Tinsley had been strong and brave until then, but with her brother and all her cousins wrapping her in a group hug, the emotions overflowed. Tears broke free and poured down her face as she cried into Ridge's chest. "It's okay. We're here. You're safe now. Are you hurt?"

"Just a punch to the face," Tinsley said as she tried to stop the out-of-control emotions.

"Thank you all for protecting her," Ridge said over her head to the Keeneston group.

"We didn't have to protect her. She took out a bunch of men, including the leader of the Myriad with a dagger throw to the heart," Ahmed told her family. "It was very impressive. I don't know many men who could make that throw. Where did you learn that?"

Ridge was speechless and it made Tinsley laugh. She looked at the faces of her brother and cousins and only Ryker and Harper didn't look shocked.

"At church," Tinsley answered simply, then laughed harder at Ahmed's reaction.

"We have a Special Forces priest and we don't learn that in church," Miles muttered.

"Yeah, we need to talk to Ben about that. I think we could incorporate that into mass," Marshall agreed.

"Whitlock!" Ryker yelled out. A man a little older than Paxton and with dirty blond hair turned and walked toward them in his FBI jacket. "This is my cousin Tinsley. We need to get her to the hospital."

"Let me shake your hand first," Whitlock said. "I'm the head of the gang unit. Thanks to you and your very, um, unique family, we arrested a hundred and thirty-seven

Myriad members. We also confiscated thousands of illegal guns, and I can't tell you how many drugs. Of course, your uncles and cousin blew up quite a bit of it, too, so the true value is unknown."

Tinsley couldn't help the small laugh that came out. "Thank you for coming to my rescue."

"Patrick!" Whitlock yelled out. "Get Miss Faulkner to the hospital as fast as possible."

"We're going with her," Ridge said.

"Take one of the SUVs," Whitlock yelled out to the young agent.

"Thank you," Tinsley said, turning back to her family. She had been told how they had rappelled from a helicopter, swum through the marsh, and the final group had come in through the front door while Whitlock's group helped round up and arrest the men and storm the front of the bar. "Thank you all. Now I just want to get to Paxton as quickly as possible."

"Watch out, Harp," Ridge called out as he held open the SUV door for her. "We have a new badass in the family."

"I've known she was a badass all along, but now I'm making her work the Clemson and South Carolina football game to stop the bar fights," Harper called out as she hugged her husband.

Tinsley sent a wink to her cousin and got into the SUV. "Patrick?"

"Yes, ma'am?" the young agent answered as Ryker, Ridge, and Greer got into the SUV with her.

"Drive fast," Tinsley ordered as all her thoughts were focused squarely on getting to Paxton.

30

Paxton was in so much pain that lights were flashing behind his eyes. Ahmed had pulled the tourniquet so tight that his leg was alternately throbbing yet somehow numb, too.

"Tell them to prepare for surgery. The femoral artery was nicked. They'll need blood for a transfusion. Lots of it," Gavin yelled out for the EMT to radio in. "We'll be there in fifteen minutes." Gavin's face was directly in front of Paxton's as he flashed a penlight into his eyes. "You'll go right into surgery," Gavin said as he took Paxton's blood pressure. "You've lost a lot of blood."

"No," Paxton said through teeth gritted in pain.

"No what?" Gavin asked.

"No surgery until I talk to Tinsley."

Gavin's grave face popped back in front of Paxton's. "Not happening. You need surgery."

"I need Tinsley," Paxton said, and Gavin huffed out an annoyed breath.

"Okay, let me see what I can do." Gavin disappeared from view as Paxton stared at the roof of the ambulance that was being escorted by the police. "Paxton needs surgery like yesterday, but he won't go in without seeing Tinsley," Gavin said into a phone. "Well, tell the agent to drive faster!" Gavin all but shouted.

"Shit," Paxton cursed and Gavin's face was instantly in front of his again.

"What is it?"

"I need a ring."

Gavin's confused look would be humorous if Paxton wasn't in so much pain. "I'm sorry, what?"

"There's no way I'm going into a surgery I might not survive without Tinsley knowing I want to marry her. I need an engagement ring."

"You can ask her without one," Gavin said, patting his hand.

Paxton grabbed Gavin's hand and squeezed. "Get me a ring. I don't care if it's a piece of string, but she's going to be wearing something after I propose."

"Okay, give me another second." Gavin disappeared from view. "Olivia, it's Gavin. Yes, we were part of that. The FBI agent who was in charge of it is severely injured and wants to propose to Tinsley before he goes into surgery. Any way you can get an engagement ring to the hospital in ten minutes?"

Gavin held the phone out and put it on speaker. "She wants to talk to you."

"Hello?" Paxton said as he clenched his teeth in pain.

"Tell me your vision and I'll make it happen," the woman named Olivia said over the phone. Paxton could hear high heels running as he thought of Tinsley and the perfect ring for her.

"Colorful and unique, just like her."

"Got it. See you in the ER."

The line went dead and Paxton looked to Gavin. "Who was that?"

"Olivia Townsend. She's Ryker's lawyer and she's the scariest woman I've ever met. If there's anyone who can browbeat a jeweler into giving her a ring this quick, it's her."

Paxton chuckled and then groaned in pain. He just needed to stay conscious long enough to propose, and then he'd let the blissful darkness take him.

"Get out of my way and let me through or that man will die and I'll have you arrested for his murder." Paxton heard the stern voice from the phone as he was being pulled from the ambulance.

Gavin chuckled and Paxton smiled. She was just what Gavin said. "Let her through!" Gavin yelled out to the police escort.

Paxton waited until a beautiful woman with a fancy updo and a royal blue suit popped into his visual field. "Hello. Do you like it?" She opened a velvet box and Paxton knew everything was going to be okay.

"You're perfect. It's perfect. Tinsley's perfect," Paxton said happily. The woman looked amused as she handed him the box.

"I gave him some pain meds," Gavin told them. "Here's Tinsley."

"Here's all of Shadows Landing," Olivia said as the EMTs wheeled Paxton toward the large glass doors.

"Tinsley!" Paxton yelled as the world spun in a very good way. He felt fantastic.

"I'm here, Paxton." Tinsley's worried face came into view and he could see her confused look as she glanced at Olivia. "Is he in legal trouble?"

"No, I'm just here for moral support," Olivia said, stepping back to join Ryker.

"Tinsley, I have to go into surgery," Paxton said as doctors and nurses swarmed the bed. Tinsley held on to his hand as they pushed him down the hall. Doctors were talking to Gavin and Paxton was being hooked up to who knows what.

"I know. I'm right here. I'll be here the whole time. I'll be the first thing you see when you open your eyes."

Paxton smiled up at her. She was the best. "I could kill Curtis for hurting you. Oh, wait, you already killed him."

"Curtis was a very bad man," Tinsley told the doctors and nurses who had all stopped and were staring at her.

"Okay, we're here. You're going to have to leave him now," ordered the doctor who had been questioning Gavin.

"No!" Paxton was running out of time. "I love you, Tinsley."

"I love you, too, Paxton." Tinsley kissed him and they began to move him into surgery, but Paxton reached out and grabbed Tinsley's hand. "Honey, you're going to do great. You have the best doctors—"

"I don't give a crap about them. I only care about you. I can't go in there until you know how much you mean to me. You're my everything. Tinsley, you're my whole world. You're my heart and soul." Paxton shoved the box at her. That probably could be smoother, but he knew he was out of time. "Will you marry me? Sorry I can't go down on one knee right now. You deserve so much more, but I almost lost you today and I can't let one more second go by without you knowing how badly I want the honor of being your husband and how proud I would be if you would be my wife."

Tinsley kissed him then. "Yes," she said as her lips were

still on his. "Yes, I'll marry you. Now get fixed up so you can carry me over the threshold. I love you, Paxton."

Paxton sighed in relief. He was going to marry the woman he loved more than life. With a smile on his face, he let the darkness take him. But instead of darkness, it was the bright future he dreamt about.

Clapping was the first thing Tinsley noticed when the doors to the operating room closed. She turned around to see almost everyone she knew and all the hospital staff, EMTs, and police applauding.

Tinsley hadn't even opened the box to look at the ring. She opened the lid and smiled. It was perfect: a square diamond in a rose gold setting with a halo of colorful gemstones around it. It was a work of art. Now she just needed her fiancé to survive his surgery.

Hours went by, but Tinsley didn't notice. She was lost in her own world of thought. Peter and the rest of her friends, family, and, heck, even the knitting club all showed up at the hospital. At some point, food was shoved into her hands. She ate but she couldn't tell you what it was.

Miss Ruby hugged her. Miss Winnie talked to her. Miss Mitzi just sat nearby and knitted while Tinsley sat quietly and waited to see how her future would play out. Would she live happily ever after or become a widow before she could even become a bride? Gavin, Ellery, Trent, Skye, Harper, Dare, Wade, Darcy, Savannah, Granger, and Kord all took turns sitting by her side.

Tinsley was sure they talked, but she couldn't hear them over the beating of her heart. When Peter walked in and stopped in front of her, Tinsley finally realized it was Ridge and Ryker sitting next to her. Ridge had his arm around her shoulder and Ryker held her hand in his.

"Tinsley, it's time to pay attention now," Ryker ordered in his CEO voice. She blinked and looked around for the first time in hours.

"I take it there's no news on Paxton yet?" Peter asked with his face set seriously. Normally he was all smiles.

Tinsley shook her head.

"There is news on the case. Do you want to hear it?" Peter asked as everyone quieted down.

Tinsley nodded, still not knowing if she could find the voice to talk.

"Paxton led the largest drug and weapons bust in history. We've found enough evidence both here and in Atlanta—at least in the places Cy didn't blow up—to connect the Myriad to the Argentinian mafia. Arrests have already been made as we captured ten associates trying to board a plane to Buenos Aires from Atlanta. The CIA is working with the Argentinian government to bring the rest to justice."

"The paintings," Tinsley said finally. "We need the whole collection together. I have to find the owners."

"You'll have the full support of the federal government at your disposal to do so," Peter assured her.

Tinsley nodded but then stopped as a tired doctor came out from the double doors. Ridge and Ryker both took her hands in theirs as everyone else stood. Peter stepped to the side as the doctor made his way to her.

"I'm sorry, I didn't get your name. I'm Dr. Evans."

"Tinsley Faulkner," Tinsley stammered out. "How is Paxton?"

"You're fiancé is a fighter. We almost lost him, but we managed to get the artery repaired. He's had blood transfusions to replace the blood he's lost, and he's stable now. He'll stay in the hospital for a couple of days for us to keep an eye on him. Would you like to see him?"

Tinsley could only nod as her knees gave out and she collapsed against her brother. "He's going to live," she said, finally breathing for the first time all day.

"Can we all see him?" Ridge asked.

The doctor looked around the packed waiting room. "Um, a limit of two visitors is our policy."

"How's this for policy?" Peter held up his badge as Granger and Kord followed suit.

"His room is very small. I don't think you will fit," the doctor stammered, trying to figure out where the hospital policy fell on this situation.

Tinsley felt Ryker stiffen. "I'm Ryker Faulkner and that man is about to become my family. Get him a bigger room."

"Ryker Faulkner?" the poor doctor stammered. Ryker simply nodded. "We'll move Agent Kendry to a suite right away and then I'll send a nurse to escort you all to him."

The doctor practically ran off and Granger shook his head. "How did you do that? I thought we had him with the badge. That usually works."

"I'm the hospital's largest donor. There's a whole new Faulkner wing," Ryker said with a shrug as if it weren't a big deal.

"Thank you. I would have never pushed," Tinsley told her cousin.

"I know. Even if you are now a dagger-throwing badass, you're still the nice one." Ryker winked at her and went to sit back down.

Energy Tinsley never imagined she had in reserve flowed through her and she began to pace. She just needed to see Paxton. She had to tell him she loved him and she needed to have him in her arms. Then she'd know it would all be all right in the end.

Paxton felt as if he were floating. That was the first thing he processed as being real instead of the dreams he'd been having. The second thing he processed was the small hand holding his. Paxton knew instinctively that it was Tinsley. The third thing was that he heard talking all around him.

Paxton blinked his eyes open and the talking immediately stopped. Tinsley's face appeared in front of his and he gave a small smile. "There's my fiancée." Paxton paused then and looked around the room. "I did propose, right? Or was that a dream?"

Tinsley smiled as unshed tears shone in her eyes. "You did and I accepted."

"Oh thank goodness," Paxton sighed and Tinsley laughed happily. He looked down at their joined hands and saw the engagement ring. His dreams had come true. Then he looked around the room and saw what might be his nightmares come to life. "Tinsley," he whispered.

Tinsley leaned forward so she could hear him. "Yes?"

"Is the knitting club sitting in the corner or are the drugs making me see things?"

"We're here," Dare said, looking up from his knitting needles.

"We made you something," Miss Ruby said.

"Give us one more second to finish it off," Miss Winnie told him.

Paxton looked around and saw groups of people all around the largest hospital room he'd ever seen. The Davies and Faulkner families were in one area. The law enforcement people were in another. Then the knitting club had laid claim to the couch area.

"This doesn't look like any hospital room I've ever been in," Paxton said, looking around.

"It's a conference room," Ryker answered. "I can't have my new cousin in some small room where his family couldn't gather."

"Thanks, Ryker. You had my back during the bust. I didn't imagine you as anything but a businessman but I was wrong."

"I'll do anything for my family. I've learned that doesn't make me weak, but stronger. Now you're going to be part of this family. But if you hurt my cousin," Ryker said and leaned down so his face was inches from Paxton, "I'll kill you."

"And then we'd bring you back to life to kill you again," Cy called out from their corner. Ridge nodded in agreement along with his cousins and uncles.

"I wouldn't have it any other way. I might ask to go on some of these guy trips in the future," Paxton said with a chuckle.

"I'm in," Dare said, shooting up his hand.

"We'll be sure to invite the wives on our spa trips," Annie said with a grin.

The guys groaned and the youngest Davies brother, Pierce, looked nervous. "You all know we were never here, right? Like, our wives can't know what we're doing or they'd kill us."

Cy, Miles, and Marshall nodded as they suddenly looked very nervous.

"This is going be a very fun wedding," Paxton said with a smile and Tinsley laughed. It was the best sound he'd ever heard.

"Here we go!" Miss Ruby said as she and the rest of the knitting club held up a large blanket with a block letter K in the middle for Kendry.

"That's beautiful," Paxton said, truly touched. Maybe the knitting club wasn't so bad. "How long have I been out? That had to take you all forever to knit."

"We each knitted a section so it was done in no time," Miss Mitzi told him as they carried it to the bed.

"We couldn't have you recovering with nothing but a hospital sheet to keep you warm," Miss Ruby told him.

"Do you think getting shot trying to save Tinsley would get me two apple pies a month?" Paxton asked innocently before reaching down to his wounded leg. "Ow. It hurts a lot and apple pie would make it feel better."

"Oh, you poor, dear boy," Miss Ruby said, glancing back to the knitting club. "We'll take good care of you."

"Thank you all. Knitting clubs are the best because they have the biggest hearts." Paxton held open his arms and Miss Winnie and Miss Ruby came in for a hug. Over their shoulders he saw the Faulkner and Davies men staring at him in disbelief. He winked at them and their mouths dropped.

"Come on, ladies, let's get baking."

The room was quiet as the knitting club left for the night.

"You're going to share, right?" Ridge asked. "I mean, I'm going to be your brother now."

"Nope. This is to get you back for what you put me through when I wanted to date Tinsley. Revenge isn't a dish best served cold. It's a freshly baked apple pie, boys."

Paxton smirked. Having brothers and cousins was going to be fun. Although it surprised him that it was Ryker who burst out laughing first. He wasn't sure if he'd ever heard Ryker laugh.

"Oh, this *is* going to be fun. Welcome to the family, Paxton," Ryker said.

Paxton reached for Tinsley's hand and ran his thumb over the engagement ring. Home. Family. Love. He had found it all right here in Shadows Landing and he couldn't be happier.

31

Three months later...

Tinsley hadn't felt this nervous since she'd been kidnapped. It had taken months, but with Olivia's legal help, Paxton's FBI connections, her Keeneston family's political connections, and a few bribes on Ryker's part, Tinsley had traced the history of the art collection they'd confiscated from the Myriad. Not only that, but she'd found the rest of the collection—another twenty pieces that had been scattered all around the world.

She'd been lucky. During her research, she'd discovered the great-granddaughter of a former local government official who had not only kept impeccable records, but had saved them from the Nazis to show the devastating destruction of life and property during WWII. There, in the documents, was a full list of paintings from a collection that a family of generations of art dealers had on display a month before their gallery was shuttered by anti-Jewish policies.

With that paperwork in hand, Tinsley had the original owners' names and began a worldwide search for the surviving members of the family.

Tinsley and Paxton had gone to battle with the FBI to get the paintings released into her custody. Then she'd gone to battle against countries to get several stolen paintings back. She'd threatened heads of states, museum directors, and even a very wealthy private collector. Some owners of the artwork had been horrified to find out their art was stolen by the Nazis during World War II and had given them back with no strings. Other times, she'd had to raise money to buy the art, or at least reimburse buyers for what they paid for it. She'd even rushed into the middle of a live art auction in New York City at one of the most prestigious auction houses to prevent a painting from being sold.

But now her was mission was complete.

"We are meeting the head of the museum," Olivia reminded them. Olivia and Ryker had come along since they'd done so much work on the case, and considering it was Ryker's private jet they were flying in. Also he'd threatened some people on her behalf and paid off others. "It's Ms. Rachel Katz. Are you ready, Tinsley?"

She took a deep breath. Paxton smiled at her proudly as they stood up.

"I'm ready."

Tinsley had been a woman on a mission. She'd delayed any talk of a wedding until she could get this collection to the rightful owners. Paxton hadn't argued once. Instead, he had helped in every way he could.

The plane door opened and Olivia went down the stairs first. A woman in a dove gray suit with a light blue silk blouse stood waiting for them by a luxury SUV.

"Olivia Townsend," Olivia said, holding out her hand as

she began the introductions. "Tinsley Faulkner, Paxton Kendry, and Ryker Faulkner."

Tinsley reached out and shook hands with the woman in her early forties. Her dark brown hair was pulled up into a twist and the excited smile on her face matched Tinsley's. "I am Rachel Katz. Shalom and welcome to Israel. It's a pleasure to meet you in person."

"You, too, Ms. Katz."

"Rachel, please. Come this way. We are very excited to be of assistance in this endeavor. Your actions to get the artwork back to their rightful owners are very admirable. Everyone in the art community is talking about it."

A uniformed driver held open the door to the SUV. Ryker sat up front, while Olivia and Paxton climbed into the third row, and Tinsley sat next to Rachel in the second row. "I didn't do this to be talked about. I did it because it's the right thing to do."

Rachel reached out and touched Tinsley's arm. "I know. That is even more reason we are excited to work with you."

Rachel pointed out landmarks as they drove through Jerusalem to the art museum. As incredible as it was, Tinsley could hardly pay attention. She was too eager to get to the museum.

When they arrived there, all the employees were lined up on the steps. When Tinsley got out of the SUV, they began to clap and she nearly lost the battle to maintain her composure. She might be dubbed the new badass of the family, but she was still sensitive. And this . . . this was as sensitive and emotional as it would ever get.

Paxton took her hand in his as they walked up the steps to the museum. She shook hands with all the employees as they made their way inside. Tinsley followed Rachel through the lobby and then into an expansive exhibit room.

Tinsley stopped in her tracks as she placed her hands over her mouth. It was beautiful. They'd cleaned the frames and replaced several of them after restoring the art by delicately cleaning the canvases. The lighting was perfect and the pieces looked . . . happy. They knew they were home.

"The family is arriving in fifteen minutes. The press will arrive in two hours."

"Does the family know?" Tinsley asked Rachel.

Rachel shook her head. "No, they do not. I couldn't find the words to tell them, so instead I told them they'd won a private tour of a new exhibit, organized by an American, that I thought they'd love. I still don't think I can find the words."

Tinsley took a deep breath and watched Olivia, Ryker, and Paxton walk a slow circle of the room. She watched them taking in the art and was moved just from that.

Tinsley took a moment to stop before each painting to talk with them. They'd been her constant companions these last months.

"Is that a Monet?" Paxton asked as he joined her.

Tinsley laughed and swiped at a tear. "Manet. You know that."

"I'm pretty sure it's a Monet."

"They're here!" Rachel gasped as she pulled herself together. "Come with me." She motioned for the group to follow her. Rachel reached back and pulled Tinsley to come stand with her in the lobby.

Tinsley didn't realize she was holding her breath until Paxton reminded her to relax. Through the open door, they saw the minivan's side door open. A man and woman in their early seventies got out of the front of the minivan to help two elderly men from the back seats. The taller of the two had a walker and the other used a cane. They were dressed in suits and smiled up at the two people helping them out of the van. Soon, several vehicles pulled in behind the minivan and a lot of people emerged from them. There were young children, teenagers, college students, thirty-somethings, and more retirement-aged couples. They all came over and hugged the two elderly men and each other. They were smiling, laughing, and several of the teens rolled their eyes and turned their attention back to their phones. Ah, teenagers, the same in every country.

Tinsley felt Paxton's hand come up to the small of her back reassuringly. It was then she realized she was shaking. It seemed an age for the large family to make it to the lobby.

"Welcome!" Rachel called out, her voice cracking as she tried to keep it together. "I'm Rachel Katz. I'm the curator of the museum and this is Tinsley Faulkner. She's a painter from South Carolina, in America. She's put together this exhibit for you to enjoy today."

"Thank you for having us. My family loves art. It is in our blood," the old man with the walker said. He held out his hand for her and Tinsley had to bite her lip to maintain her composure when she saw the old black numbers from a concentration camp tattooed onto his arm. "I'm Elek Alder and this is my younger brother, Sandor. You said it was okay to invite the whole family." Elek laughed as he gestured to the thirty-plus people behind him and Sandor. "These are our children, our grandchildren, and our great-grandchildren."

"It's an honor to meet you all," Tinsley said as a couple of heads popped up at her strange-sounding accent. "This is my fiancé, Paxton Kendry, my cousin, Ryker Faulkner, and my friend, Olivia Townsend." Tinsley made the introductions and everyone shook hands. Now it was time to finish what she'd started. "I asked Rachel to invite you here today to be the first to see the collection I've put together. Please come this way."

Rachel offered her arm to Sandor as Elek walked next to Tinsley into the exhibit room. The brothers walked three steps inside the door before they both stopped.

"Elek, is this—" Sandor sputtered as he reached out and grabbed his brother's arm. It was then Tinsley saw a matching black tattoo on Sandor's arm.

Elek turned to her, tears streaming down his face. He wavered and Paxton was there to hold him up. His son rushed forward with a chair and someone who must be Sandor's son similarly brought him a chair.

"Papa, what is it?" one of the sons asked worriedly as the two brothers clung to each other.

Elek's hand reached out and clasped her wrist. "You did this? Where did you... How?"

"Papa? What is going on? What did this woman do?" a daughter asked Elek in alarm.

Tinsley couldn't answer. She only could nod. Elek pulled her in front of him and Sandor and then tugged her downward. When she was on her knees in front of them, the men enveloped her in a hug as they all cried together. *This* is why she had done it. The paintings were finally reunited with their family. She wasn't sure how long the brothers held her and cried, but when they finally released their grip on her, her shirt was soaked with tears.

"Can we see it?" Elek asked.

"Of course, Mr. Alder. It's yours. I brought it home for you," Tinsley said softly, but it was loud enough for the family to hear.

"Ours? I don't understand. Papa, what's going on?" the daughter asked.

Elek stood up and Paxton hurried to help if need be.

Sandor followed and together they stepped farther into the room. They moved slowly, pointing to paintings and talking to each other in hushed whispers before they sat back down and addressed their family.

"I've never told you the full story, but it's time you all learn what our people went through. Not from a book or from people who weren't there, but from us. It was 1944," Elek said and his family instantly fell silent. Even the teenagers put down their phones. "The Nazis invaded Hungary. Jews were killed on the street and those who weren't murdered were rounded up and marched almost three hundred kilometers to Auschwitz. They were starved, whipped, and murdered along the way. Around four hundred and fifty thousand Hungarian Jews were killed. Murdered."

Sandor looked as if he were far away when he spoke. "A family friend gave my father forged papers and told us to run. My father went to the family gallery where we were living and ripped paintings from their frames. He took all he could carry and then we went looking for Elek."

Elek continued the narrative. "I was part of a forced labor team. That day we were beaten and worked within an inch of our lives, but then they started shooting us. Hundreds of us, just murdered and kicked into the river. I ran. I threw away my coat and walked with a group of teenagers. That's where our father and mother found me. We used those forged papers to make it to the Austrian border. Then we slipped into the countryside at night."

"We lasted nine days," Sandor said before both brothers fell silent.

Finally Elek took a deep breath. "We tried to pass off the papers when we were caught, but it didn't work this time. We were thrown on a train for Auschwitz."

Tinsley saw both brothers absently rub on their arms where the tattoos were.

"I still see it in my nightmares," Sandor said as if he were back there. His voice was small, thin, and barely above a whisper now as he relived the terror. "They took our parents away. I can still hear my mother's screams. We never saw them again. Our heads were shaved, our shoes taken, our clothes taken ..."

"We were young and strong so they sent us to a work camp," Elek said, his voice also barely above a whisper. "Death might have been better." He stopped, then straightened his shoulders and looked to his family. "We fought for you before you even existed. You're the reason we fought, the reason we lived."

"We were near starvation when the Americans and Allied forces arrived," Sandor said, his voice growing stronger. "They brought us blankets. They gave us the clothes off their backs and food from their pockets. But we weren't free yet. We went back to Budapest, thinking we could go home."

"Only there was no home left. All of our friends and family had been murdered either there on the street, on the death marches, or in the camps. We were all that was left. Even the buildings were rubble," Elek told them. "Gellert and his wife were dead. The Nazis had murdered him when they found he'd helped over a thousand Jews escape, including trying to help us. His teenage son was alive, though, and we lived with him in what had been a shed on his property filled with old papers and discarded furniture. His house had been burned down by the Nazis after they shot his father and mother in front of him."

"For three years we lived like that," Sandor said, picking up the story. "Until Israel became a state. The rest is the history you know. We came here with nothing. We worked hard, saved, and started buying art again in honor of our father. We met the loves of our lives and were blessed with our families. But every night, every day, *I remember*. I remember my father's vow to restore the family's collection, and I remember being torn from our mother's arms at Auschwitz. I remember the hunger, the cold, the degradation."

Elek squeezed Tinsley's hand. "This woman has brought back our family legacy and fulfilled my father's vow. This is the Alder Collection stolen from us by the Nazis. That Vermeer was ripped from my father in Austria. That Manet was hidden in my mother's dress and was found at Auschwitz. How?" Elek simply asked her.

Tinsley looked up from the brothers to the tear-soaked faces of their family and couldn't find the words.

"I'm not just Tinsley's fiancé. I'm an FBI agent specializing in art crimes. Tinsley is an art expert as well as an artist in her own right. She owns a gallery and one of the paintings came through her door as part of a drug deal between a gang in the United States and the Argentinian mafia," Paxton answered for her before telling them of the case and then what they did to bring the collection together and back to the Alder family.

Tinsley was so grateful he was able to tell them because she didn't know if she could speak with all the emotions going through her. So, she simply sat on the floor holding Elek's and Sandor's hands as Paxton told them how they had ended up in Israel today.

"Rozsa," Elek said, motioning to a woman who must be his daughter. "Bring me the Manet."

The woman headed straight for it and lifted it from the wall. "Here you go, Papa."

Elek gestured to Tinsley. "This is for you. A wedding gift. There are no words that can express what we are feeling right now. But when there are no words, there is art."

Sandor nodded as his niece turned to hand the painting to Paxton.

"Mr. Alder," Tinsley finally gasped. "We can't take that. It's too much. It belongs to you, to your family."

"We wouldn't have seen it or any of these paintings if it hadn't been for you. It's not nearly enough. Tell me, where did you find it?" Elek asked.

"This one was found in a private art collection in Poland," Tinsley told him. She looked up and saw movement by the door and smiled. She had decided to come after all. "This brave young woman showed them proof of your ownership and the family holding it gave it back. In fact, she was by my side fighting heads of state and powerful collectors to bring your art home."

The young woman appeared to be in her early twenties. She wore flowing linen pants and a bright yellow tunic. Her reddish-brown hair was straight and cut into a shoulder-length bob. Tinsley gestured toward her and she slowly entered the room.

"Elek, Sandor, this is Julianna Balogh, the great-granddaughter of Gellert Balogh."

"Hello, sirs. I've heard much about you from my grandfather."

Tinsley stepped back into Paxton's arms. Her job was done. The wrongs of the past could and should never be forgotten, but she could help make them right.

EPILOGUE

"You may kiss the bride," Reverend Winston said as the church full of people suddenly erupted into cheers.

Paxton lowered his lips and covered Tinsley's for a sweet kiss with all his love for her poured into it. When he pulled back, he was looking at his wife. Paxton smiled as Tinsley laughed with pure happiness. Paxton clasped her hand and together they ran down the aisle toward their future.

"Husband," Tinsley said with a huge smile as they got into the horse-drawn carriage that would take them to the Bell Plantation for their reception.

"Yes?" Paxton asked as he kissed her once again. He just couldn't stop, and to be honest, he never wanted to stop kissing her.

"Let's make a little detour on our way to the reception."

"Whatever you say, dear. I've heard that phrase is the best phrase a husband can learn." Paxton didn't tell her he'd been told that while being cornered by the knitting club last night with their knitting needles pointed at him as they gave him decades of marriage advice.

Tinsley snorted with laughter. "Yeah, we'll see how often you remember that. Even if you forget, I'll still love you."

"Where are they?" Ridge asked impatiently as they waited for the bride and groom to arrive at the reception.

Savannah rolled her eyes at him and Ryker tried not to laugh. His cousin still had a blind spot in terms of his sister.

"Ryker, a word?" Olivia was dressed in an evening gown but was never off duty. Ryker followed her off to the side of the tent being used for the reception.

"What is it?" he asked her once they were alone.

"The shared business venture is a go. The terms need to be negotiated, though," Olivia told him.

Ryker nodded. It was a long time coming. He normally didn't like to share ownership with other people, but he was going to make an exception this one time. "Set up a meeting. We'll hash it all out and sign the papers right then and there."

"Will do," Olivia said, already walking away with the phone to her ear.

"Do you ever stop working?"

Ryker turned around to see his Great-Aunt Marcy Davies standing there. He hurried over and offered her his arm to escort her to her table. "No. It's my only flaw, though."

Marcy rolled her eyes at him and Ryker chuckled. Only his family would dare tease him. He'd scared everyone else off. That's why he was taking a risk with this business venture. His Kentucky cousin had suggested it. When he looked into it, it was a solid plan.

"You need a good woman in your life and then you won't think about work so much," Great-Aunt Marcy said.

Memories of the one woman he'd loved flashed into his head. The laughter, the passion, the fights . . .

"Sorry. I'm married to my work. Besides, you have plenty of grandkids to see married off." Ryker might love his family, but he'd totally throw them under the marriage bus if it meant he was able to get out of the line of fire.

"Don't you worry about them. I have that covered. Mark my words. Your time is here."

Ryker felt a shiver run down his spine. Marcy didn't need to know what had happened to him and the vow he made to never fall in love again. He didn't deserve love.

"Ryker," Olivia said, interrupting at exactly the right moment. Ryker helped Marcy sit down and then turned to his lawyer. The normally composed young woman looked uncharacteristically flustered. Her eyes were going this way and that while she shifted from side to side on the balls of her feet.

"Did the deal fall through?" Ryker asked, taking her elbow and stepping away.

"The what? Oh, no. The deal is all set up. The meeting is next week."

"Then what is the matter? I've seen you face down the most intimidating people imaginable in court and didn't bat an eye. Now you're shaking like a leaf." Ryker glanced around to see who did this to her and how he could hurt them for it. Olivia was an independent young woman, and as much as people said they would make a powerful couple, in truth, she was his best friend.

"My brothers are moving back." Olivia managed in a strangled whisper.

Ryker blinked. "I didn't know you had brothers."

Olivia nodded as her face began to flush red with anger.

"I have them all right. Big, meddling, think-they-know-everything brothers."

Ryker didn't know what to say. Olivia was as quiet about her past as he was about his. It's one of the reasons they got along so well. They didn't meddle in each other's lives. "How many?"

"Lots. Too many. Damn it. I know what they're up to!" Olivia said after looking up from her phone. "They're moving to Shadows Landing because they think you and I are a couple."

Ryker laughed, then immediately stopped. "I'm sorry. I'm not laughing at the idea of you as a girlfriend, just as *my* girlfriend. Why would they think we're a couple?"

"Because I bought Savannah's house last week. It's right on the river and I want to use it as a place to decompress. I didn't mention it to you because it's not a big deal. I like it here. I know it's hard to believe, but I don't have many friends. What friends I have all seem to be your family."

Ryker nodded. He knew it took a lot to admit. He didn't have friends either besides Olivia and his family. "It's hard when you're us. We go after what we want come hell or high water. That tends to burn some bridges. Then you put yourself out there and learn they're only with you for the power or money."

Olivia sighed and then nodded. "Men don't like that I'm smarter than they are. They don't like that I put my career ahead of them. Screw them. I have a vibrator and it doesn't whine about how hard it is to date a woman who makes more money than they do." Olivia looked up at him as he fought a smile. "By the way, thanks for making me rich."

Ryker shrugged. "You're the best lawyer I know."

"And I'm proud of that. But now my brothers are going to come, and they're going to be the biggest pains in the ass and probably ruin the great working relationship we have all because they think I'm dating you."

"Just tell them we're not dating."

Olivia made a very agitated noise, nearly a growl, which surprised Ryker. "I did! They didn't understand why I'd buy a house down the road from you. Now they're all coming here. They've each bought a house in Shadows Landing and they're going to drive me crazy. They still think I'm a little girl who needs protecting."

Ryker looked over at Ridge lecturing Tinsley for being late to the reception. He also saw Jackson and Ryan staring daggers at Gage Bell for dancing with their little sister, Greer. Although, with her closing in on thirty, *little* was about as relevant to Greer as it was to Olivia or Tinsley.

"I don't think that will ever change," Ryker said, gesturing with his chin to the older brothers around them.

"Ugh! Your cousin Parker is with the US Marshals right? Maybe he can put me in witness protection." Olivia started to look around for Parker, and Ryker shook his head.

"You never back down from a fight. I can't imagine your brothers causing this type of reaction."

"Oh, I can beat them up. But it doesn't stop my brothers from completely interfering with my life and treating me like a ten-year-old girl in pigtails. I know they love me. Heck, they're moving here just to be with me. But, Ryker, it's going to be too much. They'll want to be involved with everything. My brothers are slightly overprotective."

"Did I hear something of overprotective brothers?" Greer asked as she joined them.

"Yes, my brothers are moving to Shadows Landing," Olivia groaned.

"Don't worry," Greer said, giving Olivia a hug. "I'll show you how to erase their tracking software on your phone. Oh,

I have all kinds of tricks to teach you. Between our fathers and brothers, we Keeneston girls have you covered in how to deal with overprotective men. Come on, let's tell the girls, and we'll give you some tips."

Greer grinned back at Ryker and he mouthed his thanks as Ridge came over to join him. "I can't believe they stopped at home before coming here. Tinsley said it was to check on their Manet. How dumb does she think I am? Then Savannah got mad at me for getting mad at them."

Ryker silently handed his bourbon over to his cousin who downed it. Thank goodness he'd never fall in love and have to go through this.

Tinsley danced with her husband as other couples began to join them on the dance floor. There was a little commotion as the crowd parted and suddenly Paxton yelped and jumped five feet in the air.

When Tinsley looked to see what had caused it, she didn't just laugh. She bent over with big belly laughs. She looked up at Gator, Skeeter, and Turtle and swiped at her tears from laughing so hard.

"That is not funny," Paxton said, shaking his head at them, but the smile on his lips told them all it was very funny.

Tinsley looked down at Bubba, all decked out for the wedding in a bow tie and shook her head. "How did you get him to walk on a leash?"

"We've been working on it since you two got engaged," Gator said proudly. "He loves it. He tries to eat us until we get it on, but then he parades around with it."

"Then he tries to eat us again when we take it off," Turtle said, causing Paxton to hide a laugh under a cough.

"We took pictures. It's our wedding gift," Skeeter said, holding out a large print.

Paxton took it and looked down at it. She could see him struggling not to laugh. "I love it."

He turned it around and Tinsley felt her mouth open. "How on earth did you get Bertha to wear a veil?" There was a picture of Bubba and Bertha as a groom and bride. Sketched out in front of them on the sandy bank was Tinsley and Paxton's wedding date.

"That was a little trickier and bloodier. But we got it," Gator said proudly.

Paxton held out his hand and shook each of the men's hands. "It's the best wedding present I could ever imagine. Thank you all."

"Shucks. We're just glad you like it. We're still going to give you crap for screaming like a girl, though," Gator said as Skeeter and Turtle nodded.

"That's fine with me," Paxton smiled.

Tinsley wrapped her arm around her husband and looked up at him. The ghosts of his past had been left behind as soon as he'd woken up from his surgery. Now they were both filled with the happiness for their future together.

"Come on, Mrs. Kendry. Let's show them how to dance," Paxton said as he spun her around the dance floor and toward their happily ever after.

THE END

Bluegrass Series

Bluegrass State of Mind

Risky Shot

Dead Heat

Bluegrass Brothers

Bluegrass Undercover

Rising Storm

Secret Santa: A Bluegrass Series Novella

Acquiring Trouble

Relentless Pursuit

Secrets Collide

Final Vow

Bluegrass Singles

All Hung Up

Bluegrass Dawn

The Perfect Gift

The Keeneston Roses

Forever Bluegrass Series

Forever Entangled

Forever Hidden

Forever Betrayed

Forever Driven

Forever Secret

Forever Surprised

Forever Concealed

Forever Devoted

Forever Hunted

Forever Guarded

Forever Notorious

Forever Ventured

Forever Freed

Forever Saved

Forever Bold

Forever Thrown (coming Aug/Sept 2021)

Shadows Landing Series

Saving Shadows

Sunken Shadows

Lasting Shadows

Fierce Shadows

Broken Shadows

Framed Shadows (coming Apr/May 2021)

Endless Shadows (coming Oct 2021)

Women of Power Series

Chosen for Power

Built for Power

Fashioned for Power

Destined for Power

Web of Lies Series

Whispered Lies

Rogue Lies

Shattered Lies

ABOUT THE AUTHOR

Kathleen Brooks is a New York Times, Wall Street Journal, and USA Today bestselling author. Kathleen's stories are romantic suspense featuring strong female heroines, humor, and happily-ever-afters. Her Bluegrass Series and follow-up Bluegrass Brothers Series feature small town charm with quirky characters that have captured the hearts of readers around the world.

Kathleen is an animal lover who supports rescue organizations and other non-profit organizations such as Friends and Vets Helping Pets whose goals are to protect and save our four-legged family members.

Email Notice of New Releases

https://kathleen-brooks.com/new-release-notifications

Kathleen's Website
www.kathleen-brooks.com
Facebook Page
www.facebook.com/KathleenBrooksAuthor
Twitter
www.twitter.com/BluegrassBrooks
Goodreads
www.goodreads.com

Made in the USA
Middletown, DE
24 May 2021

40343045R10184